He Exposed Me to the Real, Now I Hate Lames 2

Natavia

He Exposed Me to the Real, Now I Hate Lames 2

Copyright © 2016 by Natavia

Table of Contents

Desi

I walked around my other home; the home that Bishop and I conducted business in. I looked around the kitchen. Bishop was right about the person having access to my house. There were no signs of someone breaking into my home.

"Think, Desi! Think!" I shouted out loud. The clock on the wall fell to the floor. It was hanging when I first walked into the kitchen but I didn't think nothing of it until a small, black box rolled across the floor. I picked it up then looked at it. I wasn't a fool when it came down to cameras. I used to set men up back in the day with them. I used to have sex with rich men then threatened to tell their wives if they didn't pay me my money. I pushed the button on the small black box and it opened. Someone had taken the disc out. Although I didn't want to call Bishop, I called him anyway.

"It better be good, Desi, one day left," he said when he answered the phone.

"I'm at the house. You have to come over here," I said to him. He hung up in my ear and I wanted to break down in tears. I still couldn't believe Bishop didn't trust me. After all that I did to prove myself to him, he still thought about me being the same woman I used to be. I knew where his drugs were at and I had access to them. If I wanted to set him up, I could've been done it. I wasn't an amateur in that department. He slapped me and even put a gun to my head. My phone rang and it was Chasity.

"What, bitch?" I answered.

"Word on the street is that Bishop is telling everyone how you set him up. You took six bricks from him and he doesn't want your hoe ass anymore," she laughed then continued. "Looks, like you are going back to the strip club. I told you that we will never find love," she said then laughed into the phone. I thought back to the day when Chasity and I got into it at the hair salon.

"When it all settles you will see what I'm about. Bishop will be cutting you off soon. Just wait and see, so don't fall in love yet unless you already did," Chasity said. The night I was drunk, Chasity drove me home and she had to use my house key. I was passed out and I was sure she got a copy made.

"You set me up?" I screamed into the phone. She laughed.

"I rode the short, yellow bus, remember? I'm not capable of such a thing. You set Bishop up yourself! Stop blaming everyone for your mistakes," she spat.

"I'm going to let you have your moment, Chasity. But mark my words, I'm going to fuck your life up, bitch! I'm going to run it through the pits of hell. You just woke up your worst nightmare. You will have nobody by the time I'm done with you, do you hear me? No, fucking, body! So, you want to play games then, bitch, let's get to it," I said.

"I don't know what you're talking about," she said. I heard Bullet in the background then she hung up on me. She didn't want me to know she was back with him. The wheels started spinning very fast in my head. Chasity got Bullet to take Bishop's product. Bullet's careless ass was supposed to take the camera instead of just the disc. Then something else popped up into my head. Chasity's cousin, Jesula, was in town and she could've done it. While I was thinking, I heard someone walk into my house. When I turned around, Bishop was staring at me with murder in his eyes. I hated how he looked at me. He looked at me like I was his enemy—like I was against him. If only he knew how I was slowly breaking down on the inside.

"What did you find out, Desi?" Bishop asked me. I gave him the camera. He looked at it then looked at me.

"I came all the way over here for this? What the hell is this?" he asked.

"It's a camera. A nanny camera, to be specific. It was in the clock above the floor where you kept the safe. It was planted inside the clock," I replied.

Bishop sat down at the table across from me. I didn't look at him because I couldn't.

"I was set up," he said in disbelief.
"We both were, and Chasity had something to do with it. The night I was drunk, I think she got a key made. I also think that her cousin, Jesula, and her boyfriend, Chaos, might be in on it. Maybe, even Bullet. I don't know but I do know that Chasity was responsible for Bullet getting robbed and now he is with her. It's a fishy situation but all I know is I didn't have shit to do with it," I said. Bishop let out a deep breath.

"I fucked up, Desi," he admitted. He reached for my hand across the table and I snatched it away from him. Tears fell from my eyes.

"I love you too much to do something like that to you, Bishop. If I wanted to steal from you, I would've been done it. I liked you for a long time, I even went out of my way to please you. I wanted you to see that I was down for you. I changed my style and everything else that defined who I was, for you. I went through all of it to get you to notice me. Do you think I would've gone through that just to take something from you? I was feeling you before you were even selling bricks. Nigga, I was into you when you were just a street hustler and that was three years ago," I fussed. I stood up from the table then grabbed my purse.

"I'm done chasing you. How you reacted was all the evidence I needed. You never gave me a chance. You told me you were over my past but you weren't. Every time something happens to you, I will not be blamed. You can kiss my ass," I said to him.

"Can we just talk about it? I know I fucked up and I'm trying to apologize," he said.

"Because you know now that I didn't do it. But while you were choking me and threatening to kill me, I was trying to tell you that I didn't do it! You didn't give a fuck about me! All of my life I had no one; I had no friends, family, nobody! I thought I had you," I said. He tried to reach for me but I smacked his hand away.

"Don't touch me, Bishop," I spat.

"Okay, I won't touch you. But can you just listen to me for a second?" he asked.

"No, I can't. Good-bye, Bishop. My job here is done," I said before I stormed out of the house. Bishop followed me to my car. He pulled me back from getting into the car. I slapped him in the face as hard as I could.

"Leave me the fuck alone!" I screamed.

"I deserved that," he said as he backed away from me.

"I owed you that," I replied. I started up my car and pulled off. I left him in the middle of the street. I called the owner of the house and told him I was moving out and the furniture could stay. I was done with all of it.

****

Thirty minutes later...

I stopped over Ree-Ree's house and knocked on her door. Jada opened it.

"I need to talk to Ree-Ree. It's urgent," I said to him.

"Ree-Ree, Desi out here and she needs to holla at you," Jada called out to her. I stepped inside and a cute little dog ran to me. I picked it up and her collar had the name "Bella" written inside of a pink dog bone charm.

"I need one of these," I said as I held the dog.

"You can have her if you want. I think I'm allergic to her," Ree-Ree said when she came into the living room. Jada kissed Ree-Ree's cheek.

"I'll get up with you later," he said to her before left her apartment. Ree-Ree's home was nice and spacious and very neat. Her apartment had an eccentric vibe. Ree-Ree sat down on the couch across from me. Bella went to sleep on my lap.

"How much do you want for her?" I asked Ree-Ree.

"No price, but what brings you here? You and I really don't see eye to eye," she said.

"That's understandable being as though Chasity is your best friend more so like your mama. Chasity controls your life, almost like a little puppet," I said.

"She was your friend, too," Ree-Ree spat.

"She was a bitch I made money with. I didn't come here on a friendly visit. I came here because I need your help," I said.

"Why would I help you?" she asked me.

"Why wouldn't you? You hate Chasity as much as I do, if not more. You are just scared of her and continue to stick to her," I replied.

"I don't hate her. Now, can you leave?" she asked.

"Have you ever wondered why you slipped that day and got that brain injury? It doesn't cross your mind that it happened after you refused to go to a party with Chasity? Well, I know all about it. Chasity likes to run her mouth when she drinks and one night at a party a while back, she told the strippers how she put baby oil on the bottom of your shoe and it made you fall. I thought she was just talking shit because I wasn't aware of your accident until Bishop recently told me what happened to you. I didn't think Chasity was that conniving until she set me up and made it look like I stole from Bishop. I know I was screwing Bullet behind her back and I will admit to that. But the shit she done to us was wrong," I said. Ree-Ree wiped the tears from her eyes.

"Chasity would never do that," Ree-Ree said.

"Stop being a dumb bitch, Ree-Ree, and just listen to me. That bitch is not your friend! What fucking part don't you understand? The only person you need to look out for is yourself. You know what she is capable of; I'm also sure you know about some of the foul things she did to me. So, if she would do that to me, what makes you think you are special?" I asked Ree-Ree as she sobbed.

"A few years ago, Chasity was very drunk and talking out of her head. She was crying her eyes out and all she kept telling me was that she was sorry. I asked her what she meant but she never told me. I knew she had done something bad but not that," Ree-Ree said.

"I need your help," I said to Ree-Ree.

"I don't trust you, Desi," Ree-Ree said.

"Good, you are not supposed to. I didn't come here to be all buddy-buddy with you. I came because I need you to do something for me," I said.

"I'm not helping you with nothing," Ree-Ree spat.

"Okay, cool. But you do know this dog has been missing for quite some time, right? Matter of fact, isn't this the dog that was stolen

from Ashanta's house? Yet this dog is at your home. And you know
Chasity was going to blame it on you if it ever came back to her. Why do
you think she gave the dog to you? Why not just let it roam the streets?
She doesn't like animals. Let me guess, her excuse was Bullet might pop
up at her house? My God Ree-Ree, you are just a pawn, honey. The
bitch even knew you wasn't smart enough to take the dog's collar off.
She wanted them to know that you had Ashanta's dog. So, enough of
the bullshit. Are you helping me or not?" I asked Ree-Ree.

"What do you want me to do?" Ree-Ree asked.
"I want you to get her bank information. The next time you
are around her, I want you to take pictures of her credit cards and
everything else. Send the pictures to me. That's all I want. That bitch is
fittin' to pay us for our pain and suffering," I said.

****

The next day…
I laid in bed and thought about Bishop. He kept calling me but I
ignored his calls. I answered the phone after what seemed like the
hundredth time.

"What do you want?" I spat when I answered the phone.
"Open up the door, Desi. You got the locks changed on me?"
Bishop asked me.

"Nigga, why wouldn't I when you threatened to kill my black ass?"
I asked him.

"Shorty, just open up the door. I'm dirty, Desi," he said. I rolled my eyes then went to my door. I opened the door and Bishop walked in wearing all-black.

"What happened?" I asked him.

"I was ready to merk Damos at Chasity's house. As soon as I pulled up on that nigga, a police car cut me off then he got inside of it. I think the cop was his father but after they drove off, I broke into Chasity's house. That nigga had my shit in a duffel bag inside of the closet in the little boy's room. Out of all my life in the streets, I've never seen a nigga take someone's shit then take it back to where they lay their head at," Bishop said.

"Bullet isn't smart, that's why," I said. I walked into the kitchen.

"I'm putting a price on Chasity's head, too," he said. I spit my drink out.

"I don't want that bitch to die right now," I said.

"What do you have going on?" he asked.

"Something that you don't need to know about. Now, leave whatever you got to leave then get out," I said to him. He pulled a gun from out of his pants and hid it on top of my cabinets in the kitchen. I held my hand out and he looked at me.

"What is your hand out for?" he asked.

"Nigga, you want me to hold your gun, cool. But you will pay me. Don't worry, I'm cheaper than the bail and the lawyer you will have to pay if you get caught with it," I said.

9

"So, we are seriously like that?" he asked.

"You did this to us, Bishop. Sorry, I'm not one of those weak bitches that niggas are used to these days. I don't mind helping out but I would like to see my money first," I replied. He went into his pocket and peeled off a few hundreds from the stack he had in his hand. I snatched it away from him and started counting it.

"Okay, see you later," I said. He shook his head.

"I don't know what to do," he said defeated.

"Start with getting out and everything else will come to you," I said. Although I told him I wasn't weak for him, the truth is, I was still weak for Bishop. I still wanted him to hold me and kiss me with so much passion like he used to. The way he used to grip my neck as his tongue explored my mouth and the way his hands gripped my ass when he sexed me, stayed on my mind. I knew I was going to go back but I also knew it was too soon. I wanted him to fight for me as I would do for him. I wanted him to confess his feelings as much as I confessed mine.

"What if I don't want to leave? Damn, Desi. We been sleeping together every night for the past month," he fussed.

"And? We ain't in a relationship," I said and he bit his bottom lip.

"We ain't single, neither!" he yelled at me. I crossed my arms as I frowned my nose up.

"What would've happened if I didn't find your product in two days and be honest with me?"

"Honestly, I don't know, but I do know if I didn't care about you, I would've killed you already. I'm not shit for that, Desi. I know what I did was a fuck-nigga move but you got to understand my mind set. I'm a street nigga. I'm fucking with a woman who used to scheme niggas. You used to scheme niggas just like me. I know you changed a lot of your ways but, shorty, street niggas don't give a fuck about that. If someone takes from us, survival mode kicks in. Niggas out here got to feed their families. I honestly wasn't thinking of us when I saw that my drugs were missing. I didn't look at you as the woman I fell for, I looked at you as if you were a nigga on the street that robbed me. I was immature on that part, though. I went into survival mode before hearing you out. I'm sorry, Desi," he said.

"Get out, Bishop," I said as tears fell from my eyes. He wiped them away before he kissed my lips.

"I can't walk away," he said.
"But you were willing to attend my funeral?" I asked.

"Let me leave because now you are talking stupid," he said. He headed toward the door until he heard my cell phone ring. He grabbed my phone off the counter.

"What in the hell is your problem?" I asked him. I snatched my phone back.

"You hoeing again?" he asked me.

God, please send this nigga some sense, I thought.
"None of your business," I said.

11

"You got niggas coming here, shorty?" he asked with a vein popping out of his neck. Bishop was low-key crazy. I heard stories about how men could be very possessive but I never had to deal with it until I met Bishop. I was just used to saying "Fuck me and pay me." With Bishop, it was a whole other ball game. I was getting a taste of it all: the emotions, the tears, heartache, and everything else that happens in a relationship.

"My business once again," I said. He slammed the door after he left out of my condo, so hard that it put a crack in the wall above the door. My door was hanging off the hinge.

"Oh hell nawl! Muthafucka! You broke my damn door!" I yelled down the hall but he kept walking. Bella ran out to me from my bedroom. I picked her up, and as much I didn't want to give her back, I knew I had to.

Chasity

I was in the hospital for three days before I went home. I had bruised ribs, a sprained ankle, and a tooth at the bottom of my mouth was missing. My face was still bruised up. When Bullet picked me up from the hospital, he was quiet. I knew something was bothering him.

"What's the matter with you?" I asked Bullet.

"Someone stole the drugs from the house. I was only gone for an hour and when I came back home, it was gone. We are fucked," he said.

"Damn it, Bullet! How in the hell you steal someone's drugs and then it gets stolen back from you?" I asked him. We pulled up to a small house in the country.

"What in the hell is this?" I asked.

"My father hooked us up with a spot. Bishop knows we took his shit, Chasity. I don't know how he knows, but I'm sure he was the one who took it. We are fucked!" Bullet yelled as he banged on the steering wheel.

That stupid bitch, Desi, is always scheming, I thought.

"Well, he took it from you first. He was the one who started it and all you did was take your shit back. I don't know why we are hiding," I said to Bullet.

"Bishop will shoot us, Chasity! It doesn't matter if he took it from me or not. I'm starting to think he wasn't the one who stole from me. It doesn't make sense now that I think about it. Bishop spends one hundred and fifty thousand dollars when he re-ups. That nigga is getting money, Chasity. I don't understand why he would rob me and not someone like Kwenya, a nigga that got more money than all of us," Bullet fussed as I rolled my eyes.

I got on the phone and dialed Ree-Ree. I wanted to know if the hood was saying that Bullet stole from Bishop. I probably shouldn't have called Desi to rub it in but I couldn't help it even if I incriminated myself.

"Hellooooo," Ree-Ree answered the phone.
"What's going on? I'm out of the hospital," I said.
"Ohhhh, that's wonderful. I can't wait to see you," Ree-Ree said.

You need to stop playing and let me taste it, I thought. I wanted to taste Ree-Ree. I don't know what it was about her but I had these weird feelings for her.

"Can you come and spend some time with me tomorrow?" I asked her.

"Sure, do you need anything?" she asked. She was so thoughtful and, at times, I wished Bullet was as attentive as Ree-Ree was with me.

"Nope and I will send you the address," I said. Bullet was mumbling under his breath. When I got off the phone, I grilled him.

"What is wrong with you?" I asked.
"Nobody is supposed to know where we are," he spat.
"It's Ree-Ree. Do you think she will tell someone? She is my best friend," I said. I called my mother to see what Marquis was doing.

"Hey, Ma. Where is Marquis?" I asked her.

"With his father," she said.

"Bullet is right here," I replied.

"His real damn father! I'm tired of you bringing Marquis over here to avoid spending time with him! Why do you want someone like Bullet to be his father? Bullet isn't a real man! Remember how he did Marquis when you and him broke up? He didn't want any parts of him. I looked up Deron's number to his office and called him. Marquis's life is not a game! You are so busy being a whore that you don't know how to be a mother! I wash my hands of you! I know what you did to Deron and that was low, Chasity. I know I wasn't there for you when you were younger, but we were poor. I had to work three jobs to make sure we had everything. I had too much pride to show my body and screw different men! I'd rather get on my hands and knees to scrub floors than become a prostitute. I hope Deron takes Marquis away from you and Bullet," my mother yelled into the phone.

"Fuck you, *madre!* Fuck you! I swear I will spit in your face if I see you again. You gave my son to a stranger!" I cried.

"Well, that's what happens when you trap strangers. You reap what you sow. I will pray for you because you are so lost that you will never be normal again. You are a manipulator and the day you spit in my face will be the day I spit on your grave!" she said in her accent. I was ready to curse her out but she hung up on me.

"THAT BITCH!" I yelled.

****

The next day…

I wasn't supposed to be driving but I did anyway. I drove straight to Deron's office. As soon as I walked in, I limped straight to the back. I opened up the door to his office and he was on the phone. When he saw me, he hung up the phone.

"Get the hell out!" he yelled at me.

"Where is my son?" I asked him.

"With my mother. He is getting to know his other family. I'm not having this baby mama drama with you. I'm telling you straight up, so if I was you, I would leave," he spat.

"You can go to jail for kidnapping!" I yelled at him.

"Bitch, I don't care about your threats. Now, get the fuck out of my office," he said to me.

"You are just mad that your wife is in jail. She isn't getting out no time soon because of what she did to me," I laughed.

"His wife is right here," a voice said. When I turned around, my face dropped. I heard that Serene's bail was denied because of the damage she had done to me.

"You just don't learn, do you?" Serene asked me.

"This has nothing to do with you," I said.

"As long as my last name is Swain, it has everything to do with me," Serene spat. She grilled Deron when she dropped a duffel bag on the floor.

"What is that?" he asked her.

"More of your clothes. Perhaps, you can move in with your ghetto-ass baby mama," Serene said.

"Seriously, Serene? We are going through with this?" he asked her. She slammed some papers on his desk.

"I would like for those divorce papers to be signed as soon as possible. I'm not cut out for this. This nasty bitch keeps popping up at your job. She is going to drag you down and I refuse to go down with you. I'm glad I decided to come in today to give you your things. I needed a little wake-up call. The rest of your clothes are in the truck. You can either get them now or your baby mama can take them to her trap house with her," Serene said. I wanted to curse her out but I wasn't in any shape to do so. My body still ached from when she attacked me.

"Damn it, Serene! Please don't do this to me right now!" he yelled at her.

"The stress is not good for the baby, Deron," Serene said sadly. I smirked on the inside; that's probably how she didn't stay locked up long. They must have found out she was pregnant when they booked her.

"High-risk pregnancy it sounds like," I laughed. I knew she wasn't going to do anything to me at that point. I sat down at his desk.

"Missing-tooth bitch," Serene said.

"Your husband can afford to get it fix. Why can't you and I get along? Hopefully, we'll have the same baby father," I said. Serene looked at me and smirked.

"Hopefully, because you are going to be dead," Serene said.

"Bitch, don't say nothing else!" Deron yelled at me and it caused me to jump. It looked like he was going to hit me if I did.

"You are pregnant and you want a divorce? You want us to raise our baby in separate households? Why are you doing this? This bitch trapped me," Deron said.

"Ummmmm, you and I were talking about hooking up. You were drunk, but before you got drunk, you wanted it. So, tell the whole story," I spat.

"I can't do this," Serene said. When she left the office, Deron chased after her. Minutes later, he came back in with three big duffle bags. He sat them on the floor before he sat at his desk. He loosened his tie and took off his lab coat.

"I want my son, Deron," I said.

"He will be at your mother's house tomorrow, now get the fuck out!" he gritted with murder in his eyes. His eyes were bloodshot red and his face no longer looked the same. I didn't like how he was looking at me, so I grabbed my purse and left.

****

"It's spooky back here," Ree-Ree said when she walked into our house. Bullet was on the couch watching TV. He was drinking a beer and burping. Bullet was making my ass itch. He didn't have any money and he was banned from the streets. I had money in my account but I told him I was broke and that I had to pay lawyer fees for the custody battle Deron and I were going through.

"Yes, it is. I keep telling Bullet that but he likes being away from the city. It's quiet back here, though," I said. I sat on the rundown couch. I missed my leather furniture and I couldn't wait to go back home. I just had to heal first because my house had a lot of stairs and the ranch-style home we were in was convenient for me.

"Can you go inside my purse and get me my pain pills? My side is killing me," I said to Ree-Ree. I wasn't going to ask Bullet because he never got up when he watched TV.

"Sure, where is it?" she asked.
"It's on the kitchen counter," I said.

I need to figure out something quick because I'm not living like this forever. Bullet can run and hide if he wants to, but I'm not going to. I didn't do nothing; he is the one who stole it. I'm going to pump Ree-Ree's head up so she can go back and tell her cousin, Bishop. I want my name to be clear before I go back home, I thought.

My phone rang and it was Jesula.

Fuck, I don't have the money to give her since Bullet lost the drugs. I'm screwed, I thought to myself.

Kwenya

One week later…

I walked out of jail and Rakita was waiting for me. Ashanta disappeared on me again and I was stressing. All kinds of thoughts ran through my head as I thought about what happened to her. I called her the same day she visited me before I went to my cell. Her phone was disconnected and I had Yolo and Jada both looking for her. What messed my head up was when her mother came to visit me and told me that Ashanta was gone and even accused me of her disappearance. I almost lost my mind and the only good that came out of the situation was my freedom. The police made a mistake on my search warrant. They spelled my name wrong and the address was wrong, too. Poet was still baking, they released her the same day they ransacked my shop. My aunt, Lolita, was running that location. I still had a court date because they were still trying to pin those two bricks on me, but I wasn't going down for that. I'd rather serve a sentence for killing Bernie and Bullet before I pled guilty to a drug charge that wasn't mine. I wasn't thinking about my court date, though, because I needed to figure out where Ashanta was with my seed.

"What's the sad look for? Baby, you are free," Rakita said to me when I got inside her car. I leaned my seat back and rubbed my temples.

"We need to talk, Kita," I said as she buckled her seat belt.

"What is it now? Every time you use that tone nothing good comes out of it," she replied.

"I got a baby on the way by Ashanta and she and I are trying to work it out," I said. She reached into her backseat and grabbed a newspaper.

"What's this?" I asked.

"Just read it," she said. My heart almost stopped when I read the article...

Ashanta Bennett, 27 has reportedly been missing for a week. A man was out on his boat and notified the police last night around midnight after he saw a silver Lexus floating in the river. According to investigators, the car was driven off a cliff. There were also a few empty alcohol containers found on the cliff. The rescue team is still searching the water for her body. Benjamin Scott, a well-known doctor who is also Ashanta's father spoke out this morning and these are his words...

"My daughter has always been a responsible woman. She would never drink and drive. I don't believe this was a freak accident. I believe there was foul play and I want the person who is responsible brought to justice. I will not rest until I find out what happened to my daughter!"

Rakita grabbed my hand and I snatched away from her.

"Don't fucking touch me!" I yelled at her.

"Baby, I'm here for you. I'm so sorry this happened to her," she said.

"She was carrying my baby, Kita. Take me to my mother's house. I don't want to hear shit else, just take me there," I said to her.

The drive to my mother's house was a silent one. I had seen many deaths and attended many funerals but I was not accepting what happened to Ashanta—I couldn't accept it. When Rakita pulled up to my mother's house, I got out of her car.

"Thanks. I will call you later," I said. Rakita was saying something but I ignored her as I walked up the stairs to my mother's house. I knocked on the door and moments later she opened it.

"Thank God you are home!" my mother yelled when she hugged me. Afterward, I walked into her living room. The smell of fried fish filled her house. As much as I was missing eating home-cooked meals, I didn't have an appetite. I sat down on the couch then pulled out the sonogram picture Ashanta gave to me.

"What's the matter, baby?" she asked me. Tears burned the brim of my eyes and one managed to escape. My mother took the picture from me.

"You are going to be a father. You are not the only man that feels this way about becoming a father. When I told your father I was pregnant with you, he cried like a baby," she said but I said nothing.

"I need to talk to you about something, Kwenya. Bernie would never set you up like that. I know now is not the time but I need to clear the air before he and I get married. What if it was one of your friends? You are in the streets, so it could've been anybody. Can you please just leave the streets alone? You are about to become a father, so it's time to grow up," she said to me.

"What happened to you, Ma? I mean what really happened to you? You are so weak for that nigga. I'm starting to believe you knew what was up. I'm starting to believe you are against me, too. What the fuck is wrong with you? I come here for peace and you tell me that bullshit? Do I look like I want to talk about that nigga?" I asked as I stood up.

"You don't respect me," she said.

"You don't respect yourself! You are letting a nigga turn you away from your only son, Ma. How do you think I feel? I'm hurt, Ma. But it's all good, though, because I don't give a fuck what happens. You and that nigga can be together but you ain't got to worry about me and I mean that shit. My own mother, though. My shorty is dead! Do you hear me? She is dead! Floating somewhere in a river while carrying my seed! I don't give a fuck about that nigga!" I yelled at her.

"I'm sorry I didn't know," she said sadly. On any other day, I would've felt bad for talking to my mother like that but she needed to hear the truth. Bernie was using her and she was letting him.

"Even if you didn't know, you still shouldn't have brought his name up knowing he is the real reason that I might have to do twenty-five years. I'm out!" I said. I walked out of her house. Not only did I lose Ashanta but I lost my mother, too.

****

Two days later...

"You got to eat something," Rakita said to me as I laid across her couch. Yolo, Jada, and even Bishop, tried calling me but I didn't feel like talking. I had people hitting me up wanting some work but I didn't have the mindset to mess with it. I had bricks put away but I couldn't touch it. I didn't know who was watching me.

"I'm good, Kita," I said as I flipped through the channels.

"You are going to get sick," she said. I took the plate from her and sat it down on the table. My new home wasn't going to be finished for another few weeks. When I found out who Damos's father was, I bought a six-bedroom gated house a few hours away from the city. I should've been moved out of the city since I was doing dirty work. I didn't like some of the appliances or the floors when I purchased the house, so I wanted everything inside to be renovated before I moved in.

"I apologize for the other day. You did a lot for me when I was locked up as far as handling things with my lawyer. I appreciate it," I said. She kissed my lips.

"I love you and I will do anything for you. Just let me be here for you," she said. She reached for my dick but I slapped her hand away.

"I'm not in the mood for that," I said right before the doorbell rang. When Rakita opened the door, Jada and Yolo walked in.

"Speak when you come into a person's home," Rakita said to Yolo. Jada tolerated Rakita but Yolo hated her.

"I did speak, you just didn't hear me," Yolo said.

"I didn't hear you say nothing," Rakita spat.

"You wasn't supposed to hear it," Yolo said as Jada chuckled. Jada sat across from me and I knew he wasn't feeling me not answering him and Yolo's calls. We'd been friends since third grade. We went to every school together except for college.

"You come home and don't bother with nobody, huh? Damn, nigga, you do us like that?" Jada asked.

"I have a lot of shit on my mind," I said as I sat up.

"And that's why you should've hit us up or picked up the phone," Yolo said.

"Ashanta is dead. My mother is tripping on me and a nigga got drug charges. I'm not in the mood to talk to nobody," I replied.

"He doesn't want to talk to y'all," Rakita said.

"Go in the room, Kita, so I can holla at my niggas," I said to her. She put her hands on her hips and rolled her eyes.

"I'm not going nowhere," she said.

"Okay then I will leave," I responded.

"Let me know when they leave," she said before she walked down the hall. She slammed the bedroom door and the pictures on the wall shook.

"Yo, you could've crashed at my crib," Yolo said.

"I'm not homeless, nigga," I said.

"How do you know Ashanta is dead? Bishop showed me the newspaper but they didn't find her body," Jada said.

"She drove off a cliff. Ashanta can't swim. She drowned and I know she did. I'm not going to pretend that she is out there alive. I'm not trying to be in denial. There's just something off about it. The newspaper said that she was drinking and driving but Ashanta was pregnant and I know shorty. She ain't the type to do something like that. I think that nigga Bullet had something to do with it," I said.

"That nigga been MIA because Bishop is looking for him. That nigga stole bricks from Bishop and Bishop got it right back. Bullet is hiding somewhere," Yolo said.

"Bullet has to go, but with his father being a cop, we have to think. Bernie is a dirty cop, so he has to go before Bullet does. Bernie is Bullet's shield," I said.

"You kill a cop and everything shuts down. They start riding through the hoods, locking niggas up for no reason and everything else," Yolo said.

"I know and it might take a while, but I got something for that nigga," I said. At first I didn't care if Bullet made it or not, I wasn't thinking about that nigga until Ashanta told me he raped her.

"Tell us what you want us to do," Yolo said.
"Can the two of you move sixty bricks in two months? I don't want y'all faces to be seen, though. I don't want anything to be tied to us. You got to move how I move but better," I said.

"We can't make no promises but we can try. Nigga, that's a lot," Jada said.

"Put Bishop on, that little nigga move work quick," I said.

"Yeah, that's because Desi was helping him but she ain't fucking with that nigga anymore. She was breaking it down for him and even had other niggas pushing it for him. They have a whole squad," Yolo said.

"Mannnn, women don't know how to hustle," Jada said.

"A smart woman can hustle better than a man if she puts her mind to it. A woman is always the least to be expected," I said.

Jada stood up. "I will holla at you later. Be easy, and if you need anything, let us know. Sorry about your shorty," Jada said. After Yolo and Jada gave me dap, they left. I got up and walked down the hall to Rakita's bedroom. Rakita was lying on her side watching TV as she ate sunflower seeds with vinegar.

"You still eat those?" I asked her as she sat up.

"Yeah, when I'm stressed," she answered. I sat down on her bed.

"What are you stressed about?" I asked her.

"I'm catering to you while you mope around over another woman. A woman who you are in love with, a woman who was carrying your child. I just never thought that I was capable of doing something like that," she said.

"I'm not forcing you to do anything," I replied.

"What was so special about her? Why did you fall in love with her? I've known you for years and you never gave all of yourself to me. I always had to question if you loved me or not. When I was with you, I always had to wonder if I was ever good enough," she said.

"I fell in love with Ashanta because she was delicate. The way she talked, acted, and everything else about her flowed. Also, because when I was with her, I didn't think of nothing else. The streets, other women, and all of that other shit didn't come to mind. That's how I knew she had my full attention and that's what I needed. I wanted a shorty who could pull my mind from the streets and not push it into the streets," I said.

"Are you saying that I pushed you further into the streets?" she asked.

"I did love you, Rakita. I was with you before I had money. You were my first shorty but you got an abortion and didn't tell me until we got into an argument. Then, when you went away to college, you just changed. I don't know what it is but you just ain't the same, Rakita," I said. She put her head down.

"What if we can start all over?" she asked. I kissed her forehead before I stood up.

"I'm going to go check into a hotel. I will hit you up later," I said. I left out of her apartment.

Ashanta

As I sat on the bus with a bandage on my face, I thought about everything that was happening. I was on my way to Mexico with a fake name. My new name was Nala Janae Richards. My age was still the same, but according to my birth certificate, I was from Africa. The sharp pain on my cheek burned and I knew that I needed medical attention but I couldn't do it until I got to Mexico. The bus driver got on the loud speaker to announce that he was coming close to our stop.

"Are you okay, ma'am?" a middle-aged Mexican man asked me in broken English.

"Yes, I'm fine," I said to him. I knew the scar on my face was going to be ugly. A part of me wanted to break down and cry, but I was done crying. I was done being the victim and I promised myself that I was going to go back. I knew I had to go back. Flashbacks of the night I drove my car off the cliff played in my head as I rode the bus. It all happened the night after I saw Rakita outside of the prison after I visited Kwenya...

"I cannot swim!" I said to Rakita. She and I stood on the cliff with my car still running. She held two empty bottles of alcohol in front of me.

"I don't want you to swim! I want you to drive your car off the cliff," she said. She gave me the two bottles.

"What is this for?" I asked her.

"For your DNA. If your DNA is not around the crime scene, it will not look believable," she said. I put my mouth on the bottles then hurriedly wiped my mouth off afterward. Rakita looked at me and smirked.

"Your uppity little ass doesn't like to get your mouth dirty, I see. I'm still trying to figure out why Kwenya loves you. You are so opposite of what he is attracted to," she said.

"You are, too. I'm smart enough to know that a drug dealer wouldn't fuck a cop," I spat. She shoved an envelope to me.

"Here is your new identity and a bus ticket to Mexico. I will make sure you get on the bus. Do you hear me?" she asked. She went to my car wearing a pair of gloves. She took it out of park and my car slowly drifted until it went crashing down the cliff. I heard a loud splash in the water. I picked up my duffel bags before I got inside of Rakita's car.

"That wasn't so hard. You need to look happy. This is better than jail," she said.

"You do know secrets come out eventually, don't you?" I asked her.

"Bitch, I don't care what comes out! As long as your ass is gone!" she yelled at me.

"Desperate bitch!" I yelled back at her. Her fist came crashing into my face. I swung and hit her back. I wasn't much of a fighter but Damos was stronger than Rakita. If I could get Damos down, I knew I could do the same to her. I pulled Rakita's hair as I hit her again.

"Bitch, I will shoot you!" she screamed. As she and I were tussling inside her car, I felt something sting my face. I screamed out in pain. Rakita had a pocket knife on her keys.

"BITCH!" I yelled. I leaped onto her and her keys fell between the seat. She and I were going at it like wild animals. We ended up on the ground outside of her car. She sat on top of me and choked me.

"Bitch, I will kill you if you ever try that again. Now, get your ass in that car and don't you say shit!" she said.

"My baby! My baby!" I mustered out. She got off of me and pulled me up. She pushed me into her car then handcuffed me.

"The only reason I didn't kill you is because my DNA is under your fingernails," she said. My face burned as I felt blood drip onto my shirt. Rakita took me to the bus station. She un-cuffed me before I got out. I wanted to attack her but I thought about my unborn child. I hurriedly grabbed my bags and got out of her car. I went into the bathroom to clean up before I got on the bus. I tended to my wound the best way I could but there was a nasty gash across my left cheek…

The bus came to a stop. I grabbed my bags before I got off. I'd been to Mexico plenty of times with my family while on vacation. I knew where I wanted to go and that was the Four Seasons Resort in Punta Mita. In one duffel bag was my clothes and in my other duffel bag was my money. I had all of my cash on me from all of my accounts. I didn't feel comfortable traveling with a lot of money and knew I had to do something quick. I wanted to call my parents and Serene but I knew that I couldn't.

****

I sat outside of the hotel eating breakfast as I thought about what happened the week prior. I could barely chew because of my cheek but I knew I had to eat.

"Excuse me, can I sit here? I got down here late and now I have no place to sit," a woman said to me. When I looked up, it was a black woman. She was very pretty and her peanut butter skin was flawless. Her long hair was pulled up into a ponytail and she wore a two-piece bathing suit with a cover-up over it.

"Yes," I said as I chewed my watermelon. She sat down and looked at me.

"It's beautiful out here," she said.
"Very," I answered dryly.
"My name is Jesse," she said.
"Nala," I said using my fake name. When I tried to chew the bigger piece of watermelon, I winced. I had to spit it out onto a napkin.

"Is it your face?" she asked.
"Yes. Glass flew into my face," I answered.
"Do you want my nurse to look at it for you?" she asked me.
"No, thank you," I answered.
"I think you should get someone to look at that. You don't want an infection while pregnant, do you?" she asked me.

"How do you know?" I asked. My eyes followed hers as she looked at my prenatal vitamins that sat on the table by my orange juice.

"Where is your nurse?" I asked her.

"At my home, of course. She works for me on my estate. Trust me, you will be well taken care of," she said.

"I don't know you like that. I'm fine right here. I don't go to stranger's houses," I said and she laughed.

"Okay, but you will regret it. So, tell Ms. Nala, what brings you here to Mexico? You are sitting here alone, pregnant, with a wound on your face," she said.

"I'm on vacation, now do you mind? I would like to sit in peace," I said. My attitude was slowly changing and, although I didn't want to sound mean, I couldn't help it. If anyone would've had taken a walk in my shoes, I'm sure they would've been the same way.

"Has anyone ever told you that your eyes are like windows to your life?" she asked me. I dropped my fork as I thought about Kwenya because he always told me that.

"I have been told," I said.

"You are running from something. I did that before. I ran from everything until one day I got tired. I stopped running and fought back. My ex-husband used to beat me. He beat me so bad one day that I couldn't have kids after that. I mean he beat me to the point I needed plastic surgery. I got revenge and I have been standing tall ever since," she said.

"Sorry to hear that. I'm glad to see that you are not in that situation anymore," I said.

"I'm going home today. You should come and get help. I don't take well to strangers, Nala. I have not talked to a stranger in a long time," she said.

"I don't trust people and neither should you. I could be a killer and yet you invite me to your house. What's the catch?" I asked her.

"I have people around me everywhere I go. Trust me, darling, I'm not afraid of inviting you but something tells me that you are not capable of such a thing. Your bark is louder than your bite. Your attitude comes from pain, so today, I will let it pass but tomorrow, you will respect me. You will grab your things after this breakfast and meet me down at my limo. I will have two of my men escort you downstairs and don't worry about your room. I will have it put on my tab," she said. I looked at her as if she was crazy and her eyes were menacing. I went into my hotel room and laid on the bed. I wasn't going with a stranger. Her persona was off and she somewhat creeped me out.

Two days later…

I walked into the lobby with my bags and the woman, Jesse, was inside the hotel's lobby talking to the man at the front desk. I was treating my wound the best way I could but puss started to build up inside my face. I needed real medical attention and I didn't have the supplies. The cleanest hospital was more than eight hours away. I didn't want to go to the scum hospitals nearby. The bus was arriving in an hour and I had to prepare myself for a long ride to the hospital.

"I was looking for you," Jesse said as she headed toward me. I rolled my eyes at her but I couldn't help but notice her attire. She wore a white linen jumper with tan wedge heels. Her hair was flat-ironed straight down with bangs. Her make-up was flawless and I couldn't help but to eye her black Chanel purse. She resembled the actress Regina Hall. Jesse was a well put-together woman but she seemed scary.

"Why?" I asked her.

"I think you need help. Are you about to get on the bus? I wouldn't get on a bus in Mexico. A lot of these buses have men and women that come from different drug cartels. You should read the news here because there is always drugs on those buses and people will do anything to survive. Many buses get hijacked with people on them because of the drugs," she said.

I don't want to be a part of that! I shouted inside my head.

"I will find a way," I replied. I walked away and headed for the door. She followed me.

"I have a private nurse that can help you. I run a lucrative business and I don't want a bad name for myself by doing something to a pregnant woman. My limo is right there and you can take a picture of the tag and give it to the front desk. Your wound is infected," she said.

"Okay, fine," I replied. She waved a few men over and they came to get my things. I held onto my money bag. I followed Jesse to the stretch white Rolls Royce limo.

****

I sat in the backseat of Jesse's limo as she rambled off on her phone in Spanish. The two men that sat across from us were armed. I

saw the mafia in movies and always thought they were exaggerated.
Truth is, we don't believe in things we don't see but that doesn't mean
they don't exist.

"My maid is getting your room ready, and don't worry, the
room is the size of an apartment," she said. I sat quietly as I stared out
of the window. We rode through the slums of Mexico on our way to her
estate. An hour later, we pulled up to her estate and my mouth dropped.
Her house was beautiful and she had a waterfall in the middle of the
circular driveway. She had gardeners planting flowers in front of her
house. When I stepped out of the car, I just stood and looked at her
land.

Her husband was probably a very wealthy man, I thought to myself.

"Nala, come. We can watch later but the nurse is waiting for you
in your suite," she said. When I walked inside of her house, it was like a
museum.

She is wealthy like Oprah Winfrey, I thought to myself. I slowly
followed her as I looked around. She pressed a button on the wall and
the elevator opened. I stepped on with her and it went up to the fourth
floor. When she and I stepped off, there was a suite. She was right, it
was bigger than an apartment. It had a kitchen and everything else inside
of it.

"This is so beautiful," I said.
"Thank you. Someone dear to me stays inside this room when
visiting. The nurse will be with you shortly, so make yourself at home,"
she said.

"Why are you being this kind? Are you looking for something in return?" I asked her.

"I find myself very concerned for your baby. I was in your shoes at one point and, like I said before, I even lost a few babies behind it. You don't have to trust me but if you want proper care in Mexico, this is best for you. Now, I will see you later," she said and exited the room.

I walked into the master bedroom and sat down on the bed.

I need you Kwenya, I said to myself.

Bishop

"Come on, baby, just put the tip in," Monie said to me. I smacked her hand away.

"Yo, chill out! If you can't cooperate then I'm leaving," I said to her. Monie was a broad that was taking over Desi's spot. I was feeling Desi and I didn't want her out in the streets, so I stopped her from packaging up my work. Monie wasn't bad but she wasn't about her money like Desi.

"Why are you acting brand new?" she asked.

"Shorty, you need to just get over it on the real. I'm not sticking nothing up in you," I said as I headed to her front door. Yolo and Jada said they needed to holla at me about something so I was on my way out to meet them.

"But you were banging Desi, though? You were banging a bitch that screwed every nigga in this city," Monie said. Monie was a sexy lil' broad. She was light-skinned and she stayed with a fresh weave on her head. The deep, wavy sandy brown hair came down above her apple bottom. She was twenty-two years old and a college student. She had a good head on her shoulders but she loved the hood life. I used to mess around with her back in the day but she started tripping on me about everything. She was cool as long as I kept my dick away from her.

"Why y'all females hatin' on shorty? So what she been around. She sexy, her pussy is bomb, and she is down for a nigga. She has all the qualifications y'all broads be lacking nowadays," I replied.

"I knew you liked hoes when you were fucking with Emani," Monie spat.

"I'm gone," I said. I left out of her apartment and headed to my crib before I met up with Yolo and Jada. Thirty minutes later, I was pulling up to my new four-level townhouse. It was semi empty because I was barely staying home. I was always at Desi's crib. I knew I had to push my pride to the side for Desi. She wasn't the type to take shit and be cool with it. I called her and she answered on the second ring.

"What, nigga?" she answered and I chuckled. Desi's attitude was the worst but I was used to it.

"Can I take you out?" I asked her. She turned the radio down before she answered.

"Take me out where? To kill my ass in the woods somewhere? Hell, nawl, Bishop. I'm not being alone with your scary ass anymore," she fussed.

"Stop being dramatic, damn."

"I will when you leave my ass alone, but as you must know, I'm ready to meet up with someone and your call is interrupting me," she spat. I bit the inside of my cheek to keep from exploding on her.

"You are on some bird shit, I see," I said. Desi started yelling and cursing me out. I sat the phone down as I got undressed for the shower. When she stopped, I picked the phone back up.

"You know I didn't hear shit you just said, right?" I asked.

"That's because you don't care," she spat.

"What time will you be home?" I asked her.

"When I leave the strip club," she spat.

"Oh yeah, you really showing off. Okay, do you. But if I walk into a strip club and see you shaking your ass, it's a rap after that," I said before I hung up. After I showered, I got dressed and headed out the door to meet up with my niggas. When I met up with Jada and Yolo at a low-key bar, we discussed business. I was going to be a part of their team. The bricks were going to be cheaper from doing so and I was down with that.

****

After I left the bar, I headed to my mother's house because she needed to talk to me about something. As soon as I pulled up in front of her house, I noticed a Ford Explorer. I got out of my truck and headed straight into the house. I heard laughing coming from the living room and I knew that laugh. It was Liana. She was the shorty I told Desi about when she asked me if I had ever been in love. Liana was the only female I caught feelings for in the past but she left me. I wasn't on the path she wanted me to be on. She ended up getting married and having twin boys by her husband. She messed my head up on that one because I found out the news the same day I found out my sister was dying. I been a hoe nigga since then but when I started messing with Desi I chilled out. When I was with Desi, I didn't have a chance to see other females like that. I had only been with one other female while me and Desi was kicking it but that was before I caught feelings for her.

"Look who came home," my mother said as she smiled happily at Liana. I wasn't too pleased to see her. I was busy on my grind and she just had to show up. Liana was cute in the face. She had pretty brown skin and big button eyes. Her butt was never big but she had sexy hips and a small waistline. She was also on the tall side at around five-foot-ten and weighed one hundred and seventy pounds. She always wore her hair hanging down her shoulders. She used to live with me, my mother, and my sister. Her parents kicked her out when they found out she was in love with a "thug". I knew she wanted to go to the military but I didn't think she would come back to break up with me for someone who was in the military, too.

"What's good with you?" I asked her. She stood up and hugged me.

"I missed you," she said. She kissed my face and I backed away from her. I eyed my mother as she smoked a cigarette.

"That's what's up. But what's going on?" I asked but she didn't respond.

"What's going on, Ma?" I asked my mother.

"Liana is coming back to stay with me for a while—her and the twin boys. They are upstairs asleep and you should see them. Her husband has a hand problem and I was worried that he might hurt her and the kids," she said. My mother was too nice and always had been.

She said she only looked out for women and small children. I knew no matter what I said my mother still wasn't going to see it from my point.

"Where are your parents?" I asked Liana.

"You know my parents are not the easiest people to get along with. You know this house is like my home," she said.

"So, that nigga kicking your ass, huh?" I asked her.

"BISHOP! Have some respect," my mother said. I went upstairs to my old bedroom. I opened the door and the two little boys were stretched out on the bed. They were only two years old. That was my first time seeing them because when my mother tried to show me pictures, I never looked at them. I still couldn't believe that bitch gave birth to another nigga's kids.

"I'm sorry, Bishop," a voice said from behind me. When I turned around, Liana was staring into my face.

"It's too late for that shit, shorty. You do realize that this shit is a smack in the face. The first time you left, you came back engaged and months after that you were giving birth. Now, you want to come back? Why bring this shit to my mother's house? You ain't no kin to her," I said.

"She is still like my mother. She was in my life for ten years. I knew if I ever needed advice, I could call her. This is not about you, Bishop, and regardless how you feel, I'm always going to be in the picture," she spat.

"Bitch, I—" I stopped when one of her sons woke up. He got down off the bed and walked to his mother as he rubbed his eyes.

"This is Kwan and the other one's name is Twan," she said and I just looked at her.

"What's up, Kwan?" I asked. I didn't have any kids and I had never been around them like that. I didn't know what to say so I kept it short.

"Hi," he waved. He hugged his mother around her neck. He looked exactly like Liana but I could tell by his hair and skin tone that his father was a different race.

"So, you got knocked up by a white nigga?" I asked her.

"Not now, Bishop," she said.

"Yeah, you are right. Be safe," I said as I headed back down the stairs. She followed me.

"I noticed the truck you are driving and I can tell by the expensive jewelry you have on that you are still out there in the streets. Not too many people our age have that luxury so I already know what you are doing," she said.

"I guess your life is better, huh? Don't seem that way to me. Look where you are at, shorty. You are back where you started. Your dreams turned to nightmares but my nightmares will soon turn into dreams. I do what I want to do and how I want to do it. Now, go tend to your kids," I said before I walked out of the house.

46

****

Later on that night…

I met up with Yolo and Kwenya at the club. Kwenya wasn't himself but Yolo got on the nigga's nerves so bad that Kwenya agreed to come out. It was messed up about Ashanta, though, because shorty was a good person and I knew he was feeling her heavy. Kwenya drank the whole bottle of Henny as he rolled blunt after blunt in our VIP section.

"Slow down, my nigga," I said.

"This is grown man shit," Kwenya replied.

"Where is that nigga Bullet at? I can't wait to see that nigga, though. I got almost every nigga in the hood looking for that nigga," Kwenya said.

"Scared niggas hide but I want that nigga, too. Him and that bitch for touching my shit," I said.

Chasity's cousin, Jesula, and her boyfriend, Chaos walked through the crowd and passed our VIP section. They sat in the section next to ours.

"Them two are the ones that robbed Bullet and Ashanta," I said.

47

"Oh, word? They are up to something and I bet them niggas are trying to figure out how much we got in our pockets. I'm ready to leave," Kwenya said. He stood up and gave us dap before he walked out of the club.

"What is this nigga up to? He parked around back in the dark," Yolo said. The man that was with Jesula followed Kwenya outside. Yolo and I got up and followed him as he followed Kwenya. I pulled my gun out and so did Yolo. The bouncers at the club were shady; for a few hundred dollars they would let you slide through with your burner. The nigga that was following behind Kwenya pulled out his gun as he walked further into the darkness where Kwenya was parked. Yolo and I could no longer see much.

"This nigga parks in the weirdest places," Yolo whispered.

"To avoid club cameras," I replied. I heard a crashing sound then a grunt but we couldn't see nothing. The only light that shined through the dark alley was the infrared. I heard another sound and it sounded like someone fell. Yolo and I wanted to shoot but we had to be cautious because we didn't want to shoot each other.

Kwenya's truck started up and the headlights came on. Blood ran down the alley and that's when I noticed the nigga, Chaos stretched out with two bullets to his head. Kwenya had a silencer so nobody heard him kill Chaos, but I knew if we didn't get out quick someone would've spotted us.

"Yo, you merked a nigga outside of the club," Yolo said.

"That nigga was trying to rob me. What you thought?" he asked. I shook my head because I knew Kwenya knew what Chaos was up to and he lured that nigga right in. Chaos wasn't a smart nigga because he was being set up and didn't realize it. Yolo and I hopped in the backseat of Kwenya's Escalade before he pulled off. I knew there was about to be a lot of bloodshed because Kwenya was out for blood. I heard stories of him when he was young and wild but when he got older he chilled out. I guess that Ashanta situation triggered that part of him again.

******

Four days later…

I read the newspaper and the body that was found outside of the club was unidentified. The article stated that the body's DNA wasn't in any records and they had a reason to believe the person was an illegal immigrant. He was a John Doe and I knew the case was closed.

Where is Chaos from if he is an illegal immigrant?
I asked myself after I sat the newspaper down on the couch.

Kwenya's new operation worked out better than he thought. It hadn't been a week and we were moving work around the clock across the DMV. Jada had the D.C area, Yolo had the Baltimore area, and I had the Annapolis area. Those were the areas we were supplying and had to build a team within.

"Ma, you ready?" I called out to her. My mother hated driving although she owned a car. She always wanted me to take her to run errands. Desi was still giving me the cold shoulder so I decided to cool off on her.

"Wait a minute! I'm trying to check the lottery to see if I hit," she said. Moments later, she came into the living room with a cigarette in her hand. She didn't pick up that habit until after my sister died from AIDS.

"You want to move in with me?" I asked her.

"I like it here, Bishop," she said.

"But, Ma. This is the hood and it's time to leave it. I been trying for a year to get you out and you still refuse to," I replied. I wanted my mother to move into the crib that I moved Desi into but she changed her mind. With all the dirt Desi was doing in her old crib, I thought it was best for her to move in instead of leaving it empty.

"That's because I knew Liana was going to eventually come back and I knew you wasn't going to approve of her living someplace you paid for," she said.

"You knew for a minute?" I asked.

"Yes, she been going through a lot and been planning on leaving him. I just feel sorry for her," she replied. Liana came in the house with two grocery bags.

"Can you get the rest of the bags for me, Bishop?" Liana asked me.

"I told you Bishop was going to take me to the store," my mother fussed.

"So, I came over here for nothing?" I asked. My mother rolled her eyes at me. My mother was a petite woman in size and in height. She weighed around 110 pounds and she stood at five feet. I got my height from my father. I looked like my mother, same complexion, eyes, mouth, and nose. My father left after my sister died and we haven't heard from him since. I wasn't tripping, though, because that nigga didn't think I belonged to him so he treated me like a stepchild. Apparently, my mother stepped out on him but I looked just like that nigga.

"Aight," I replied. I went to her truck and grabbed the rest of the bags.

"Where are the boys?" my mother asked Liana when I walked back inside.

"With Ree-Ree. She called me and told me to bring them over her house for a little bit. I'm going to get them after I take my work clothes off," she replied. Every female I messed with was cool with Ree-Ree and they always kept her in something. Emani was only her friend to find out information on me but Ree-Ree and Liana were actually close before she left. Ree-Ree and I are first cousins; our mothers are sisters.

"Bishop, do you mind picking the twins up for me?" Liana asked.

"Shorty, do I look like their father to you? What in the hell is wrong with you? Don't ask me some fuck-nigga shit like that again," I said. My mother walked out of the kitchen and Liana grilled me.

51

"You don't want me here, do you? Is it because of a woman or something? Your mother told me that you weren't serious with nobody," she said. My mother still wanted me and Liana to work it out even after she cheated on me.

"I don't care what you do but don't ask me to help you with anything, and you better not be having my mother watching yo' kids, neither. My mother isn't a damn nanny," I said then she started crying.

"Damn it, Bishop! Stop patronizing me," she screamed. My phone rang and I answered it.

"When are you getting this shit out of my house?" Desi asked me talking about my gun. I walked out the kitchen so that Desi couldn't hear Liana, although it wasn't nothing serious but I knew Desi and shorty wasn't wrapped too tight.

"Is it bothering you?" I asked her.

"Yes, it is. Now, how long are you going to be?" she asked me.

"Bishop, I know you didn't just walk away from me," Liana yelled at me. I wanted to slap the hell out of her.

"You sure move fast, don't you? It's only been two weeks and you are already messing around on me?" she asked.

"So now we in a relationship again?" I asked Desi.

"Nigga, I don't give a damn if I tell you that I don't want to talk to you for a year! You are not allowed to do what the hell you want to do! Is it that bitch, Monie?" Desi started yelling into the phone.

"I'm on my way over there," I said. Liana was asking me something but I walked out of her face and out of the house.

****

When I walked into Desi's crib, she was lying on the couch, smoking a blunt with a glass of wine in her hand. She was only wearing a bra and a thong with a scarf wrapped around her head. Her body was covered in pretty, colorful ink and it made her chocolate smooth skin look even better. Desi was gorgeous and I wasn't saying that because I loved her—she was really gorgeous. Her lips were nice and full and her eyes were round, but they slanted in the corners. Her cheekbones reminded me of an Indian's and her teeth were straight and white.

"So, who was that in the background?" she asked me.
"A friend of the family," I replied. I sat down on the couch and put her leg across my lap. I rubbed her leg and squeezed her feet. My hand slid up between her legs until I got to her red lace thong. Desi smacked my hand away.

"Who was that bitch?" she asked me.

"Shorty, I just told you. Damn, why are you bugging and you know you wanted me to come over just so I can touch you. You know

53

my gun doesn't bother you. Why do you have this on?" I asked before I leaned forward to kiss her and she slightly moaned. Desi's body was used to sex and she couldn't go long without it. She and I were fucking two to three times a day. I took the wine glass from her and sat it down on the table. I laid her blunt in the ashtray.

"What are you doing?" she asked as she crossed her arms. I slid her thong to the side then slipped my finger inside her. I leaned forward and kissed her again and this time she accepted me. Desi was dripping on my fingers and my dick was straining to bust out of my shorts.

"Can I have it?" I asked as I slowly slid her thong down. She didn't answer me but the way her juices glazed over her pussy lips confirmed what I already knew—she wanted me inside of her. I took her bra off before I pulled her up so she could straddle me. I grabbed her breasts and licked them. She gripped the back of my head as she sucked on my lip. She slid her tongue down my throat for me to suck on it. Desi was a stone-cold freak.

She reached into my shorts to pull my dick out. I slid my shorts down along with my boxers and kicked them off with my shoes. She pulled my shirt over my head. I gripped her by the hips then slowly slid her down on my dick and a groan escaped my throat from the way her muscles choked my dick. I sucked harder on her breasts to keep from groaning louder. Desi licked on my ear and sucked on my earlobe. My hands moved up and down her back as she rode me. Her wetness was drizzling down my dick and onto the couch.

"You feel so good," she said as she rotated her hips. I thrust upward then grabbed her around the neck. I pulled her nipple into my mouth as I gripped her neck a little tighter. She liked when I was rough while being deep inside of her. I felt her body trembling and she started moaning.

"Damn, I don't want to love you!" she moaned as she started cumming. I lay her down on the couch and lay down beside her in the spooning position. I lifted her leg up and as I slid back into her, I sucked on her neck.

"UMPPPPPPPPPPPPPPPHHHH! I FEEL EVERYTHING!" she screamed out. I reached to the front of her to fondle her clit as my tongue traced up and down her neck. I pushed myself in deeper and I went faster as her pussy made gushy, wet sounds.

"DAMN IT!" she moaned as she threw her ass back into me. I held her leg up higher as my dick stretched her open. She started playing with her pussy as my dick drilled into her.

FLAP! FLAP! FLAP!

The sounds of me slamming myself into her echoed throughout the living room. I tapped her butt so that she could stand up. When she did, I leaned her forward. I smacked her ass again.

"Touch your ankles, shorty," I said to her. She bent forward to grab her ankles. Her dark and round, tatted ass was up in the air and her pussy was open for me. She made her ass cheeks bounce before I plunged back into her. She knew that position drove me crazy and it didn't matter how hard I fucked her, she took every inch of me. I gripped her hips as I leaned back a little to keep my balance. I slammed her down onto my dick as hard and as fast as I could until she started yelping.

"You better not fucking run!" I said while I smacked her ass. I gripped the back of her neck and went harder until I felt my nut build up. Desi was cumming again and I was cumming with her.

"ARRGGGGGGHHHHHHHHHHH!" I grunted as I let loose inside of her.

"Let's get in the shower," I said.

Later on that night...

I woke up to Desi making noises. I sat up and wiped my eyes and she was packing the clothes I had at her crib. I got out of bed.

"Yo, I will smack the fuck out of you! Do you know it's too late for this bullshit and I'm tired? Take yo' crazy ass to bed!" I yelled at her.

"I wanted the dick and that's it. I didn't want a sleepover with you lying next to me like you care about me," she said.

"I never been the type of nigga to beg a bitch. If you wanted me to leave that's all you had to say," I said. I grabbed my clothes.

"Crazy-ass bitch," I said as I got dressed.

"What did you just call me?" she asked me.

"You heard what I called your crazy ass. I'm tired of kissing your ass. I said I was sorry more times than I can count. Do I look like a fuck nigga to you? You want me to crawl to your ass? Bitch, you lost your rabbit-ass mind. You keep playing with my head and shit but it's over! I'm done," I yelled at her.

"Get out!" she yelled back as I put my shirt over my head. When I walked passed her, she mushed me in the back of my head. I pushed her in the closet and she tripped over shoe boxes.

"I got a lot of shit going on, shorty, and your mind games I ain't got the time for. Play by yourself because you knew what you were doing," I said. I walked out of her bedroom and out of her door as she yelled behind me.

Desi

I knocked on Ree-Ree's door. She said she had a lot of information for me. As soon as she opened the door, I was greeted by two little light-skinned twin boys with greenish eyes.

"Whose twins? They are cute," I said.

"It's a friend of the family. She moved back into town and she wants me to watch them until she finds a daycare with an opening," she said.

"Did you tell Jada where Bullet was hiding?" I asked Ree-Ree. I didn't want anybody to know because it would've messed up my plans. I knew if they went to Bullet, Chasity would've got killed, too.

"No, but Chasity told me that she was coming back home because Bullet wants to move out of state," Ree-Ree replied.

"The money out of her accounts should be gone by tonight. You got a lot of information out of her purse. Are you sure she doesn't expect you are up to something?" I asked her.

"I'm sure. She asked me to grab her pills, so I had a reason to go into her purse," she replied.

"I know this hacker and he is a genius. Chasity had sixty thousand dollars in her bank account and twenty thousand in her savings. That bitch was really racking up on her baby's father's money, wasn't she?" I asked.

"Yes, and she is also in the process of a custody battle," she replied and I smiled.

"Oh really?" I asked as a plan formed in my head. Someone knocked on Ree-Ree's door and she opened it. A caramel-toned, tall woman stepped inside her apartment wearing dress pants and a dressy top.

"Hey, Liana. I was just about to call you and tell you that I was dropping them off at home," Ree-Ree said. Liana looked at me.

"Hello, I'm Liana and you are?" she asked.

"Hi," I said and rolled my eyes. I wasn't a fan of meeting people.

"So, did Bishop come over? I don't know why he doesn't want to interact with the twins," she said to Ree-Ree as she grabbed the boys' small backpacks.

"What in the hell does Bishop have to do with these damn kids? And, bitch, you better not say he is the daddy. I know damn well those light-green-eyed babies ain't his," I said. Ree-Ree pulled me to the side.

"That's his ex-girlfriend. She moved back to town. That's the one that was in the military," Ree-Ree whispered.

"The bitch that left him and got married?" I asked and Ree-Ree looked away.

"Who are you because you seem to know too much about me. Ree-Ree, who is this bitch?" Liana asked.

"I'm Desi, your ex-nigga's new bitch," I spat. She laughed as if I said something funny but the only thing that was funny was that the joke was on her.

"As if you are his type," she said while she frowned her nose up.

"Honey, please don't take it there. I'm trying to save you in front of yo' kids," I spat.

"But you haven't met his mother? His mother is like my mother-in-law. You can't compete with that even if you tried. So, if Bishop felt like you were worthy then she and I would've met you already," she said.

"You don't know me and that's okay because I'm about to tell you a little story about myself. There's only two things I care about and that's Bishop and my money. Meeting families and all of that other bullshit ain't really my thing, and a little fake-ass friendship with mamas ain't on my agenda. You might have his mama but I got him, plus the big dick. Oh, and my hands are always in his pockets," I replied.

"Hoodrat," she said when she grabbed her kids.

"Giraffe," I spat back before she left. Ree-Ree looked at me.

"Do you always have to be so mean?" she asked.

"Yes, I do. I'm only nice if I'm getting paid for it," I replied.

****

I walked into Smithson's with Bella. I got attached to the dog so I held off on giving her back. I knew after what happened to Ashanta that he needed something special from her. He didn't seem like the type of man to deal with a toy dog but it was better off with him. When I walked in, I was greeted by a light-skinned girl who looked to be in her early-twenties.

"Hey, my name is Poet. Welcome to Smithson's, and how may I help you today?" she asked cheerfully.

Honey, if your ditzy ass don't lay off the coffee, shat! I thought to myself.

"I'm looking for Kwenya," I said.

"I will be right back," she said. She walked to the back of the shop. Moments later, he walked out with a scowl on his face. I heard in the streets how his attitude had changed. Kwenya never had a good attitude but at that point it was horrible. Even his employee seemed uncomfortable around him.

"What do you want, Desi?" he asked.

"I want to give you, Bella," I replied. He looked at the dog and his mood softened.

"Ashanta's dog?" he asked when I handed her to him.

"Yes. Chasity had the dog at Ree-Ree's house. Ree-Ree didn't know what was going on," I replied. Bella went to sleep in Kwenya's arm as he held her. I wanted to laugh because his stocky figure almost swallowed the dog.

"Good looking out," he said. After I left his shop, I headed downtown to press charges on Chasity. Ree-Ree took a camcorder from Chasity's car and snuck it in her purse. I told Ree-Ree when she texted me telling me she found her camcorder for her to not touch it. I needed all of Chasity's fingerprints on the camcorder. I had all of her phone records from when Ree-Ree was calling me and texting me from Chasity's phone, threatening me. I made sure Ree-Ree deleted it before Chasity saw it. I had a note someone forged in Chasity's handwriting. The handwriting was identical to Chasity's. She messed up when she tried me. I touched myself all night on the camcorder with my dildo and every other toy I owned. I made sure it was hidden in my bedroom. I wanted the police to know that Chasity had been stalking me and even recorded me. I was going to run my lie until I couldn't anymore. She was going to be broke and humiliated by the time I was done with her.

"How may I help you today?" an officer asked me from behind the front desk of the police station.

"How can I file a complaint on someone stalking me? My ex-girlfriend and I broke up a few months ago and she has been calling me nonstop and even threatened me. She has been writing me letters saying that she is going to kill me. I found her camcorder in my bedroom and she has been recording me. She will not leave me alone and I'm very scared because she owns a gun," I said. I was laughing on the inside.

"Fill out everything on this report and we can take it from there," the officer said. She was a middle-aged white woman and I knew she was gay. As soon as I said my ex-girlfriend, the bitch looked like she hit the Mega Millions. After I filled out my report and left the camcorder with them, I left the police station. I headed to the other side of town. My job was never done.

****

I pulled up to the broad Monie's building. Bishop's truck was out front. I got out of my car and sat on my hood. It was summer time. I wore a pair of jean shorts and fitted, white V-neck shirt. My diamond choker he bought me fit perfectly around my neck and, like always, I didn't wear a bra. I wore a pair of platform brown clogs and I had on a pair of leopard-print YSL shades. My short hair was styled to perfection and my make-up was natural and it made my face glow. A few niggas were trying to get my attention but I popped my gum and waited for Bishop to come outside. I didn't care about what we were going through, I still wanted to meet this bitch, Monie. I called his phone and he declined my call. I called his phone again and got the same thing. I sent him a text telling him I was outside of Monie's building and two minutes later, he was storming out of the building wearing a sleeveless, white shirt with a pair of jean shorts. His tall, solid frame bopped over to me and the scowl on his face made him appear even sexier.

"Have you lost your damn mind, shorty?" he asked me.

"You miss me, baby?" I asked. I slid down from the hood of my car to hug him. The cologne he wore caused my nipples to press against the fabric of my shirt.

"Cut the bullshit out. What do you want?" he asked.

"I want to meet this bitch that you spend your time with. I met your fake baby mama earlier. You know the one that is living with your mama and shit. Oh, nigga, I got all the tea. So, I figured since I'm in the mood for introductions today, why not meet the other bitch?" I asked him.

"You have lost all common sense. Yo, I'm not entertaining you today. It's too hot for the bullshit, Desi. Take yo' ass home and what's up with the shorts?" he asked. I knew it was going to make him jealous.

"Easier for me to give people my ass to kiss. Now, I want to meet her," I said. Bishop didn't know what the real issue was. What Liana said to me hit a nerve. Why wasn't I good enough to meet his mother? He'd been staying with me every night and we did almost everything together and not once did he mention anything about his mother. Not only did I have an issue with that, there was also the fact that he didn't tell me Liana was back. I also wanted to know why Liana felt like Bishop had to interact with her kids. It was just too much on my plate.

"That's uncalled for, shorty," he stressed.

"Just like it's uncalled for me to meet your mother? What's the matter, Bishop? I'm too much of a tramp to take home to the family? You don't want nobody to know about my freaky ass? What the hell is it? The whole time I been trying to show you the real me but guess what? You been showing me nothing but signs of a lame-ass nigga. What happened to being a real nigga?" I asked him.

"If I was a lame, you wouldn't be on some stalking shit, and I know for sure it ain't all because of my dick. So, you can speak out of anger but I'm not arguing with you outside. My business is my business and it's never meant for the streets, ya' feel me?" he asked. A girl walked outside wearing a skirt and her shirt was tied in the front, showing off her flat stomach. She was cute in the face but she was nothing special.

"What's going on? Is that Desi?" she asked Bishop.

"It ain't a ghost. Bitch, you see me," I spat and Bishop shook his head.

"Why is she in front of my building?" she asked Bishop.

"Ask me questions, boo. Not him because he is just as surprised as you are and I'm the only one entitled to questioning him," I said.

"Monie, just go back up so you can finish doing what you were doing for me," he said to her. Monie sucked her teeth before she hurried off.

This hoe must've had some of my "yes daddy" dick because ain't no bitch moving that fast if she ain't fucking a nigga, I fussed inside of my head.

"I'm not banging her. I used to back in the day, but I don't look at shorty like that. Now, why are you really trippin'? I been trying to see what's good with you and you kept brushing me off. Now, because my ex-shorty came back home, you want to show me some attention," he said.

"Just because I don't want to be bothered does not mean you are single. I say my best shit every day and you know me. Don't play with me because I'm telling you right now that my games are always more interesting," I said and he smirked. He walked closer to me and pressed his body into mine which trapped me between him and my car.

"Oh, yeah? What kind of games, shorty?" he asked rubbing on my legs.

"You know what kind," I said.

"Can I come back? Damn, you act like I pistol-whipped you or something," he said and I almost laughed.

"I'll think about it. Do you still love that tall bitch?" I asked.

"Naw, I'm loving on this other shorty but she pissing me off, so can I get some wet-wet?" he asked me and I pushed him.

"I love you," he said as he stared into my face. I grabbed his face to kiss his lips.

"I like you, too," I joked. "But your ass still ain't spending the night," I said. He pulled away from me.

"Call me later," he said as he headed to his truck.

"I will and don't forget my ring!" I shouted behind him. Bishop turned around and looked at me like I was crazy.

"You told me you loved me so now we are getting married," I said and he fell out laughing. I went overboard at times but he accepted it all.

"Let me see what those pretty lips do first," he joked back. He smiled and the gold diamond fronts he had in his mouth beamed underneath the sun. He was overly sexy and I couldn't get enough of him.

"Suck my nipples first," I replied.

"Anything you want, beautiful," he flirted. Butterflies formed in my stomach. It amazed me how love could cause different feelings inside my body. He winked at me before he got inside his truck.

I need to change my panties, I thought to myself.

Ashanta

I was in Mexico for almost three weeks and I was already homesick. I missed everyone back home. I stayed in my room eating and writing. The story I was writing was titled, *His Love Was the Death of Me*. It was about a woman who was killed but she came back as someone else to seek revenge on those who she thought killed her. The more I wrote, the more it seemed like it was becoming my life. There was a knock on my door so I closed my laptop. It was lunch time and Jesse always preferred that we ate our meals together. She was a very busy woman and I barely saw her at times. She always had a house staff member to check up on me. Jesse was difficult, perhaps even weird, but for some reason, I was starting to feel safe around her. I grabbed my sun hat before I walked out of my room. I followed the butler to the beach where Jesse sat at a table waiting for me.

"Come and sit. We need to talk," she said. I sat down across from her. My stomach grumbled as I thought about the beef tacos, black beans, and cilantro rice that was on my plate. The glass of freshly-squeezed lemonade looked even better.

"Yes, ma'am," I answered.

"Leave us be, Malone," she said to the butler before he scurried away.

"I don't ask for much but when I do I expect to get it. I want to know the real you," she said.

"I told you everything you needed to know. My husband ruined my life and I ran away," I answered.

" I ran away, too, and never looked back. I should've stayed home and stuck up for myself but I didn't. I came to another place because my husband was a fugitive. I thought because we were in a new area the problems were going to go away but when you run you are not escaping. You are taking your problems with you and that's what happened to me. Now I'm a single woman with no family or friends. All I have is the people that work for me and that will be your life if you don't get revenge on those who did you wrong," she said.

"I don't know where to start right now," I replied.

"What is your real name? Don't tell me Nala because I know that's not your name. Every time you say your name, you pronounce it different each time as if you are not comfortable with it. I have seen a lot and you can't fool me," she said.

"Ashanta," I answered.

"That's a start. Now why did you leave home?" she asked. I told her everything but I didn't give her any names. I didn't want to incriminate Kwenya by telling a stranger that he was a drug dealer.

"Eat your food, and when you finish, come to the front of the house. There will be a limo waiting for us," she said before she scurried off.

****

I thought Jesse and I were just going around the corner but we ended up in Hollywood on a private jet.

"I told you everything. Now can you tell me what you do?" I asked her.

"My husband was a rich man and when he died, his riches were passed down to me. I have vacation resorts, restaurants, boutiques, and a cruise ship. I have been a business woman for many years," she said but I wasn't buying it, so I didn't respond. We rode through a neighborhood in Beverly Hills until our limo stopped at big house that sat on top of a hill. The house looked like it was made of glass.

"Come," she said. The driver opened the door for us and Jesse grabbed my hand. We stood in front of a gate as she buzzed the intercom. A few seconds later, it opened and a weird-looking Chinese guy with yellow pants and a white shirt came outside to greet us.

"Heyyyyy, my lady. I'm so excited to see you," he said. He was a little feminine in a way. His hair was slick back into a ponytail.

"It's nice to see you, too, Jonju. This is Nala and Nala this is Jonju. He and I do great business together," Jesse said. I shook Jonju's hand. Jesse and I followed him into his house. As soon as we walked in, I was in awe. His décor was very feminine and immaculate. Jesse took her pumps off and I took off my sandals. She and I followed him down a long hall until he pushed open a set of metal double doors. Inside, the

71

room was creepy. It had human-sized figures with scary faces. He had a life-size bigfoot statue that looked too real. I started to get paranoid.

"What is going on, Jesse?" I asked her.

"Jonju is a very popular man in Hollywood. Everything in this room is his creation," she replied.

"I'm not following," I said.

"I will let you two talk," he said before he walked out of the room.

"What the fuck is going on? I'm not trying to star in a movie role," I spat.

"Watch your tone, Ashanta. I'm teaching you to become a strong woman. I'm teaching you how to have a lot of tricks under your sleeves. I am teaching you how to fight back. You will thank me later," she said.

"What does showing me a weird-ass room have to do with anything?" I asked. She walked away from me then came back with a mask. It creeped me out because the mask looked like real, human flesh.

"This is how you get revenge. A wolf in sheep's clothing, Ashanta. You will go back home and face everybody who crossed you as someone else. To protect your baby, you will need to keep a low profile and what other way is better?" she asked me. I took the mask from her and held it in my hands. It was the same skin tone as me and it felt like real skin.

"I just want to wake up from this nightmare. My life has got to be a dream," I said as I gave her the mask back.

"I read your book and so far, it's good," she said.

"You went through my laptop? How is that possible?" I asked.

"I have ways of hacking into things. Don't worry, I was just a little curious about you. The woman in your book was very, very devious. Where did she come from?" she asked me as she pointed to my head.

"She came from your mind. It's there but you need to stop being a bitch. You need to wake up and realize that only the strongest survive and the weak are preyed upon," she replied.

"Is this a joke to you? What I write is what I write!" I shouted at her.

"You are so lucky you are pregnant or else I would whip your ass myself. I think your story reflects what you want to do but I'm trying to help you. Anything is possible but you have to get your tail from between your damn legs. I wish I had someone to show me what I'm trying to show you before my life spiraled out of control. I wish someone cared enough to tell me but I didn't have that luxury. I want to envy you because after it's all said and done, you will have your life back. I will never get my life back! I will never see my da—," she stopped talking. A look of sadness appeared on her face and her eyes watered.

"You can't live through me," I said.

"I'm not a writer. You have the gift to live through your words. I can't do that but I will live through you. I will make you do what you have to do because I couldn't. When reality kicked in for me, it was too late," she said.

"I think you need to get some help. I'm not a psychiatrist but I studied some of it in college. You can talk to me," I said and she laughed at me.

"There goes that innocence that I like," she replied. Jonju came back into the room with a tray of wine. There were three glasses and he tried to give me one but I declined.

"Rude, aren't we?" he asked me.

"No, I'm pregnant," I spat. He grabbed his chest.

"I'm soo sorry, darling. No wonder your attitude is bitchy. Please forgive me because I was about to tell the queen that you needed to get out. I don't like rude people in my home," he said.

"Shut up, Jonju," Jesse said in a serious tone. He cleared his throat.

"Go out in the living room and let me and Jonju finish discussing business," she said. I hurriedly rushed out of the room. I headed to the living room. I sat on the couch and closed my eyes.

Wake up, Ashanta! Wake the fuck up! This is a dream! I yelled into my head. My stomach growled and I needed to eat something. I placed my hand over my stomach and thought about the life that was growing

74

inside of me. Jesse was right, I couldn't run from my life back home. It was my third time leaving Kwenya and that's what hurt the most. I told him about our baby before Rakita faked my death. I faked a death just so Rakita could be with my man—my child's father. My fist balled up and tears stung the brim of my eyes.

"Are you ready?" Jesse asked me. She had a way of sneaking up on me without me hearing her. I wanted to know more about her and I knew there was more to her than what she wanted me to see.

"I been ready," I said. Jonju came out of the room and his eyes looked glazed as if he was high. He appeared more friendly and he kept wiping his nose.

I always heard that people in Hollywood did some type of drug, I said to myself.

"I apologize for snapping at you earlier but the queen has come to my rescue. Is there anything I can get you?" he asked me.

"No, I'm fine and I apologize, too," I said. He kissed Jesse's cheek before he handed her a suitcase.

"If you have any issues with that, let me know. I will catch a plane out to you with a new one. It's my newest creation and there are instructions inside of the suit case. You have to stay away from the heat. The mask's only purpose is to change your cheeks and nose, so some features might still be visible if you don't add make-up to it. Make sure you wear foundation over it to blend the outline of the mask into your skin. Do not get it wet because it will peel off. It's like a sticker that is made out of fake skin," Jonju said. Jesse kissed his cheek.

"I will call you soon. Nice business as always," she said. Jesse grabbed my hand to help me up. I wanted to tell her that she didn't need to treat me like a child but I thought better of it. After she and I put our shoes on, we exited the house and the limousine was still outside waiting for us.

"We are going back home. I don't like to stay in other places for too long. I do what I got to do then leave," Jesse said as the limo driver opened the door for us.

"I think it's only fair that you tell me everything about you since you know enough about me. I will not stop asking you until you tell me what the hell is going on with you. You have me riding with you and it's my right to know who I'm with just in case something happens," I said. Jesse sipped her glass of champagne.

"I don't like to tell much because our own words can come back to us like weapons. Just pay close attention to your surroundings, that's all," she said. I looked out the window.

"Thank you," I said. I owed her that much. Even though she seemed deranged and dangerous, I was just glad that I was still alive.

"Thank me after I teach you everything you need to know. It's just the beginning," she said.

"I don't want to wear that thing on my face over my wound," I said.

"It's your call. By the time I finish telling you what to do, you might not need it," she replied.

Kwenya

There were still no signs of Ashanta but I wasn't giving up. I hired a private investigator because I knew that Ashanta was not a heavy drinker. The liquor at the crime scene wasn't something she would drink. New evidence was found at the scene and it was dried blood that belonged to her. Her parents were doing interviews with different news stations and they refused to say that she was deceased. I sat on my couch with a bottle of liquor in my hand. I was slipping further and further into the streets. I hadn't heard anything about the broad Jesula since that night I killed her boyfriend. There were no signs of her or Bullet. My court date was in a few months for the two bricks they tried to pin on me. I was pulled from my thoughts when Ashanta's dog started barking at me. I hated small dogs but it was the only thing I had left of her. The intercom buzzed because someone was at my gate. Bella must've heard the visitor's car outside.

I went into the kitchen to look at the small monitor under the light switch. I had cameras set up at different angles around my new house. It was the private investigator I hired. When I opened the door, he walked in. He was a white boy around age thirty. My lawyer recommended him to me; he was my lawyer's younger brother.

"What do you got for me, Chase?" I asked him when he walked in.

"I checked out the scene myself and even used an old beat-up car. I wanted to stage how she drove off the cliff to get a better image. The cliff is surrounded by trees, and in order to drive off, you have to maneuver your way through the woods. If Ashanta was drunk, she would've at least hit several trees before she landed in the water. I checked every tree in that area and none of them have marks on them," he said. He handed me the pictures.

"Those are pictures of the car I used. The car left paint on the trees I sideswiped on my way to the cliff. A drunk person would've sideswiped a tree or more," he said. I sat down on the couch as my head started to throb.

"You said she was married right? Do you think her husband had something to do with it?" he asked me.

"He could've but that nigga ain't built like that. That muthafucka ain't smart. Ashanta would've tried to fight him off," I said. I took another sip of my liquor.

"The police stated some of her blood was found at the scene but it wasn't much. I think someone planned this and I hate to tell you this but I think she was in on it. Her body still hasn't been found and according to the tire tracks at the scene of the crime on the night it happened, the car drifted off as opposed to speeding off the cliff. If she was drunk and speeding or even swerved off the road, she would've crashed before she made it to the cliff and the tire tracks would've proved that she was speeding but she wasn't. The story has many gaps because blood was found on the dirt. So, was she out of her car before it went into the water? See, what I mean? There are too many gaps, Kwenya," he said. He sat down on the couch across from me.

"I have dealt with a case like this before. Women in abusive relationships run away all the time. Her records state that she was going through a divorce and her husband was abusive. Maybe she got tired and he scared her off. I don't know what to think at this point but I do know that this was planned," he said.

"She left while carrying my baby," I said in disbelief.

"I will look further into this. I will get back to you as soon as I find something else," he said.

"I will be right back," I said. I went into the basement to grab a few stacks out of my safe. I walked back upstairs and handed him the money. Chase looked at it.

"You already paid me," he said.

"I know but hit me up when you find something else," I said to him. He thanked me before he left the house. Bella followed behind him to the door. I picked up the dog so she wouldn't run outside.

"If your owner played me again, she is going to be a dead bitch for real," I said.

****

I pulled up to a barber shop and waited for it to close. I sat in my old Lincoln Town Car until the owner came out. The nigga's name was Kev and he owed me ten thousand dollars. I'd been dealing with him since I started hustling and that nigga never shorted me my money. I fronted him something extra and he always paid me for it when it was time for him to re-up, but the nigga hadn't called me in a few weeks. Niggas thought because my mind was somewhere else that I was slippin'. I waited in the cut as he closed his shop down. I got out of the car and headed toward him. It was dark and I wore dark clothes with a hat pulled down low over my face. When he turned around he spotted me, and as soon as he did, he took off running. I pulled my silencer out then shot him in the leg. When he made an attempt to keep running, I shot him in the other leg.

"AWWWWWW, FUCK!" he screamed out. I walked up to him and dragged him in the alley.

"Where is my money at, nigga?" I asked him.

"Come on, man. All of this over ten g's? We are better than this, man. We been niggas since you were a little nigga," he said.

"We ain't never been niggas. We did business together since I was a little nigga. Now, where is my bread at?" I asked him.

"I was robbed," he lied.

"Oh, yeah?" I asked him.

"Come on, man. I got you next Friday," he said.

"Your funeral is next Friday, nigga. What you think word wasn't going to get back to me? What you think I don't know what's going on in my city? You been gambling with my money, muthafucka'," I said.

"That's a lie," he said. I heard someone walking and I hurriedly shot Kev between the eyes. I dragged his body behind the dumpster and waited until the person walked passed the dark alley. I peeked around the corner and the coast was clear. I got inside my car and pulled off.

****

The next day...

"Is everything okay with you? I got everything down pact now. Maybe you should take a few weeks off," Poet said to me as I sat at my desk in the back of the shop.

"My aunt doesn't like to keep track of the books so I have to come in to do them," I replied.

"I'm really sorry about what happened to Ashanta," she said. The front door of the shop opened and the bell chimed.

"Helllloooooooooooooo! Is someone in here?" a voice called out.

"I will get that," Poet said before she walked to the front. Moments later, there was loud fussing and cursing. I walked to the front of the shop and it was Ashanta's mother pointing her finger in Poet's face.

"You tell that muthafucka' to come out here and face me. I want to know what happened to my daughter," she screamed with her wig in her hand.

"Can you please put your wig back on. I don't want any problems," Poet said. We were ready to open and I didn't want Ashanta's mother yelling and screaming when the customers came in.

"I might have to fight and you don't know how much I paid for this good hair. Now, tell that thug to come out and face me like a real man," Ashanta's mother screamed.

"I'm right here," I said.

"Where is my daughter? I will not rest until I find my daughter! Did you cut her up and stuff her inside of one of your deep freezers? Is she buried somewhere in the woods? I know all about your kind," she said.

"I loved your daughter. She was carrying our baby. But you can bring your voice down at my place of business. Now, if you want to talk to me we can go in the back," I stated calmly. She put her wig back on and it was crooked. She pulled a small canteen from out of her purse and took a sip from it before she followed me to the back.

"I want my daughter. I know you know something," she replied.

"I want her, too," I said.

84

"I know Damos isn't capable of such an act but I know you are," she said. I chuckled because Mrs. Scott was a delusional drunk.

"Go ahead and laugh. I bet you will not be laughing in jail," she said.

"What is my type, Mrs. Scott?" I asked her.

"A thug who hides behind his fake identity. You charmed my daughter, swept her off her feet then killed her because she found out what you were up to. I know about your dealings in the streets," she said.

"You don't know nothing about me because if you did, you wouldn't be disrespecting me in my place of business. I will let it slide this time because you don't know me, yet. Would you like another drink?" I asked her. I pulled out a fifth of Henny from the file cabinet.

"I don't drink with murderers. Can you please just tell me where my daughter is?" she said.

"If you think I did something to your daughter, do something about it. Truth is, you don't believe it yourself," I replied.

"Did you kill her because you think the baby belonged to Damos? I know about her pregnancy but I promised her I wouldn't tell anyone," she said. I wondered where Ashanta's hood mother came from because Ashanta was very opposite from her mother.

"I know for a fact that I knocked her up, Mrs. Scott. Now, are you done questioning me? If not, maybe I should call my lawyer and have him present," I said. She balled her fist up.

"I will stab you in the throat, you arrogant, black muthafucka! You will answer everything I ask you!" she yelled at me. I took a sip from my Henny bottle. I leaned back in my chair.

"You will have to kill me then because I don't have shit to tell you," I replied.

"Do you need me to call the police?" Poet asked when she walked back to my office. Ashanta's mother turned around and eyed her.

"Bitch, I will beat the skin off your ass if you called the cops on me. I'm a Scott, and I come from a decent family. Are you trying to fuck up my family name?" she asked Poet. I wanted to laugh but I held it in. Ashanta's mother was all the way hood.

"Ma'am, I can hear you from the front and so can the few customers who just arrived," Poet said with attitude.

"Good! Let them hear me so they can know what you murderers are up to. Matter of fact, why are you even here? My daughter's only been missing for a month and you are acting as if you and Kwenya got something going on," Mrs. Scott said.

"Kwenya, I'm trying to keep my job, but if she disrespects me one more time, I'm going to knock her old, drunk ass out. I've been nothing but nice to this woman and I cannot take it anymore," Poet said.

"I got it from here," I said. Poet walked away.

Mrs. Scott stood up and grabbed her purse off the desk.

"I want my daughter and I don't believe that it was an accident. Someone intentionally hurt my daughter. She was so sweet and fragile and I ask God every night, who can do something like that to her? Ashanta has never bothered anybody and always tried to help someone if they needed it. She was a good woman with a heart of gold. I miss her so much. Damos is missing, too, and I'm sure you had something to do with that, too," she said.

That nigga ain't missing. He is hiding with his bitch ass, I thought to myself.

"Have a nice day, Mrs. Scott," I said to her. She stormed out of my office. I closed the door and rolled up my blunt. I needed something to clear my head. I was becoming angrier because I felt like Ashanta purposely played me. I hoped she was alive so that I could squeeze her throat. I pulled out my silencer and placed it on my desk. I had a few more bodies to drop. Bernie thought he had me but that nigga wasn't ready for what I had in store for him.

****

I sat on Rakita's couch and listened to her ramble on and on about why she and I should be together. She begged me to come over to her crib and as soon as I went, the questions started coming.

"Rakita, what is the issue?" I asked her.

"We need to work on us. I'm ready to settle down and have a baby," she said. I brushed my hand down my waves because she knew that's what I was looking forward to but I was only looking forward to it with Ashanta.

"You should've had the two I knocked you up with a few years back," I said. I stood up and she grabbed her purse.

"What restaurant are you taking me to?" she asked me.

"It doesn't matter but I know my stomach is touching my damn back. You sitting up here asking me shit when you know I can't function when I'm hungry," I said.

"Let's go," she said.

Rakita

I was smiling on the inside as I watched Kwenya slowly lose his mind. I felt sorry for him but he needed to know how I felt when he was running around with that other woman. I was going to do everything I could to get him back because I knew Ashanta was long gone. I still couldn't believe she fell for what I told her, although half of it was true. I was a federal agent and I was on an undercover case in New York. I was investigating a man named Chaos. I was fired because I wasn't doing my job; I ended up catching feelings for Chaos. After they fired me, I came back home and never looked back. I had a friend that still worked for the FBI and she helped get me my badge back, which I used for my own personal use. Chaos ended up getting locked up for a drug charge and his twin brother took on his identity. As Kwenya and I sat at the dinner table, my cell phone vibrated. I excused myself.

"I'm going to the bathroom. I will be right back," I said but Kwenya waved me off because he was on the phone. I rolled my eyes at him when I got up. I rushed to the bathroom because Chaos was calling my phone from the cell phone he had in jail.

"My fuckin' brutha is dead! I want that nigga Kwenya's head on a stick! He is from your hometown and I want to know more about that nigga!" Chaos yelled into the phone with his Jamaican accent.

"What?" I asked.

"Bitch, you heard me! I know you heard of him. He is the big man in your city and I want to know everyting about him," he said. My stomach turned and my knees started shaking. Chaos didn't know I was a FED and that I was the reason he was locked up. They fired me right after I gave them evidence to put him away.

"How am I supposed to get information? I don't know him," I lied.

"Well, get to know him. I want his head for murdering my brutha in an alley. His girlfriend is coming back to Annapolis. She had to get his body to ship him back home. I'm going to send her to you and you will take care of her. She is going to help you with everyting I need," he said with venom dripping from his voice.

"I don't want to get involved!" I yelled into the phone. If Kwenya found out what I was up to, he would've had me killed. I had done a lot of damage and I didn't mean for it to go as far as it went. I buried a deeper hole for myself when I answered for Chaos.

What reason would Kwenya have to kill Chaos's brother? I asked myself.

"I'm not done with you, Rakita. I will call you later," he said before he hung up. I hurriedly walked out of the bathroom. Bishop and the girl I heard about whose name was Desi, walked over to our table. I used to see Bishop in my old hood when I was younger but I didn't know much about him. Desi and Bishop looked like a modern-day hood rich couple. Desi's diamonds were overkill and the way she walked to our table, you would've thought she was Princess Diana. I looked at Kwenya but he didn't look at me. I was pissed he invited his friends on

90

our date. Bishop spoke to me and Desi waved at Kwenya. Bishop whispered something in Desi's ear and I heard him.

"Be nice, damn," he said to her. She rolled her eyes at him.

"Hi," Desi said to me.

"Hi," I answered with the same tone. Bishop and Kwenya started talking about getting into the real estate business because Desi was trying her hand in it. As they talked, I sipped on my martini and waited for our waitress to come back to get our food order.

"So, Rakita. What have you been up to?" Bishop asked me.

"Nothing, just working," I said not wanting to share much information about my job. I was a leasing manager for a luxury community out in the suburbs.

"I can dig it," Bishop said.

"What's the matter with you?" Kwenya asked me.

"I just thought it was going to be you and I?" I asked.

"They are a part of my circle, so get over it," he spat.

"We can leave because I told Bishop I don't like to be around females like that," Desi said.

This fake Joseline Hernandez-acting bitch, I thought.

"She will get over it," Kwenya said.

"Are you trying to embarrass me?" I asked him.

"No, but I will," he answered dryly. The waitress came and took our food orders. I just wanted to eat and go home.

"So, how long have you and Desi been dating?" I asked Bishop trying to make small talk.

"Six months," he answered.

"Me and Kwenya been on and off since high school," I told Bishop.

"Ummmm, and y'all don't have no kids or nothing? Fuck that because I will be damned," Desi said as she sipped her drink.

"I said we been on and off," I replied. She rolled her eyes. I wasn't feeling her funky attitude at all.

After the food came, we ate and talked. Desi started to loosen up but I still wasn't feeling her attitude. A few hours later, everyone was tipsy. After we parted ways, I got inside of Kwenya's BMW. I leaned the seat back and lifted up my maxi dress. I slid my panties down and started to touch myself. Kwenya and I used to have sex anywhere. He was rough and words couldn't explain what he did with his tornado-like tongue.

"What are you doing?" he asked.

"You know every time you are behind the wheel, I like to put on a show. I know you want some pussy, baby. It's been a while for you I'm sure," I said. I knew him like a handbook, and when he drank, he was like a sex machine. I unzipped his shorts and pulled out the thick, long, black dick that I loved so much. I kissed the head of it before I slid it to the back of my throat.

"Ughhhhhhh," he groaned as I deep-throated him. I wanted him to surrender to me. I wanted him to come back to me so that he and I could have our happily ever after together. Kwenya pulled over on the side of the road. He turned his car off.

"Get out the car," he said. I hurriedly got out to sit on top of the hood of his car. He spread my legs and my pussy clenched as I thought about how he was going to stretch me open. I popped my breasts out of my bra and fondled them as he slid his girth between my wet slit. When he slowly pushed himself inside of me, I lay back on the hood. Kwenya pulled me down to the edge of the hood and spread my legs wider. I was dripping wet as the pressure from his dick pushed into me and I could feel it traveling all the way up to my stomach. I dug my nails into his forearm as he buried his big dick inside of me.

"OOHHHHHHHHHHH!" I moaned out. He pulled my dress up and leaned forward so that he could suck on my breast. His strong hands massaged my thighs as he grinded into my spot. Seconds later, I was coming on him. He wrapped the dress around my neck and pumped harder into me.

"You like this rough shit? Huh?" he asked as he slammed into me. He pushed my legs further back to go deeper, his strokes were angry. I knew deep down inside he felt like Ashanta left him, but I didn't care what he thought. I just wanted the bitch gone.

"KWENNNYYAAAAAAA!" I screamed as his dick plunged into me. He was screwing me so good that my pussy was gushing and my nipples were harder than before. I was passed aroused; I was so horny that I started playing with my pussy and grinding back on his dick. The noises I was making sounded like it came from an animal but I didn't care.

"Go deeper! Go deeper! Fuck me harder!" I yelled as I slid up and down on his dick. My legs trembled and the rest of my body jerked as his dick painfully pumped into me but I still wanted more. As I played with my clit, I felt it jump and a hoarse moan escaped my lips as I came. The tip of his girth was ramming into my spot as I came back to back. When a groan escaped his lips, I knew he was on the verge of busting. He tried to pull out but I wrapped my legs around him and grinded onto him.

"Bitch, let me go!" Kwenya yelled at me. He tried to push me off but his body gave in and he released inside of me.

WHAP! He slapped me on the side of my head. I rolled off the car. He put himself back inside his shorts. He stood over me with murder in his eyes.

"Have you lost your mind?" he yelled at me as I stood up but he pushed me back down in the grass.

"What is your problem?" I asked him.

"I swear I'm too fucked up to think. I got to be sober around your simple-minded ass. Are you trying to trap me or something? Get your dumb-ass in the car!" he said before he mushed me in the back of my head. If it wasn't dark outside, he would've left me on the side of the road by the woods. Kwenya was an arrogant and evil bastard at times. I fixed my dress before I opened up the passenger-side door.

"Get your ass in the backseat," he said.

"Are you serious?" I asked him.

"As you just were about trapping me," he spat. I opened up the door and got in the backseat. Kwenya pulled out onto the main road. We were the only ones on the road at that time of night.

"You have changed," I said. He turned up the rap music on the radio. I drifted off to sleep.

****

I was yanked out of the backseat. I fell asleep and forgot that I was in the back of Kwenya's car. My butt came crashing down onto the pavement.

"I will fuck you up!" I yelled at him as he walked away from me.

"I been in your corner and this is the thanks I get? I been by your side when your black ass was locked up. I accepted everything about you and we are still living in two different places. We occasionally fuck and

95

you give me money here and there, take me shopping when you want to be nice, and that's it! I want more!" I yelled and he burst into laughter.

"You think because my shorty ain't here, that means you can replace her? You think because she was pregnant that I want you to carry my child? We could've had a few but what did you do, Kita? You took your wanna-be happy ass to the clinic and got rid of both of them. I appreciate all you had done for me, but I did shit for you, too. I remember when you didn't have a bed and slept on a blow-up mattress in high school. I hustled sun up, till sun down for you to sleep on something. Not only did I take care of you, but I did shit for your family, too. All you have ever done for me was pick me up from jail, suck my dick, give me some pussy, and call my lawyer," he said before he got inside his car and pulled off. I stomped my feet and screamed at the top of my lungs.

"BITCH!" I yelled.

After I walked into my apartment, I headed straight to the fridge for my wine but there was a knock on the door.

"He must want to apologize," I said as I strutted to the door. When I opened it, I tried to close it, but he grabbed me by the throat and pushed me into the wall.

"I have been waiting for your call. I did what you wanted me to do, now I want you to tell me what's going on about the private investigation on Damos," he said. I had my friend in the FBI set me up a fake file about Damos dealing to an undercover cop. It was the same fake file I showed Ashanta. Bernie thought Damos was being investigated. I bribed him and told him that I could help him with the case if he helped me. Bernie knew I was a FED but what he didn't know was that I was fired. Bernie set Kwenya up for me. He really didn't want to, but he thought I was going to help Damos out. If only his old ass knew it was a lie. I wanted Kwenya to get locked up so I could be there for him. I wanted him to see that I was down for him and I showed him that.

"I don't know what you are talking about," I said. I pulled away from him.

"Excuse me?" he asked.

"I don't know what you are talking about. What investigation and what set up?" I asked Bernie.

"I will—"

"You will what? Reporting me is like reporting yourself. You made your stepson look like a drug dealer. I didn't force you to do it and what proof do you have that I know about an investigation?" I spat.

I grabbed at his dick. Bernie was fine and his nice body did him a lot of justice. He looked like an older version of his son with a speckle of gray hairs in his beard. I met him a few years ago at Kwenya's family reunion. He was passing glances at me. Kwenya and I had a big argument that day so I was being spiteful. I knew by the way Bernie stared at me that I was in control of what I wanted to do with him. One day I caught a flat tire and Kwenya wasn't answering his phone. I called his mother's house and told her that I needed a ride because my tire was flat. Kwenya was out being a hoe so the dumb bitch ended up sending Bernie to pick me up and he and I ended up at a motel.

"Do you miss how good I used to make you feel?" I asked him. I pulled at the collar on his uniform and he pulled away from me.

"You must have forgotten that your drug dealer boyfriend doesn't know that you are a FED," he said to me and I laughed.

"Oh, Bernie, what am I going to do with you? Tell Kwenya because I'm not a FED. So, like I stated before, if you tell on me, you are telling on yourself," I said. He backed away from me.

"You will pay for this. You are very lucky that someone saw me walk up here or else I would've killed you," he said before he stormed out of my apartment door. A U-Haul truck pulled up to the building and I didn't have nothing else to do. I sat in my window with my glass of wine waiting to see who was moving in. A loud-mouthed girl got out of the truck. She was cursing someone out on her cell phone.

"Why would they move a ghetto bitch into this building?" I asked out loud. I sat my glass down and went to open my front door. She dragged her luggage up the stairs as she talked on the phone.

"Excuse me? Can you lower your voice? It's late," I said.

"Let me call you right back," she said into the phone. She wore short booty shorts with a stretch V-neck, white T-shirt. She wore a pair of Jordans on her feet and her hair was in Crochet jumbo twists. She had half in a bun and the other half hung down her back. I studied her face and there was not one flaw; she was beautiful but I frowned when I saw the gold teeth at the bottom of her mouth. I hated when women did that.

"Bitch, who you talking to?" she asked me. I didn't want to argue with her because it was obvious that she didn't have an ounce of class. I could get ghetto at times but I didn't want my neighbors to hear it.

"Can you keep the noise down?" I asked her.

"Since I will be paying rent like everyone else, I will think about it. But do you got some weed because you just blew my high," she spat. I rolled my eyes and slammed my door. My cell phone rang and it was Chaos. I needed to figure out what to do with him because it was Kwenya that I wanted. Kwenya was wasn't a dumb hoodlum. He was heavy in the streets but he was educated. Chaos was street-smart but lacked knowledge—a whole lot of it. I needed to come up with something and quick because I was not helping him take Kwenya out.

Chasity

I paced back and forth with tears running from my eyes.

"My damn money is gone. The bank investigated it and there is nothing they can do about it! They stated that I was the one who took the money from my accounts. They said people try to pull that scam off all the time to get double the money," I fussed. Ree-Ree sat on the couch as she stared at me. I went to the grocery store a week prior and my card was declined. I called my bank and told them that someone stole my money. I had to file a report for them to investigate it and it took them a whole week just to tell me it was completely gone.

"For a week I've been broke and now they are telling me there isn't shit I can do about it. I have nothing! Deron is trying to take my son and I can't pay a lawyer! Damos hasn't been home in two days," I said.

"It's okay. It will come up. Some banks make mistakes," Ree-Ree said and I wanted to slap her.

"Damn it, Ree-Ree, just think sometimes. Someone took my damn money and I think I know who did it," I said. I grabbed my phone. I called Desi's phone and she answered with music blasting in the background.

"Helllooooooooo, a rich bitch is speaking," she answered the phone.

"You took my money?" I asked her.

"What are you talking about?" she asked.

"My money from my bank account is gone! Did you take it?" I asked and she laughed.

"Bitch, you got money? I didn't know that. The way you were walking around looking, I thought the worst of life had caught up to you," she replied.

"I know you and what you are capable of. Look, Desi, I really need that money. I will lose my son," I said.

"You never have him anyway, so he is better off without you. Now, get your broke ass off my line," she spat before she hung up. I threw my phone into the wall.

"How am I supposed to pay my bills? My car payment is due and Bullet is broke. Bullet is fucking broke!" I screamed.

"Hit the strip club," Ree-Ree said as she scrolled through her phone.

"I'm in a custody battle! I can't do that!" I screamed at her.

"Well, I don't know what to tell you but I'm ready to leave. Jada is taking me somewhere tonight," she said.

"I get the point. You don't have to keep throwing him up in my face!" I said as she stood up.

"What have I ever done to you besides be your friend? I have been coming to see you almost every day and you live an hour away from me. I drive to this country side of town almost every fucking day and all you do is bitch and complain. Well, I'm not coming to see you anymore," she said. I was about to lose my mind.

"I'm sorry, Ree-Ree, please just stay with me." I caressed her face, but she moved away from me.

"Bye, Chasity," she said as she tried to leave. I didn't have anyone but I always had Ree-Ree.

"What am I supposed to do without you?" I asked her.

"I don't know, Chasity. Maybe you should put some baby oil all over me so I can slip back into your life again," she said and my heart started to beat faster.

"What?" I asked her.

"I didn't say anything," she said and walked out of the door.

"What did you just say? Who told you that?" I asked her.

"Told me what?" she answered as I followed her.

"You know what I'm talking about," I replied.

"I'm slow, Chasity. I don't know shit but I forgot that's what you wanted, right? You wanted to pull wool over my eyes and don't think I haven't noticed the lust you have for me," she said.

"You will regret this. Do you hear me? You will regret this!" I cried. I felt like she was breaking up with me. I felt suffocated because no matter what I did, Ree-Ree was always there for me. She cared more about me than anyone and maybe I read too much into our friendship, but I knew I was in love with her and I didn't realize it until she tried to walk out of my life.

"Don't do this to me!" I screamed as I pulled on her shirt but she pushed me away.

"You did this to me and it's because of you I went through what I went through. You will meet your karma and when you do, I want to be long gone," she said before she got in the car. She started it and sped off. As she was leaving, Bullet was pulling up in his pick-up truck. As soon as he stepped out of the truck, I fought him.

"Son of a bitch!" I screamed at him as my fists pounded his chest.

"What is wrong with you?" he asked.

"Where have you been? I needed you!" I screamed at him.

"I've been at my mother's house," he said but I knew it was a lie. He was back to messing with anything that walked, but the truth is, I didn't care what he did. I stopped loving Bullet after I realized that he couldn't give me the love I wanted. Bullet was a user and so was I, and that just didn't work.

"Well, go back," I said as I pushed him away from walking up the stairs to the run-down house.

"Get your dike ass out of my face. You think I haven't been noticing the way you be staring at Ree-Ree? And I kept telling you that I didn't want that bitch here because you know they are looking for me!" he yelled at me.

"Ree-Ree does not run her mouth," I spat. He walked into the house. I went down the hall and grabbed the small amount of clothes and shoes I had. I came back down the hall and he eyed me.

"Where are you going?" he asked.

"Back to my house," I said.

"What house?" he asked.

"Excuse me?" I replied.

"What house? That house was in my mother's name and I'm going to sell it," he replied.

"You got it in your mother's name? I thought it was in your name!" I yelled at him.

"Why would I do that when I was married, dumb-ass? I talked my mother into doing it. I gave her the money so they could close on it and that's what happened," he said and I cried.

"Why would you do that?" I asked him.

"So I can get money from it. Do you think I'm going to just sit here with you? I'm tired of looking at you, too. Look at you, Chasity. Your hair ain't done and you been wearing the same funky-ass leggings for the past two days, and the sex is horrible now. Let's just part ways peacefully," he said.

"You will pay for this because you used me. That's why you called me over to your mother's house that day. You don't love me," I spat.

"I used to until I saw that you were a sneaky bitch," he said and went into his pocket. He pulled out an envelope and gave it to me. I snatched it from him to open it up.

"I had my mother check the mail at your house and it looks like someone is taking you to court," he said. The more I read the letter the angrier I became. Desi was suing me because she stated that I exposed naked videos of her.

"Your mother called my phone a week ago and told me that an officer was looking for you because you had a warrant. I forgot to tell you," he said. I slapped him as hard as I could. Since the day I came home from the hospital, my life had been out of control. I'd been in a small house in the country with Bullet for a month and I was going crazy.

"You are just mad because your wife is dead and they can't find her body," I said. He pushed me on the floor.

"I don't care if they never find her. She and I ain't divorced, therefore I can get her life insurance money. They haven't ruled her dead just yet, but once they do, I will be paid," he bragged. Desi was right about one thing; Bullet was selfish and he only cared about people he could use.

"I will see you later," I said. I stormed out of the house. I put my things in my car and got inside. I wanted to call my mother to see how Marquis was doing but she wasn't talking to me and I wasn't talking to her. My mother didn't want Marquis around us but I couldn't sweat it at that moment because my living condition was a mess. I knew I had to find a place quick before I went to court. I was broke and Desi was suing me. I had to find a way to get back on my feet. I called Jesula and hoped she answered my phone call because I had been ignoring her.

"About time you called me back," she said when she answered the phone.

"I'm sorry, I was out in the country and my reception was very poor," I said even though I knew she knew I was dodging her because I still owed her money.

"My boyfriend is dead. He is fucking dead and I used almost all of my money to send him back home for a proper funeral. You should've answered your phone!" she yelled.

Didn't I just tell that bitch I didn't have any service? I asked myself.

"I'm sorry to hear that. But are you back in the area?" I asked.

"I'm on my way back now. Chaos is sending me to a friend of his. I did too much in New York to go back," she said.

"Wait, you just said Chaos was dead," I replied.

"Look, just meet me at the address that I'm about to text you. I will be there in an hour," she said before she hung up.

****

An hour and a half later...

I pulled up into a nice community. The apartments were new and upscale. I parked next to Jesula's two-door Benz. I got out and walked into the building. As soon as I walked up the stairs, a woman came down with long, thick twists. She looked at me and rolled her eyes. She wore a short skirt, pumps, and an-off-the-shoulder top. She reminded me of a prostitute. She slightly bumped me when she passed me.

"Excuse you," I said.

"You saw me first, but anyways, I like that purse. I got one just like it. I bought it from this nigga I met on the corner a while back," she said as she popped her gum. I noticed the gold teeth at the bottom of her mouth and she talked like she had an accent.

"Where are you from?" I asked her.

"Texas," she replied. I could tell by her accent that she wasn't from the area. I wanted someone to do parties with because I knew I had to go back to stripping. Desi used to be the person I made money with. I had to find someone else because I knew Jesula wasn't cut out for that. I pushed my pride to the side even though I wasn't feeling the woman's attitude.

"So, what type of profession are you in?" I asked her.

"The same one as you, trickin' niggas," she replied.

"How you figure I do that?" I asked.

"I know a hoe when I see one. I been around them all of my life but look, I got to go. I will see you around," she said before she scurried off. I walked up the stairs and knocked on the door. When the woman I saw Kwenya with a while ago opened the door, I was puzzled.

"I'm here for Jesula," I said and she let me in. I walked into the spacious apartment and looked around. It was furnished nicely and had plants everywhere.

"I have not known this girl for a whole hour and she is already sending people to my door," the girl Rakita fussed. Jesula came out of the bathroom and her eyes were bloodshot red.

So this evil bitch does cry? I asked myself as I held in my laughter. Jesula wiped her eyes.

"I still can't believe Kemar is gone. We were going to get married," Jesula said.

"Who is Kemar and what is going on here?" I asked because I was the only one Jesula really knew in Annapolis, yet she was in Rakita's home.

"Chaos's twin. He was over here illegally and I didn't want him to get caught, so we just called him Chaos," she replied.

"You never told me Chaos had a twin," I said.

"Nobody was supposed to know. I met him through Chaos but this is Chaos's girl," Jesula said. I looked at Rakita and she looked uncomfortable.

"Who killed him?" I asked.

"Kwenya. He shot him in the head twice. That bastard blew half of my baby's face off and I want him dead. I'm not going to the police because this is personal. I want to take him down myself," she said then Rakita cleared her throat.

"Can we not talk about death?" Rakita asked.

Jesula doesn't know that Rakita was sleeping with Kwenya. This is going to be one big mess, I thought.

"Why would Kwenya want to kill him?" I asked.

"I told Kemar not to do it but he didn't listen. He wanted to rob him, and when Kwenya walked out of the club, he followed him. I told him it wasn't the right time but he said that Kwenya was hard to get

110

close to so he tried it anyway," she said as she wiped her eyes. I knew she was stressed out but I was glad because I didn't want her asking me for the money I owed her. I also knew that without her muscle, which was her man, she was weak.

"My phone is ringing, I will be right back," Jesula said. She walked to the back of the apartment.

"So, Jesula doesn't know how close you and Kwenya are, and let me guess. She isn't supposed to know because Chaos thinks that you are his woman and that would mean you are cheating. I wonder how Jesula would feel if she knew that you were fucking the enemy, or better yet, how would Kwenya feel if he found out that you are messing with someone who wants him dead? Damn, now I see the problem. You just don't want Kwenya to find out. The other one is in jail so you don't care if he does, right?" I asked her.

"I will beat your ass up in here," she said.

"No need for that. All I want is a room and your secret is safe with me," I said.

"This isn't a boarding house and I don't know you," she replied and I shrugged.

"I don't know you, neither, but I'm homeless. But I do know that Kwenya would pay me for the information I have," I spat and she rolled her eyes.

"The den is down the hall. Go straight back then make a left," she gritted.

"You must really love him," I replied. I went down the hall then made the left and the den was big enough to be a bedroom. It was actually fixed up like a bedroom. I had to think of a plan because I was only staying until I got my money back up. I wanted to break down because of how much money was taken from me but I held it in. I had things to do and crying wasn't going to fix it.

****

Two days later...

I was leaving Rakita's apartment and I ran into the same chick from upstairs. She was dressed in a tight dress with a pair of pumps. Within those two days, she and I talked a few times. She wasn't that bad, but at times, she could get a little snappy. She almost reminded me of Desi but wasn't as mean.

"What's going on, Katrice?" I asked her.

"Nothing. About to hit this club. Are you going?" she asked me.

"I don't have the funds for that. I don't hit the pole until tomorrow night," I replied.

"Don't worry, I will treat you. I need someone to show me around because I don't know this town," she replied.

"Let me shower and get dressed," I said. I went to my car to grab my make-up bag. When I walked into Rakita's apartment, she was sitting on the couch watching TV.

"Do you want to go to the club with me and Katrice?" I asked her.

"I don't like that bitch," Rakita said.

Your fat ass doesn't like nobody but the refrigerator, I thought to myself.

"It doesn't matter. What else is there to do but sit around?" I asked Rakita.

"Well, I guess I can tolerate the skank for a few hours," she said before she went inside her bedroom. Jesula was stuck in the room losing her mind over her dead boyfriend.

****

Rakita, Katrice, and I sat at a table inside of club Aces. I was supposed to be careful of running into Bishop but he didn't have proof it was me who set up the camera. I had a feeling that Desi was screwing Bullet, so Bullet acted on his own because he was jealous. That was my story and I was sticking to it. Bullet was going to take the blame for everything. I had an alibi; I was in the hospital because of what Serene did to me. My ankle still ached at times and it took a few weeks for my

113

bruises to heal. They were so bad that you could see them through my make-up before they healed.

"Look at that fine-ass man that just walked in," Katrice said. When I looked, it was nobody but Jada, and Yolo was following behind him. Rakita stared at them hoping she was going to see Kwenya.

"Who are you looking for?" Katrice asked Rakita. Rakita rolled her eyes and sipped her drink.

"None of your business," Rakita said.

"She is looking for her boo thing," I teased. I didn't really like the bitch but I was staying with her, so I had to be nice. Rakita was weak and I knew she would've done anything to keep Kwenya. She seemed like the type of woman that would go above and beyond, and I was going to use that as much as I could. A local rapper was performing so the hood was out. My face almost cracked as I watched Ree-Ree and Desi walk in. Ree-Ree had a weave in her hair and the silk romper looked like it was painted on her. Her make-up was flawless and she looked happy. Desi always went overboard. She wore a white blazer with nothing underneath it and a pair of white shorts. The diamonds around her neck looked like they were dripping between her cleavage. Her short, jet black hair was styled to perfection as always. I didn't understand why Ree-Ree was with Desi but then I saw Bishop walk into the club.

"Those niggas are finer than Baby Face's baby hairs," Katrice said and Rakita chuckled. My eyes stayed on Ree-Ree and I started to wonder if she helped Desi set me up, but I thought better of it. Ree-Ree couldn't do nothing like that. She was mad at me but I knew her heart.

"Ummmmm, so you are a carpet-muncher?" Katrice asked me.

"Excuse me?" I asked.

"Bitch, you like pussy. There is nothing wrong that. But that broad with the white on is about to make me go gay. That ass is ridiculous," Katrice said talking about Desi.

"Desi is hot but the bitch's attitude is disgusting," Rakita said.

"I hate her with a passion," I said.

"So, what's the deal with the light-skinned one? Were you messing with her or something? She walked in and you almost passed out," Katrice said.

"Ummmmm, let me find out," Rakita said. I rolled my eyes at them.

"She and I were best friends. Been friends since middle school and she is mad at me," I said.

"Well, get ready because Desi is walking over here," Rakita said. When I turned around, Desi was strutting in my direction with a smirk on her face.

"Heyyyyy, best friend," Desi said to me.

"I should beat your ass for everything you did to me! You took my money and I have a warrant because of you," I screamed over the loud music.

"See you in court. I would love to put my foot up your ass but I'm looking too cute tonight and a queen never leaves her throne for a peasant. I pay people to handle that for me. So, I hope your broke ass got lawyer money ready because I know I do," she said. I picked up a drink from off the table and tossed it on her. Desi swung on me and she and I went at it inside of the club. We were going blow for blow but she was getting the best of me. I slid under the table and Rakita tried to help me up. Desi hit Rakita in the face. Desi had always been that way. If someone helped out someone she was fighting, she would attack them, too. She said that the person was against her because if they weren't, they would've never stopped her from whipping ass. Rakita and I jumped on Desi at the same time. Ree-Ree was trying to get in but Jada pulled her back. Bishop choke-slammed me on the table and he yanked Rakita off Desi.

"Y'all bitches ain't fittin' to jump my shorty. Fuck is wrong with y'all?" he asked. The bouncers pulled at Rakita and I. They tried to escort us out of the club but I was still trying to get to Desi. Desi reached over the bouncer and clocked me in the eye. A bouncer put her in a choke hold. Bishop swung and hit the bouncer in his face.

"Nigga, get the fuck off of her like that!" he said before he slammed his fist into the bouncer's face again. Yolo tried to calm Bishop down as the bouncer lay stretched out on the floor. Rakita and I was kicked out of the club. Katrice walked out with our purses.

"Y'all bitches straight?" Katrice asked.

"You could've helped us out!" I yelled at her.

"For what? It was two against one. Bitch, that ain't fair. Y'all jumped shorty in the white," she said. I snatched my purse out of her hand.

"We only been in there for thirty minutes," Rakita said before she smiled at me.

"It felt good socking Desi, though," she said. We laughed as we headed to my car.

"I leave my state to come here and it's the same mess. Females fighting over nonsense," Katrice said. I got in my car and started it up. As I was leaving the parking lot, a guy wearing a bandana over his face was standing in the street with a gun pointed at me.

PSST! PSST!

The bullets from the silencer came through my windshield. I ducked down as my car spun. I backed up and went in the other direction. Rakita was crying and Katrice was panicking.

"What in the hell was that?" Katrice screamed.

"Someone just tried to kill me!" I cried. I had glass all over my dashboard and Rakita's arm was bleeding because of the glass.

"Was that Yolo?" I asked Rakita.

"I think it was that crazy muthafucka'. I don't know how it slipped my mind but rumor is that you had someone rob the guy name Damos and his wife, Ashanta. If it was Yolo, then Kwenya had something to do with it. That nigga lost his marbles behind that dead bitch," Rakita fussed.

"Who is Damos and Ashanta?" Katrice asked. I felt comfortable around Katrice because she didn't know anyone in the area so I told her everything. I was tired of keeping secrets because with every lie I told, I had to tell another one to cover it up. I was tired of it all and I had to fix it. I came to the conclusion that I wasn't going to fight the battle with Deron. If he wanted Marquis, he could have him. My life was dangerous and I couldn't raise a child.

Bishop

Desi and I argued all the way to her apartment. Desi was mad because I was mad that she put us on the spot like that. We went to the club to support our city's young rappers and shorty couldn't just sit back and relax like everyone else.

"That bitch set me up!" Desi yelled at me.

"She set me up, too, but I'm not sweating it because I got my shit back. She ain't in this circle so she can't do it again. As for Bullet, that nigga got ghost. You knew where he was at the whole time. You told us a little bit too late because by the time Kwenya and I got to where he was staying, he was gone. I'm not sweating it, though, because it's moves to be made. You give people power over you when they see how much they can get to you," I said.

"You can get over it but I'm not. It's because of her that you held a gun to my head. And I didn't want to tell you where he was at until Ree-Ree and I were finished with that bitch. I didn't want y'all to kill Chasity before we paid that ass back," she fussed. I pulled up to her building.

"Get out, Desi. I'm sick of talking about that shit. I apologized and we made up. We been good lately and now you want to go into Desi-mode? I apologized so much, I learned how to say 'sorry' in every damn language because you act like you don't understand," I said.

"Fuck you!" she yelled at me.

"Fuck you, too, now get your drunk ass on before I slap the taste out of your mouth!" I yelled back at her. Desi was bipolar or something. I don't know what Desi's real issue was but there was more to how she felt.

"Don't call me and I mean that! I'm done with you because everything I do is never good. I feel like you are always judging me and I hate it," she said.

"Goodnight, shorty. Call me tomorrow when you are back to normal," I said. She mushed me.

"I deserve better," she said as she got out of the truck. I got out and followed her.

"What is that supposed to mean? Every time we argue, you are quick to throw another nigga up in my face. If you want to go back to being a hoe, then go ahead. I ain't force myself on you," I said.

"You know what my issue is. My issue is that it has never been about me selling my ass. Your problem is with Liana. You are scared to let all your guard down because she hurt you and it still hurts you. You are mad that she came back to your mother's house with HER kids. She was your first real love and you still can't get over that she left your black ass for another man. That's your issue, so stop making it seem as if it's mine because it's not. How do you think I feel? You are still in love with her!" Desi said. I saw the sadness on her face and I had to take a step back.

"I just don't know, shorty," I said.

"Are you still in love with her?" she asked me.

"I'm in love with you," I replied.

"Well, do you still love her?" she asked me. I didn't want to tell her but she wasn't going to stop asking until she felt like she heard the truth.

"I love her," I replied.

"How can you love two women and expect for one of them to take you seriously?" Desi asked me but I couldn't answer that. I kissed her lips.

"Goodnight, shorty," I said and she backed away from me.

"You keep hurting me," she said.

"I'm not trying to," I said and she walked away from me.

"Damn!" I said out loud as I walked back to my truck. I was in a messed-up situation.

****

Two days later...

Desi wasn't answering my phone calls. I sent her flowers and everything else I knew she liked. She loved diamonds, so I sent her a new necklace and the bracelet to match.

"What's up with you?" Kwenya asked when he walked into my crib. I was sitting on my couch thinking and I wanted to holla at him about it. He was an older nigga and knew more. I was only twenty-four and all the different emotions Desi was feeling was new to me.

"I need to holla at you about something," I said. He sat on my couch and pulled a blunt out of his pocket. He placed his gun on the coffee table before he lit his blunt up.

"What's good, lil' nigga?" he asked me.

"I'm caught up," I said and he looked at me.

"Not with the police, nigga. I'm talking about between Desi and my ex. The broad that's staying at my mother's house," I said.

"Desi your shorty, right? She holds you down and she loves you for you. My nigga, fuck that other bitch you are talking about. I can't say much, though. For the longest time I been holding on to Rakita's simple ass but when Ashanta came along, shit changed. That night after dinner, Rakita and I fucked on the side of the road. That hammerhead shark bitch tried to trap a nigga. But I ain't trippin'. That dumb broad thinks a nigga can't hold off on his nut. I was starting to tell her that after I had Ashanta's pussy that her pussy couldn't work my nut like that. I dropped the bitch off and ain't look back since. She calls me nonstop and texts me. I don't answer the phone," he said. He stared at the gun on the table.

"Ashanta ain't dead, though. She wants us to think she's dead but she ain't dead. Her friend Serene calls me every day about her to ask if there are any leads to what happened. I can't fix myself to tell them that shorty just bounced. Then she bounced with my seed. Nigga, when I say that my mind is gone, that's what I mean. I don't give a fuck about nothing else, that's how mad I am. That naïve little bitch skipped on me and if she come back and tell me she left because Damos or someone else made her do it, then I will kill her dumb-ass," he said before his phone rang. While Kwenya was on the phone with his lawyer, I was texting Desi's phone. It seemed as if I couldn't get nothing right with her.

"I need to meet up with my lawyer. I will holla at you later," he said. He stood up and tucked his gun in his shorts. I walked to the door with him. He gave me dap before he left out of my crib. As soon as he left my crib, my mother was pulling up and she had Liana with her. I walked down the steps and met them in the driveway. My mother got out of the car with Liana.

"Oh my, this home is beautiful! It's a nice family home," Liana stressed.

"Ma, what are you doing?" I asked her.

"Liana wanted to come over. I'm surprised that you haven't showed her your home yet," my mother said as they walked into my house with me following behind them.

"Oh, please, Bishop. You have to let me decorate. This home is too beautiful to be so plain," Liana said.

"Do you ever shut the hell up? It's my home, something you ain't got, so don't worry about what I got going on over here," I said and my mother looked at me.

"I raised you to be polite," my mother said.

"You also raised me to speak on how I feel and I feel like she needs to shut the hell up about things that don't concern her. Where are her bad-ass kids anyway?" I asked.

"Ree-Ree is going to bring them over. I just got off the phone with her. She took them to see my parents because my parents don't want to see me. I gave her the address to where we were coming if you don't mind," Liana said as she looked around. I never disrespected my mother but I felt like kicking her out, too.

"How in the fuck are you going to bring another nigga's kids to my crib? My own damn shorty hadn't been here yet. You got to bounce," I said.

"I have groceries in the car. I'm cooking dinner like I normally do for you once a month. You never complain," my mother said.

"Ma, do you hear yourself. Liana and I are not together. Why are you and the rest of the family treating her like she is my wife or something? When I cut her off, the rest of y'all was supposed to cut her off, too," I said as I heard a car pull up. I walked outside and it was Ree-Ree pulling up in her silver Cadillac CTS. She jumped out of the car.

"I'm so sorry. I didn't know you lived here. I told Desi to meet me here. She and I are going to a concert and she was going to park and ride with me. I thought I was meeting Liana at the store or something. I didn't figure out it was your home until I saw your truck. Oh my gosh, Bishop. I don't want to be in the middle of this. Desi and I have been hanging out for the past few weeks and I'm cool with Liana," she explained. Ree-Ree really didn't mean any harm. Ree-Ree was cool with everybody but at times she got caught up in the mix because of it. Liana walked out the house and Desi was pulling up blasting her music.

Fuck! I thought.

"What's the matter with you?" Liana asked me.

"Did you do this on purpose?" I asked her.

"What are you talking about?" she asked. When Desi got out of the car, I knew it was going to be something. I knew she was going to stop messing with me after that. She didn't meet my mother, she didn't know where I lived, and Liana and her kids were at my house. Everything about the situation was foul.

"Oh lord," Ree-Ree said. Desi snatched her shades off. I wasn't feeling shorty's choice of clothes. Her linen shorts were too short and it looked like she didn't have any panties on underneath them. Her jean shirt's V-neck line stopped just above her navel. Her sandals strapped up her thick and oiled thighs. Shorty knew she was bad.

"What do you got that on for? What are you trying to do, Desi?" I asked her.

"Nigga, you ain't my man! Now, what is this? Is this your home, and if so, why in the hell is she here?" Desi asked me.

"I'm here with his mother," Liana said.

"Well, let me go and meet Mama," Desi said. She tried to walk in but I pulled her back.

"Shorty, don't bring that stuff around my mother when you go inside," I said to her and she snatched away from me.

"Fuck you!" Desi yelled before she punched me in the face. Liana grabbed her kids and took them in the house.

"You ain't shit!" Desi yelled and punched me again. I grabbed her as she swung on me. Ree-Ree tried to pull Desi away from me but it wasn't working. My mother came out of my house with a frying pan.

"Get the hell away from my son!" my mother yelled. My mother was ready to hit Desi but I pushed her back.

"Chill out, Ma. This is between me and her. All of y'all can go back inside," I said.

"Who is this woman?" my mother asked.

"She is my shorty," I replied. My mother didn't respond. She grabbed Ree-Ree's hand and they walked into the house.

"Why am I just finding out where you live? Then you had the nerve to send me flowers and all of those other gifts, like, nigga, are you fucking serious?" she asked me. She tried to hit me again but I squeezed her a little harder.

"Let me go! Let me go so I can beat your ass then beat that bitch's ass for trying me!" Desi yelled.

"Bishop, my sons are in the house and they can hear this woman's ignorant mouth," Liana said when she walked outside.

"Bitch, fuck you! Those ain't his goddamn kids!" Desi yelled.

"We are having a family dinner," Liana said as she crossed her arms.

"Shut the fuck up!" I yelled at her.

"I'm calling the police," Liana said.

"If you send the police to my house, honest to God I will split your dome in half. Now, get gone before I TKO your dumb ass!" I yelled at Liana. She went back inside of the house and slammed my door. I let Desi go and she backed away from me.

"I don't think you are ready for me. Matter of fact, I know that you aren't. I should've been known after how fucking hard I had to prove myself to you. I'm done with you and I mean that from the bottom of my heart. Stop calling me and you better not think about coming over," she said. She started walking to her car.

"I ain't do shit!" I said to her.

"That's what fuck niggas say. You are a little boy that is trying to play a grown man's game. But, honey, I'm grown and you don't want me to play because I will mess your whole life up," she said to me.

"Yo, get the fuck out of my driveway. I'm trying to tell you that I didn't do nothing. Is it because you didn't meet my mother and didn't know where I live? Give me some time to adjust to this new situation but now it's fuck me? Okay, bet. If I see you stuntin' with another nigga, just watch how I move," I said. She got into the car and backed out of my driveway. I headed straight in the house. I walked in the kitchen and Liana was peeling potatoes like she didn't do nothing. I snatched the bowl of potatoes from her and threw it in the trash. I threw everything that they were trying to make in the trash. My mother was mad but I didn't care.

"What is your problem?" my mother asked me.

"Why are y'all acting like what y'all did was right?" I asked.

"That girl you were just talking to is nothing but trouble. I used to work in the group home she stayed in years ago. She used to sneak out, smoke weed, and all of that other stuff. She was a whore then. I cannot believe you, Bishop. Liana made a mistake but she loves you and you still love her, so what is the problem?" my mother asked me.

"The problem is I don't want her," I responded. Ree-Ree cleared her throat.

"Aunt Rashonda, Desi is not that way anymore," Ree-Ree said.

"So now y'all are best friends?" Liana asked Ree-Ree.

"That's none of your business, Liana. Desi is cool once you get to know her. She sticks it out with Bishop in any situation," Ree-Ree replied.

"You said the girl Chasity had a good heart, too. You think everyone has a good heart," Liana said. Her sons ran through the kitchen with chocolate all over their hands and faces and Liana acted as if she didn't see it.

"Yeah, y'all definitely got to bounce. I want all of y'all to leave my crib, and Ma, from now on when you visit, leave them behind," I said and walked out of the kitchen. I sat on my couch as they left out of the door.

Ashanta

I sat in my rental car across from Kwenya's shop. I didn't want him to see me just yet but I had been following him. I couldn't resist, I just had to watch him. He got off his bike and when he did, his muscles flexed. I wanted him more than ever. It was almost like a game of looking but can't touch. I looked on the passenger seat of my rental car and stared at the newspaper. They were still trying to find my body. I wanted to reach out to my parents but I had an agenda. In order for me to do what I had to do, I had to keep a low profile. After Kwenya walked inside the shop, I pulled off. I knew who I needed to see. I drove to Serene's house and prepared myself for a cursing out.

When I pulled up to her house, I got out of the car and my stomach growled.

"Hopefully Serene will forgive me then fix me something to eat," I said out loud. I rang the doorbell twice before I heard someone unlock the door. When Serene opened the door, I almost didn't recognize her. Her hair was all over her head, she had bags under her eyes, and she just didn't look the same. Tears stung the brim of my eyes because I knew my friend's spirit was gone.

"Where have you been?" she asked me.

"It's a long story," I replied.

"I thought you was dead. I should slam the door in your face," she spat.

"Can I come in?" I asked her and she stepped to the side. I walked into her big house and I could feel the sadness it possessed. I followed her to the living room.

"What happened to your face?" she asked. I had a small bandage on my cheek.

"I will get into that after you tell me what is going on," I replied.

"I thought you was dead, and on top of that, I asked Deron for a divorce. I cannot stomach that he has a son and the fact he wants custody over him. Where do I fit in with that? He must've thought I would accept it," she said.

"I had to do what I had to do. I'm very angry and those who crossed me need to get dealt with. I'm sick and tired and before I bring my baby into this world, those people need to be gone. But I'm here for you," I said and sat down next to her. She wiped the tears from her eyes.

"You seem different. I don't know what it is but you don't seem like my Ashanta," she said.

"Life, that's all. I was living a fake life and I got tired of it," I replied.

"When I first saw you, I didn't know if I wanted to be happy or mad," she said.

"I'm glad you didn't curse me out. I was prepared for that," I replied.

"Tell me everything, Ashanta," she said. I told Serene everything from the moment I visited Kwenya in jail to how I ended up in Mexico. I also told her about Jesse and the Chinese guy in Hollywood.

"Wow, you've been adventurous. But wait till after I have this baby. Rakita is going to get her ass kicked for cutting your face," she said.

"Baby?" I asked.

"Yes, I'm pregnant and alone in this big house. Deron calls me and stops by every day and I ignore him. He broke into the house last night and I didn't know. I woke up and he was standing over me. He said he just wanted to hold me. It felt so good to be wrapped up in his arms but I told him he had to go before I called the cops. He is not allowed to be around me and he doesn't understand that," she said.

"Oh my, Serene. This is all too much. You need your husband. He didn't mean to do it and you never know. You might love Marquis as if he is your own. Deron needs to be here with you. Even if you still want a divorce, at least he will get to experience the pregnancy with you. You are taking that away from him," I said.

"Stop being so damn sweet, shit, but I will think about it. We've been trying for years and it finally happened. His mother and my mother came over a few days ago. My family and his family are so close that's it

133

tearing everyone apart that I want to divorce him. If I do take him back, isn't that a sign of being weak? Is that telling him it's okay to have outside children? Is he capable of doing it again? I have a lot of questions but I don't believe the answers he gives me to them. He and I can be friends and that's it," she said. I knew Serene was a woman who stood by what she believed in. It was hard to change her mind.

"Kwenya was so worried about you. I talked to your mother last week. She called me crying because she accused him of doing something to you. She said after she sobered up, she felt so bad. Your father has paid people to look for your body because police gave up their search for you. Everyone is devastated," she said.

"I know but there is nothing I can do about that. It's better this way. If I tell my parents now, they will never understand and it will mess me up. I don't want nobody else to know until I'm done," I replied.

"So Rakita is a FED?" she asked me.

"Apparently so, but she won't be nothing by the time I'm done with her," I said. After I spent the day with Serene, I headed back to my hotel. Serene wanted me to stay but I didn't want Deron to pop up and see me. As soon as I got to my room, I opened my laptop and started typing. Jesse was right; I lived through my characters when all I really wanted to do was live through me. As I was done typing up a murder scene, my cell phone rang.

"Yes," I answered because only Jesse and Serene had my number at the moment.

"How is everything coming along?" Jesse asked me.

"Good," I answered.

"Remember what we discussed? Well, he will be arriving tomorrow morning. I will call you with further details when his plane lands," she said.

"Okay," I answered.

"You forgot to send me what you typed so far. I miss your work already and you haven't been gone long," she replied.

"Sure will and let me know if my story isn't flowing. It's more urban than I expected," I said.

"Once all of this over, promise me that you turn this into a movie and don't stop from there," she said.

"I won't," I answered.

"Goodnight," she replied. After I hung up, I dialed a number. The number was still the same, and after the fifth ring, his voice came through the phone. I didn't say anything because I just wanted to hear his voice.

"Yoooo," he answered. I sat on the phone and surprisingly, he didn't hang up. He sat on the phone, too.

"Where are you Ashanta?" he asked me and my heart fell down to my stomach. My palms started to sweat but I couldn't hang up.

We are really connected. He feels it is me even though I'm supposed to be dead, I thought.

"Where and fuck are you? Do you think this shit is a game? You want to call my phone like some crazy-ass serial killer? This ain't the *Scream* movie," he said then he calmed down.

"Why are you doing this, shorty? Is that not my baby? Did you go back to that nigga? What is it?" he asked me. I hung up on him. I wasn't doing what I was doing just for myself but I was doing it for Kwenya's freedom. I knew he had a court date coming up and although it seemed selfish of me, I was going to end up with my man in the end. I put that on everything. I went back to typing my next chapter which was titled, *Fake It till Make It.*

Kwenya

I stared at my phone and thought for a split second I lost my mind. I had a feeling that was Ashanta and she was playing games with me. I got down on the floor in my bedroom and started doing sit-ups to burn off some steam. Afterward, I headed to the shower. Once I was done, I got into bed.

"Baby, wake up," Ashanta said to me.

"Chill out, shorty. Damn, go to sleep," I fussed and rolled back over.

"I want you inside of me, Kwenya," she said lustfully. She climbed on top of me naked. Her stomach was and full like a basketball. Her breasts were swollen and her nipples stuck out like missiles. I sat up and took her hardened nipple in my mouth. Her moans filled the room as her pussy dripped on me. My tongue traveled up to her neck and along her chin. I reached down to my hardened dick and slowly pushed it inside of her. Her tight walls gripped me as I went further into her. A painful gasp slipped from her lips as she took all of me inside of her. I wrapped my arms around her as she bounced up and down on my dick. When she parted her legs further, I brushed my thumb across her clit.

"Yessssss, baby!" she screamed as I drilled into her. I sucked harder on her nipples and her body trembled. She dug her nails into my shoulders as her pussy exploded onto my dick. I plunged further inside her, digging my fingers into her hips to make sure she wasn't going anywhere. I wanted her to feel everything I was giving her.

"What other nigga can fuck you like this?" I whispered in her ear as I jabbed at her spot.

"Nobody!" she screamed out.

"Why in the fuck did you leave me?" I asked but she didn't respond. I pulled out of her before I rolled her over on her back. I pinned her knees against the headboard. My hands gripped her thighs as my tongue plunged inside of her.

"OOOOHHHHHHHHHH!" she moaned. I pulled her clit into my mouth and sucked on it. After I released her swollen bud, I pressed my tongue flat on her pussy. I pulled her pussy lips together as I sucked her orgasm from her and she squirted into my mouth. Pre-cum dripped from my dick as the taste of her teased the appetite I had for her juicy center...

When I woke up, I felt nut drizzling down my dick. I tossed the covers back and nut was everywhere. My dick was still hard.

"Fuck!" I groaned out as I jerked myself off while I thought about Ashanta's tight pussy squeezing my dick as I stretched her open. Bella jumped on my bed, sniffing around my dick and I hurriedly knocked her off the bed.

"Get back!" I yelled at her and she ran out of my bedroom. I looked at the clock and it was midnight. I pulled everything off my bed and stuffed it in the washing machine. I took a shower and got dressed. I opened the door to my garage and decided to take my motorcycle out to cruise through the city. I revved up my engine and put my helmet on. I took off without a destination.

****

I sat at a bar with a glass of Henny. A woman sat down beside me. She looked older but she carried her age well. Her hair was styled in a high bun with a bang. Her eyes slanted and her face was round; she looked like she was mixed with black and Asian or Hispanic. She wore a romper and the scent of her Marc Jacobs perfume tingled my nose. I knew the scent because Ashanta used to wear it.

"Was someone sitting here?" she asked me.

"Naw," I answered. She asked the bartender for a menu.

"What are you drinking if you don't mind me asking?" she said.

"Henny," I replied.

"A man's best friend." She giggled.

"That's what it is," I replied. I focused my attention on the TV above the bar. The news channel was on and Ashanta's face appeared on the screen. They were still looking for her.

"That is so sad what happened to that young woman. I told one of my friends that it sounds like someone killed her and tried to cover it up. I don't know nothing about her but from what it seemed, she was a well put-together woman. She had a good education, proper upbringing, and she was a doctor. I don't believe she was drunk," the woman said.

139

Her ass ain't dead. She's busy playing on a nigga phone, I thought to myself.

I ordered another drink and the woman sat and stared at me.

"You look stressed. Do you want to talk about it, young man?" she asked.

"Young man, huh?" I said.

"Yes, I might be old enough to be your mother. How old are you? Twenty-five?" she asked me.

"Naw, twenty-eight," I answered.

"Well, I'm forty-one," she replied and I nodded my head. My phone rang and that time it was Rakita. I didn't answer for her. A few minutes later she was texting me and telling me to come over. As tempted as I was to bust a nut, I decided to just stay away from her. I didn't know what Ashanta was up to or if she was really dead and I was denial. My head was spinning thinking about Ashanta.

"It's better to talk to someone. Let me guess, are you having woman problems?" she asked.

"Naw, I'm good on that," I answered. I didn't want to tell her about Ashanta. It wasn't her business to know about what happened to her.

"You are thinking about something. Are you married? Any children?" she asked.

"Naw and I have one on the way," I answered.

"Congratulations. Is that what you are worried about? It's okay, trust me. After the baby comes into this world, all of those feelings go away," she said. She and I talked for a little bit and she told me her name was Shantel. I paid my tab and Shantel's tab.

"I'm out of here," I said and stood up. She grabbed her purse and stood up, too.

"I'm leaving, too," she said before she followed me out. I got on my motorcycle and grabbed my helmet.

"Here is my business card. I'm a promoter and if you need help with getting your business out there, I can help you with that. I've actually been to the Smithson's in DC. I heard there were more but I live in the DC area. Smithson's is a very laid back and peaceful place. Have you ever thought about expanding?" she asked.

"Yes, I just got sidetracked with a few things," I said and took her business card.

"Well, I look forward to hearing from you," she said.
"How about you set something up with me later on this week. I just need a little help with advertising."

"Okay, I need to see if my schedule is clear and I will contact you with a date and time," she said. I gave her my number before I headed back home.

****

Three days later...

"Yo, what do you want?" I asked Yolo when he walked into my shop. He had been coming into my shop every other day.

"Where is Poet?" he asked.

"She doesn't get here until noon today. Yo, you really want her, don't you?" I asked him. Shantel walked into my shop before Yolo responded.

"I'm sorry I'm late. The traffic was ridiculous," she said. She sat at the table with her briefcase. She wore a pink skirt with the matching jacket and a pair of nude pumps. It reminded me of the way Ashanta used to dress.

"Nigga, you smashing Stella?" Yolo asked me.

"What do you think?" I asked him.

"Hell yeah. I would knock the gray hair off that pussy. After she gets done jerking me off, that Carpal Tunnel will be gone," he replied.

"Shorty my aunt's age. She ain't that old, though, she's still young to me," I replied.

"So what? I'll smash your aunt. I swear your aunt Lolita can carry my seed. I mean that, too, because you know I had love for her when I was a little nigga," he said. I looked over at Shantel to make sure she couldn't hear Yolo.

"Nigga, you ain't smashing my aunt," I said.

"You smashed mine and I'm still mad about that shit," Yolo fussed.

"It ain't my fault your aunt's the same age as us," I replied.

"I'll get up with you later. I will be back when Poet gets off. She's acting like she ain't feeling a nigga," he said. I gave him dap before he left out of the shop. Shantel had a few papers on the table.

"So, are you ready?" she asked me when I sat down across from her.

"Yeah. What do you have for me?" I asked and she blushed.

"Are you straight? You need something to drink?" I asked her.

"No, I'm fine," she answered. Shantel and I were going over a few ideas when my phone rang. I excused myself and walked to the back of the shop. I answered the phone and it was from an "Unknown" caller.

143

"Yoooo," I answered. I didn't answer blocked calls up until Ashanta disappeared on me.

Silence.

"Come on, shorty. This shit is getting ridiculous," I said but there was still silence on the other end. The caller sounded like they were moving around. I listened closely to hear the sounds of something dangling. Ashanta wore those Alex and Ani bracelets and they used to make a lot of noise. I heard the same noise over the phone.

"You think this is a joke, don't you? Your face is all over the news and in the newspapers. Your parents are worried about you. What type of shit are you on? I swear, shorty, wherever you are, you better stay there. Next time you call, take those annoying bracelets off," I said into the phone and she hung up. I went back to the front and sat down at the table to listen to Shantel ramble on. I was only thinking about wrapping my hands around Ashanta's neck.

****

The next day…

After I got off the phone with my connect, I dropped my phone in the sink which was filled with water. I had another shipment coming in. Yolo, Bishop, and Jada were moving bricks into the streets faster than I thought. Money was coming in, I was getting another part added to my house, and Shantel was helping me expand my business with her ideas. I was supposed to be carefree at that point but I wasn't. When I left the house, I headed to my mother's house. It had been over a month since I last talked to her. When I pulled up, Bernie's car was in the driveway. The nigga moved in when I got locked up, I heard from one of my aunts. I used my key and it still worked. I stepped inside the house and it was quiet. It was too quiet for my liking but I saw the basement door open. I walked downstairs to the basement and turned on the light. Bernie had my mother handcuffed with a muzzle over her mouth while she was stretched out on the guest bed. Bernie jumped off the bed wearing a thong and tube socks.

"What the fuck is this? *Fifty Shades of Grey*?" I asked. I remembered the movie Ashanta made me watch with her a while back. Ashanta had me doing all kinds of things that I wasn't used to.

"Kwenya?" my mother asked. She couldn't see me because she was blindfolded. A nigga was glad she still had her robe on. I pulled out my phone and called Yolo.

"My nigga, you won't believe this shit," I said. Yolo turned his music down.

"What happened?" he asked.

"I'm over my mother's crib. I came down to the basement and the nigga Bernie in here looking like he is about to strip at the strip club. Nigga's ass is all out and his socks look like rain boots," I said. Yolo laughed so hard he started choking.

"Get the fuck out, Kwenya!" my mother screamed as she tried to yank away from the handcuffs. Bernie was getting dressed while tripping over his clothes. I hung up with Yolo who was still laughing and headed back up the stairs. I headed to the kitchen and there was a stack of unpaid bills sitting by the fridge. I gave my mother money every month and I paid the mortgage. She had never been late paying a bill. Bernie walked up the stairs with scowl on his face.

"What's good, my nigga? What's up with this?" I asked him.

"What are you talking about?" he asked me as he balled his fists up.

"You are fucking my mother and you can't pay her bills? My nigga, you got to do better than that," I responded. My mother came up the stairs and she didn't look too happy to see me.

"What and the hell are you doing here, Kwenya?" she asked.

"I stopped by to drop some money off to you, but being as though you got this nigga over here, he can pay your bills from now on. I love you to death, Ma, but if I ain't welcome to a house I paid for then I'm not responsible for your bills. From now on, this fuck nigga can pay them, but then again, I forgot toy cops don't make much. Put his lil' fruity ass on the corner so he can sell some ass since he wants to wear thongs and shit," I said.

"Watch your mouth," she said to me. The whole situation crushed me but I couldn't let her see that it did.

"This nigga set me up and you still wanna lay up with him? What type of mother are you, Ma? I got a court date! Twenty-five fucking years if I'm found guilty and you don't care about that? This nigga more important? Yo, I swear I'm done," I said and Bernie smirked. I whispered to him on my way out of the kitchen.

"Laugh now but when I'm done with you, those thongs you were wearing are going to come in handy. A nigga named Buddy fittin' to tap that fruity ass. Punk bitch," I said before I walked out of the house. My mother called out to me but I kept walking. I couldn't sweat it because I had my own agenda and shit was going to hit the fan soon.

****

Three days later...

    I sat outside of a sports bar and waited for the last nigga that owed me money. When I got locked up, he figured he didn't have to pay me. His name was Capo and he'd been ducking Jada and Yolo, too, but he ended up tagging his location on Facebook like he was forgotten. I got out and walked inside of the sports bar. I sat in the corner wearing a black T-shirt and black cargos. I had to go back to the person I was years back. When I was a young nigga, I merked anybody who didn't pay me my bread. When Capo got up, he headed to the bathroom. I waited a few minutes before I walked in. He was at the sink washing his hands. My snapback cap was pulled down low over my eyes. When he turned around, he was staring down the barrel of the gun. He backed up into the sink and I grabbed him around his neck. I shoved the gun down his throat and he started gagging. I pulled the gun out so he could talk.

"I got your money in my trunk. Please, yo, just don't do this," he pleaded.

"Oh word?" I asked him.

"Yeah, man, please don't do it," he said as his body trembled.

"Walk out, and you better not say shit to nobody," I gritted. He rubbed his neck as he walked out of the bathroom and a few niggas were walking in but I kept my head down. Capo wasn't moving fast enough.

"Nigga, hurry up," I said from behind him. He picked up his pace as he walked through the crowd. Once we got outside, he headed straight to his car. He popped the trunk and pulled out a small backpack.

"Just take it," he said. I opened up the bag to look inside. I didn't have time to count it but I didn't care if he shorted me. Capo was going to die that night no mattered what.

"See, now, nigga, was that hard?" I asked him.

"Come on, Kwenya, man. We been dealing with each other for a minute," he said.

"I know but just because I got jammed up, didn't mean your debt was gone. I still need my money and you've known for years that I'm all about my money," I spat. He was ready to say something else but I shot him in the head. Capo slid down his car with his mouth wide open. Blood dripped from the wound in his forehead and down his face. His eyes were lifeless.

"Good doing business with you," I said and dropped the gun. I got back inside my car and hurriedly pulled off. I caught three bodies and they were all on Bernie's gun—the gun he had in my mother's room that he didn't think I knew about. I stole the gun a few days after I came home from jail. I sat outside my mother's house and waited for her to leave that day.

I wore gloves on all three murders; Chaos, Capo, and Kev. I wasn't a stupid nigga and knew it was going to be hard killing a cop. Killing a cop was bad for business in the neighborhood. A lot of hustlers lose out on money when police patrol the area 24/7 looking for answers. It was eye for an eye. If I was going down for those bricks, that nigga was going down for murder. Without Bernie, Bullet didn't have any protection.

****

Two hours later...

I lay in bed watching TV. My phone rang and I hurriedly picked it up.

"Are you done playing, Ashanta?" I asked the caller.

"Ummmm, excuse me?" the caller said. I sat up in bed and scratched my head.

Ashanta got me acting like she had cocaine in her pussy. A nigga is strung out for real, I thought.

"Who is this?" I asked. I looked at the clock and it was two in the morning.

"This is Shantel. I know it's late but I've been having problems sleeping at night," she said.

"Yeah, me, too," I replied. Bella jumped up on the bed and laid on my leg. I rubbed her head and I didn't know why because I hated small dogs.

"My husband's been dead for over a year and sometimes I think I hear him downstairs making a sandwich. He died from a bad heart," she said.

"Sorry to hear that, shorty," I said as I yawned.

"I know this is a bit tacky but can I invite you to dinner tomorrow night?" she asked.

"I'm going to be busy tomorrow night," I lied and the other end got quiet. I heard a dog bark in the background.

"Shut up, Kimba!" she yelled.

"Yeah, I'm definitely going to send my dog over there with you," I said.

"What kind of dog is it?" she asked.

"Hell if I know. It's small and got little, beady eyes. It's the size of a rat," I answered and she laughed.

"Sounds like a toy dog. You don't take me as the type to want something so feminine," she said.

"Wait a minute, shorty. This is my baby mama dog. She dipped on me and left her behind," I answered.

"How about we go to the dog park tomorrow?" she asked.

"Aight, that's cool, but you can walk her while I make some phone calls?" I replied. Ten minutes later, after I got off the phone with Shantel, my phone rang again.

"Yeah," I answered when I realized it was my mother calling.

"Kwenya! They locked him up! They just came and got Bernie. The police are tearing up my house! They are looking for evidence to a murder," she cried.

Damn that was quick, I thought, but then again, the gun I dropped at the scene was registered so it didn't take long to find its owner.

"Sorry to hear that, Ma, but I'm tired. Keep your head up," I said and hung up. She tried to call back but I let it go to voicemail.

****

I turned up the rap music as Bella barked. I wanted to throw the dog out of the window. When I pulled up to the park, Shantel was waiting for me on the bench. She had a German Shepherd.

"Damn, Bella, I hope those little legs can run. Kimba is going to snack on you," I said and she barked at me. I got out of the car with the dog in my arm. I put a leash around her neck when I sat her down on the grass. As soon as I let the leash go, she charged into Shantel's big dog. Shantel's dog was scared of Bella.

"I thought those were watch dogs?" I asked Shantel.

"I think Kimba is a little sweet at times. He is scared of everything," she joked. Bella ran around in circles as Shantel and I talked. She was cool and in some areas, she reminded me of Ashanta. They both had a relaxed attitude.

"It's been almost two hours and Kimba is hungry I'm sure," she said. Bella sat on Shantel's lap and her dog laid on the side of the bench.

"Yeah, I got shit to do," I said and stood up. She carried Ashanta's dog in her arm while she walked her dog as we headed toward her car.

"Oh my God! I have a flat tire," she said out loud. I looked and both of her tires on the driver's side were flat. There was a note on her windshield. She pulled the paper off and read it.

"Stay the fuck away," she said as she read the note.

Sounds like Rakita's crazy ass, I thought.

"Who would do something like this. Do you think it's your child's mother?" she asked me.

"Naw, trust me, I know it's not her," I said. She called the tow-truck company and after they came, I took her home. After I dropped her off, I headed back to my crib.

Damos

"My daughter isn't dead! Where and the fuck have you been? You disappeared and now all of sudden you want to show your face?" Ashanta's mother yelled at me as her husband tried to calm her down. She snatched away from him.

"Don't you touch me!" she screamed at him. I knew she was drunk because the bitch was always drunk. Her husband pulled her down into the chair. We sat in a lawyer's office going over Ashanta's will. It was officially ruled that she was dead. Ashanta forgot to take me out of her will and being as though we didn't get a chance to get divorced, she was still my wife.

"You put your filthy hands on my daughter and you think you are going to get her hard-earned money?" Mrs. Scott asked me.

"Ma'am, we will ask you to leave if you have another outburst. Mr. Scott, can you please inform your wife that we cannot do anything about this?" the lawyer asked Ashanta's father. Mrs. Scott sat down and crossed her arms.

"Damos Bennett is entitled to 500,000 dollars plus the house that's up for sale. I'm sorry but there is nothing we can do about that. Even if Damos and Ashanta were divorced, he would still be entitled to this money because his name is in the will. Him being her husband has nothing to do with it," Katie, the lawyer said. I started sweating bullets because I was finally getting something out of my miserable marriage.

"It takes a while for someone to be declared dead. I'm talking about years," Mr. Scott said.

"Yes, but according to the report, there is no way someone would've survived that crash. It's the evidence that supports this decision. If Ashanta just vanished that would've been a different story but that isn't the case," the lawyer said. Ashanta's mother stood up.

"You will not get away with this. You will not sleep as long as I'm alive. You disappeared and you came back on the same day her will is read. Sounds pretty fishy to me," Mrs. Scott said.

"I will sleep peacefully because I'm moving out of state just to enlighten you," I said. Ashanta's father leaped across the table and choked me.

"I will kill you! Son of a bitch, I will kill you!" he yelled. The lawyer called for security while Ashanta's mother stood there cheering him on.

"Goddamn it, Samuel. Strangle his ass harder! Let me show you," Mrs. Scott said. I tried to push Ashanta's father off of me but her mother was choking me, too. We all fell onto the floor and the door burst open. Two security guards pulled her parents off me.

"I'm suing the both of you!" I shouted. Ashanta's mother took her wig off and threw it at me as they tried to pull her through the door.

"I'm going to kick your ass! You did this to my daughter!" she screamed. I fixed my shirt and grabbed my truck keys off the table. I walked out of the door and down the opposite hall in the building. Her

156

parents were still yelling at me but I laughed to myself. As soon as I received my money, I was leaving Maryland and never coming back.

****

I went to visit my father. He had been in jail for a week. He had three murders pinned against him. After I went through the visiting process, I sat in the waiting area for him. When the C.O. brought him out, he looked broken down. He didn't look the same. He sat down in front of me.

"What's up, Pops?" I asked him.

"You got to get me out of here. Some of these men I put in here," he said. Kwenya knew what he was doing when he set it up so that my father could go to jail. Soon as niggas find out you was a cop it was nothing but a death sentence.

"Your bail was denied. I will be coming into some money soon and I will get you a good lawyer. I promise you I will do whatever it is that you need me to do," I said.

"How is your mother?" he asked me.

"She left for New York a few days ago. She said she hoped for the best for you but she wasn't taking any of your phone calls," I said and he put his head down.

"Life is a long time, son," he said.

"I'm doing my best but I got to keep a low profile. There's a bounty on my head," I said and he nodded.

"Why couldn't you just do right by your wife? If you didn't make the same mistakes I made, you wouldn't be running and I wouldn't be in jail," he said.

Nigga, shut your crybaby ass up. You been a fuck nigga all your life and now you regret it? I asked myself.

"I got to tell you about Rakita," he said but visiting was over because a fight broke out between two girls inside the visiting room. I gave my father the head nod as he was being escorted out. I headed back to a different house that I was staying in. When Chasity left the other house, I left too because I had a feeling Kwenya or Bishop was going to pop up. It was late and the house sat down a long, dark road; it was almost in the woods. The porch light was on and I put my key inside the door to unlock it. I turned the light on by the door inside the house and there was a man whom I'd never seen before sitting on my couch. He had a gun in his hand and he looked to be in his thirties.

"Who are you and what are you doing in my house?" I asked him but before he could respond, I was struck in the back of my head…

****

Someone threw cold water on me. I was dizzy and my mouth felt dry. My stomach ached and I felt the need to throw up. I could barely hold my head up. It wasn't just the blow to the head that had me feeling that way; I was drugged also. My vision was blurry but I could make out where I was. I was sitting in the living room in someone else's house. The guy smacked my face to give me something to drink because I was nodding off. I didn't know what it was but it tasted horrible and it took some of the sluggish feeling away.

"Who are you?" I asked the man. He was around five-foot-ten and he was black as night. He had a deep gash in his cheek.

"Did you miss me?" a voice came out of nowhere. When I looked to the side of me, Ashanta was standing in the hallway wearing all-black. I tried to get up but I was tied to a chair.

"What is going on? Let me go!" I yelled.

"Thanks, Mondo. I got it from here," she said to the man and he left out of the living room.

She grabbed a metal folding chair and sat it down in front of me. She took a seat then crossed her legs.

"My dear, dear husband," she said to me.

"I thought you was dead," I said.

"I been dead. The moment you raped me and humiliated me, time and time again. I died a long time ago," she replied.

159

"You never was a smart man. I found you because you gave your address to my lawyer. I bet you couldn't wait to collect my insurance money. You do know when a bank issues a check, they need all your information, right? What a dummy," she said. I hulked up a glob of spit into her face. She wiped it off and slapped me as hard as she could.

"How did you get my information?" I asked her. If she knew that much, I was for certain she knew more.

"I have someone who knows someone with connections. This is a very crooked world," she replied. I studied her and her hips spread a little. Her breasts were nice and round. Her face, also was nice and round. She was beautiful even with the small patch on her face. Her hair was styled into an up-do.

"A baby does the body good," she said.

"What baby? Is that my baby?" I asked her. I forced myself on my wife and I actually felt bad about it. I was mad she was screwing around with Kwenya. It angered me that another man was able to take her away from me.

"No, it's Kwenya's baby. But enough of that, let's talk," she said.

"About how much of a whore you really are?" I asked her.

"I'm not a whore but I can get a little nasty," she said and licked her lips.

"Are you high? Bitch, you lost your damn mind! Get me out of here! Help! Help!" I yelled as I hopped up and down in my chair. Ashanta laughed at me.

"There is nobody here. Did you know I have a million-dollar life insurance on you? I could have someone gut you like a fish right now. That man Mondo is here for me and he is going to do whatever I tell him to do to you, so if I was you, I would shut the fuck up," she spat.

"You have really lost your mind. You faked your death and now you are talking out of your head. This doesn't sound like you. Whatever you are going through has nothing to do with me," I pleaded.

"But you are the one who started it all. What's the matter? I'm not naïve enough for you now? I'm sick of being bullied by everyone because they think they can get away with it but they thought wrong," she said.

"Okay, congratulations on finding your inner woman. Now, let me go!" I yelled at her. She balled her fist up and slammed it into my face.

"Shut up and listen to me and listen to me good. There is a guard in the very same jail that your father is in. One phone call to the guard and something might happen. Inmates hate cops, so just think what would happen if he was out of solitary confinement?" she asked me.

"My father has nothing to do with this!" I yelled at her and she slapped me.

"Shut the fuck up! He set Kwenya up, so he has everything to do with this! The both of you are going down. But this is what I want you to do. You are going to sit in this chair for three days. You can shit yourself and pee yourself but you will sit in this chair. You will think about everything you did to me," she said and stood up.

"NOOOOOOOOOOOOOO!" I yelled. The guy Mondo walked out into the living room with a combat knife in his hand.

"I'm leaving because I have things to do. Mondo will sit here and watch you," Ashanta said before she left. Mondo looked at me and my stomach started to turn because he looked at me like I was fresh meat.

"I'm going to have fun with you," he said as he caressed my face. I screamed at the top of my lungs and he laughed.

"Nobody will hear you," he said to me.

"Why are you doing this? How much do you want? I'm coming into some money and I will give you half," I pleaded.

"It's not the money I'm here for. It's the entertainment, my little damsel in distress," he teased. A tear fell from my eye. Ashanta needed to hurry back. I was glad she was gone but I regretted feeling that way as Mondo openly stared at my crotch area.

Jesus help me! I shouted inside my head.

Desi

I walked around my new home admiring the work that was being done to it. I couldn't wait to sell it because it was a brand new door for me. Bishop tried to call me two days after the altercation between the two of us, but I didn't answer him. Every time I wanted to escape my past, something always popped back up reminding me of who I am. His mother Rashonda, worked inside one of the homes I lived in for troubled teens. It was a place I had to go to because all the foster homes rejected me. I was a whore back then and all the counselors knew about it. It would be just my luck that one of them was Bishop's mother and I knew she wasn't going to accept me. She had her mind made up on who she wanted her son to be with. My phone rang bringing me out of my thoughts.

"Yeah," I answered dryly.

"I'm just calling to see how you feel," Ree-Ree said. After I got to know Ree-Ree a little better, she wasn't as dumb as I thought she was. She was just too good to people. She was a sweet girl and I knew it was hard for Chasity to lose her as a friend.

"I'm okay, just maintaining," I said.

"You don't sound good," she replied.

"I'm fine," I answered.

"How about we go out tonight? Jada had to go out of town and I don't have nothing to do besides reading. I'm getting bored with that," she said.

"Okay, I will be ready by ten," I answered. After I locked up my house, I got into my car. A black Lincoln Navigator with tints stopped on the side of my car. The window came down and it was Ro—Rohann. I put my window down and took my shades off.

"What do you want?" I asked him. He got out of his truck and leaned into my window.

"I want you, Desi," he said.

"Are you following me or something?" I asked him.

"No, you know I'm from Baltimore. I have family that lives a few blocks away from here. Are you moving here?" he asked me.

"No, I'm fixing it then selling it," I replied.

"Let's grab some lunch," he said.

"Call your wife and tell her," I said and he laughed.

"She and I are separated. I don't know if it's permanent or not but I moved out a few days ago," he said. I rolled my eyes because a nigga would tell you anything.

"Umph. Sorry to hear that," I replied. His eyes grazed over my thighs.

"You don't miss me?" he asked.

"Ummm let me think—hell no, I don't miss you. Now, back away because I got shit to do," I spat.

"I will pay you for your time," he said. I slapped him in the face and pushed open my car door. The door pushed him back into his truck.

"I am sick and tired of muthafuckas telling me what they are paying for! I'm not doing that shit anymore, so leave me the fuck alone before I go to the press and have them release your dirty secrets on the same day you get drafted on. I will tell them all about how you ate my pussy and my ass. I will tell them every damn thing," I yelled at him. He held his hands up.

"Whoa, whoa. This is not called for. I know you are about your money and all I wanted to do was spend some time with you. I'm not thinking about the sex but ain't shit free with you," he responded.

Well-trained, I thought to myself. I put my windows up and turned off my car. I locked my car up before I got in the passenger's seat of his truck. He got in and looked at me.

"Damn, you hit hard. Why are you so mean?" he asked me.

"Why are you so damn nosey? I'm mean because I want to be. Now drive or else I will get out," I spat.

He placed his hand on my thigh. Ro wasn't hood but his swag was still attractive. He had his own style which was also attractive but his sex was too gentle. I liked it rough and demanding. Hair pulling, smacking, and choking. I wanted to be overpowered in the bedroom and Ro didn't have that. He was fully equipped and he knew what he was doing but it just wasn't my taste. I wanted to smack his hand off my thigh but I couldn't. I secretly wanted that type of affection. He caressed my thigh as he drove through the streets of Baltimore.

"Why do you keep playing with me?" he asked me.

"I don't take niggas seriously. You cheated on your wife with me. What makes me so special?" I asked him.

"I can't answer that but all I know is I stuck it out with my wife for the kids. I haven't told anybody else but our first child ain't mine. I should've left when I found out but I love that little girl. I stayed and stuck it out with her and had more kids, but in the back of my mind, I can't trust her and will never trust her. I still love her but I know she and I will never be happy. The damage is permanent," he said.

We arrived at Mo's Seafood downtown Baltimore. Ro got out and opened his truck door for me. I walked inside of the restaurant and he had his arm around my waist. I believed him at that point when he said he was separated. He and I never went out in public in fear that his wife would find out about it. We were immediately seated. The waiter set our menus down then took our drink orders. I ordered a glass of wine and Ro ordered Cîroc on the rocks.

"What's up with you and the dude with the diamond grill? The one I saw you with down in Ocean City?" he asked.

166

"He and I were in this complicated relationship but we decided to take a break," I replied then he looked at me.

"What happened?" he asked.

"Why do you want to know?" I responded.

"Come on, Desi. I been around you long enough to know the nigga did something to hurt you. You know everything about me, so I want you to allow me to know everything about you," he said.

"His ex-girlfriend and his mother are close. She is staying at his mother's house. He didn't feel like I was special enough to meet his mother and know where he lives. I would've done anything for him but he let me down. It goes deeper than that but I don't want to go much into details," I said.

"You got a man that appreciates who you are but you fell for one who doesn't?" he asked. I could see by the look on his face that his feelings were hurt.

"I felt something different when I was around him. It's hard to explain. But I told you enough and that's all you need to know," I said.

"Can I take you on a vacation for a few days? It seems like you and I both need it," he said and I smiled.

"If you are paying for everything. The only thing I should be pulling out of my purse is my lip gloss," I replied and he burst into laughter.

"I got you. You don't even need to bring your purse," he said. I heard someone's voice and it sounded familiar. When I turned around, it was Liana and two other women.

"Great," I said out loud.

"You know them?" he asked me.

"The tall one is Bishop's ex-girlfriend," I replied.

"She looks good," he said. I kicked him under the table. Liana and I locked eyes and she smiled at me. I rolled my eyes at her. I turned back around to focus all of my attention on Ro.

"What are you getting to eat?" I asked him.

"Hopefully you. I miss that little piercing down there," he said talking about my pierced clit.

"You can keep on missing it because I'm not letting you down there just yet," I replied.

"I'm up for the challenge. When a man got to work for it, it makes the pussy even better," he said.

Is this what I been missing? I asked myself. Ro and I ate and talked. He brightened my mood because I couldn't stop smiling. He dropped me back off to my car after lunch. He kissed me with so much passion I had to pull away from him.

"I will call you later. Thanks for lunch," I said as he towered over me. He had me trapped between him and my car. His dick was pressed against my center. He pecked me on the lips before he pulled away.

"Stay beautiful," he said before he got back inside his truck.

****

I wore a pair of tan linen pants, nude pumps, and an-off-the-shoulder top. I didn't feel the need to dress up because I wasn't in the mood. I parked my car and met Ree-Ree at the club entrance. She was dressed casual but cute, too. She gave me a hug and I almost pushed her off. I wasn't used to that type of affection from a friend. I never had a real friend.

"It's okay. You will get used to it," she said after I didn't hug her back.

"I guess you want me to chase after your pussy, too," I said and she laughed.

"Oh hush. I didn't think Chasity was going to fall for me," she said. We entered the club and Future's song, *Commas,* blared through the loud speakers.

"Liana and I got into it the other day. She cursed me out because she said I was taking sides and I was supposed to be loyal to her," she said and I somewhat felt bad because I didn't want her to get dragged into the situation.

"You have known her longer than me so it's only right she feels that way," I replied.

"I like her as a person but I don't want her with Bishop. She just comes back home and thinks that shit is supposed to stop. My aunt gives her too much authority," she stressed.

"Excuse me," someone said. When I turned around, it was a light-skinned girl with braids that came down to her butt. The denim jeans she wore hugged her thick hips and the top she wore complimented her breasts.

"Oh my God, I didn't realize that was you, Ree-Ree," the girl said.

"Hey Poet. Poet, this is my friend Desi. Desi, this is Poet. She works at Kwenya's bakery," she said.

"I've seen her before, but hello," Poet said to me.

"Who are you here with?" Ree-Ree asked her.

"Damn, shorty. You just left a nigga," Yolo said to Poet when he walked over.

"What's good with you Diamond?" Yolo teased. He called me Diamond from the movie *Player's Club*.

"Don't start with me, nigga," I said.

170

"This is what I have to deal with," Poet said.

"Stop lying. I'm nice to you, shorty," he said to her.

"Threatening my landlord for my house key is not nice. It's crazy as hell," she said to him.

"That's what niggas do when they want something. We go above and beyond, and I know the nigga, so it was cool," he said.

"How did he get you to come out with him?" I asked Poet. As fine as Yolo was, he wasn't working with a full deck.

"He kept coming to the shop around the time I get off and I gave in," she said and blushed.

Bitch, you blushing. That nigga is a damn fool! I yelled in my head. Bishop walked through the crowd and I couldn't believe who was trailing behind him; it was that bitch Monie. As soon as he saw me, he stopped in his tracks. I grabbed my drink from the bar and walked off. Ree-Ree followed me.

"It's nothing like that, Desi," Ree-Ree said defending her cousin.

"I don't care," I replied.

"Why did you walk off? You didn't get a chance to see that Monie had a few of her friends with her and she was probably just following him," she said. I looked over at the bar and she was right but it didn't matter to me because I wasn't feeling him at the moment.

"Annapolis' finest, Desi is in the building! Let's see if she is going to shut the dance floor down tonight!" the DJ yelled into the mic.

"Don't ask me to come to the club on Saturday's anymore," I told Ree-Ree.

"Why not? You know you can't turn down twerking music," she replied. Bishop walked over to me but I didn't walk away. I was curious to see what he wanted.

"Can I holla at you for a second?" he asked me. I thought it was pointless that he asked because he was dragging me off the dance floor anyway. We stood in the hallway next to the restrooms.

"What is it?" I asked him.

"You going on dates already?" he asked.

"I don't get the point of this conversation and where it's trying to lead to," I said. He gripped the neckline of my shirt and pushed me into the wall. My drink slipped out of my hand.

"I don't like your fucking games, shorty," he spat and I pushed him away from me.

"Being fed up is called a game to you?" I asked.

"I was practically living with you. I didn't think where I lived mattered to you because I came home to you every night," he said.

"Liana is a part of you," I said.

"So you want to say 'fuck me' over a bitch I'm not with, but you want to fuck with a nigga who is married? You jumped into another situation without trying to fix ours. Yo, are you serious?" he asked me.

"Rohann is separated," I said.

"I don't give a fuck! That still ain't your nigga and you ain't his shorty!" Bishop yelled at me. Bishop had anger issues and I often wondered if that was why he was so laid back. Most people hid behind their frustrations by being silent.

"I'm not doing this with you right now," I said as I tried to walk away from him but he grabbed my arm.

"We will catch up later. Go and have your fun," he said. He kissed my lips and walked away from me. I wanted to pull him in the bathroom. My pussy was dripping and I was horny.

When I walked back onto the dance floor, Monie and her friends were watching me. When the song *Panda* came on, I started dancing.

"Awww, shit who got Cocoa started?" the DJ asked, calling me by my stage name. I leaned forward with my hands on my knees as I started twerking in front of Monie and friends. I made sure both of my ass cheeks took turns bouncing. I stood up and held my hands straight up in the air as my ass went crazy. I leaned forward and made it clap to the beat.

"GOT DAMN!" the DJ yelled into the mic. Monie and her friends grilled me and I gave them all the finger.

"That's what that ass do when I'm on top of him! Bitch, stop staring because you can't compete!" I yelled at her over the music. I walked off the floor and headed to the bar. Bishop was talking to Yolo and I could tell they were clowning each other. I smiled on the inside because his face was so handsome when he laughed. I sipped on my drink as I tried to find a flaw but there wasn't one. He was perfect to me and I craved him. He caught me staring at him and he blew me a kiss which caused me to blush. I rolled my eyes at him and he licked his lips; my pussy started to throb. The way he sucked on my clit flashed through my mind. My nipples hardened and I had to leave. I couldn't be around Bishop. I told Ree-Ree to call me later. She was partying with Poet so I didn't feel bad leaving her. I walked out to my car but something didn't feel right. It felt like someone was following me. I turned around and didn't see anyone. I hit the unlock button to my car. Before I got in, someone yanked me by my shirt and I felt a blow to my face.

"Bitch, you thought you was going to steal my money?" Chasity screamed at me. I swung back and my fist slammed into her nose. She pulled out a razor and sliced my arm. I grabbed her by the throat and slammed her onto my car. I banged her head on my hood and she dropped the razor. I felt a sharp pain pierce through my side. I screamed out and Chasity hit me in the face. I fell on the ground. While I was down, I saw Jesula standing next to us holding a knife. I didn't know she was with Chasity.

"When you stole from her, you stole from me!" Jesula said. She was about to stab me again but shots rang out. One bullet flew past Jesula's face. Another shot rang out and Chasity ducked. More shots fired and a few bullets went through my driver's side window. Chasity and Jesula ran off and seconds later I heard them pulling off. I lay on the ground clutching my side. Someone stood over me but I couldn't make out their face. The stranger helped me into my car, snatched up my purse and car keys from off the ground. He started up my car and sped off. I was screaming for help because I was being kidnapped. The stranger took a black ski mask off and looked at me. I gasped at the person who sat behind my steering wheel.

"Those bitches were going to kill you," she said as she sped through the streets.

"Ashanta?" I asked.

"This put a huge dent into my plans! Fuck!" she screamed.

This bitch is every bit of crazy! I said to myself. I noticed her hands were trembling. I winced in pain as I sat up.

"Are you okay?" I asked her.

"I shot at real people. I practiced at a gun range but what just happened scared the hell out of me," she said. She almost crashed when she cut a car off. She was speeding through the streets of Annapolis. You would've thought she just got finished robbing a bank. She turned off onto a back road and got out of the car. Sounds of her throwing up caused me to gag.

"I think you might want to get in and drive me to a hospital," I said to her once she was finished. She wiped her mouth off and got back in my car. She didn't look too good. She looked worse than me and I was the one that was stabbed.

"I'm pregnant," she said.

"Ooooohhhhh, congratulations," I said.

"I'm a doctor. Well, I was a doctor. I have a medical bag and I can look at your wound myself," she said when she pulled back onto the street.

"Everyone thinks that you are dead. I gave your dog to Kwenya," I said.

"Thank you. I'm aware of how you got her," she said. Minutes later, she was helping me out of the car. We were in front of a trailer in the woods.

"So, you are cool with living like the Dukes of Hazzard?" I asked her.

"For the time being. Trust me, I can live wherever I want," she spat. She helped me walk into the trailer. It was very neat on the inside and it reminded me of an apartment. I sat down in a chair. She came from the back with a small metal box. She lifted my shirt up.

"It isn't bad. I can fix this myself," she said.

"Kwenya isn't the same," I said as she cleaned my wound.

176

"Me, either, so I guess that's makes the both of us," she replied.

"He thinks you are dead," I said.

"I am," she replied coldly.

"This is weird," I said.

"It will all be worth it in the end," she replied.

"You staged your death," I said. I wanted to get away from her because she was scaring me.

"I had to choose. Either I go to jail with Damos or leave Annapolis. At the time, I didn't know what was going on but to be on the safe side, I went along with it anyway. I met a woman and she told me that I needed to stop letting people control my life. I came back to clear Kwenya's name so he wouldn't get locked up and to expose everyone else," she said. I never knew a person could go through so much. It almost seemed surreal.

"Thank you," I said to her.

"I was following them. I knew what they were going to do and I couldn't live with it. Chasity has messed up a lot of people's lives," she replied. Thirty minutes had passed and she was finished stitching me up.

"The wound was only four inches long and it wasn't deep. The stitches will dissolve," she said before she stood up.

"I'm going to trust that you will not tell anyone about this, Desi," she said.

"You saved my life. I'm not telling nobody shit. What does it feel like?" I asked her.

"What does what feel like?" she replied.

"To feel born again? I always wondered because life dealt me bad hand," I said. She sat back down.

"I feel lost, trapped, and alone, but at the same time I feel free. My life, at first, was like a box and I accepted it, but when Kwenya came into my life, that box slowly started to open. I started to see that there was another life for me. I never wanted to be a doctor. I always wanted to write because it took my mind into different stories; it was like an escape from the real world. When you are writing, you are no longer in your body. It's like the book sucks you in. But now I'm writing my own life story," she said. I felt my eyes water up but I hurriedly wiped them. I felt sorry for someone other than myself and it was as if I could feel her pain. Her eyes looked empty and before I knew it, I was hugging her. Maybe I needed the hug, too, but I felt like her. She hugged me back and I pulled away.

"Everyone needs a hug every now and then," she said and smiled. She almost reminded me of Ree-Ree because underneath all the layers she developed, it was still that innocence she held.

"How did you know what Jesula and Chasity was up to?" I asked her.

"I live in their building," she laughed.

"Huh?" I asked. She got up and came back with a mask that looked like it came from someone's face. I jumped up because it looked weird.

"This guy that works for a special effects team gave this to me. It sticks to my face like tape and it feels very real, almost like real skin," she said and I just stared at her.

"Black folks do shit like this?" I asked her.

"Just think as if I was in a movie, that's all. I wasn't going to use it but I wanted to get close to them. I wanted them to share things with me so this was the only way," she replied.

Bitch, you are crazy! I thought.

"So, you live in their building as someone else?" I asked in disbelief.

"Yes. I stay in their building as someone else. Chasity and I are like BFF's. Rakita is warming up to me but she still doesn't trust Katrice. Jesula doesn't like me but I don't care about her. I have nothing to do with her. I overheard them talking about coming to see you at the club. A girl named Monie called Chasity and told Chasity you were there. I was curious to know what was going to happen, so I followed them," she said.

"I have a headache. This is crazy. But what do you need my help with? You ain't telling me all of this just because, so what is it?" I asked her.

"Chasity thinks that you have connections to hackers, bank hackers I should say. If you do, I need a huge favor," she said.

"Ummm, okay," I said.

"I need your help to cash a check," she said. There was a knock on the door.

"Who else knows you stay here?" I asked.

"My friend," she replied. She opened up the door and the woman I saw Ashanta with at the strip club a while back, walked into the trailer.

"I had to get out of the house. Deron will not leave me alone. I need to stay here for a bit," she said and dropped her bag on the floor.

"Serene, this is Desi. Desi, this is Serene," Ashanta said and I waved. Serene waved back and looked at Ashanta. My cell phone rang as they started talking. It was Bishop calling me.

"Yes," I answered.

"Where are you? Someone said that there was shooting outside of the club and that the bullets were coming toward you. What's going on, Desi? I need to come and get you," he said and I rolled my eyes.

"I'm at the hospital and I'm fine. Someone tried to rob me," I said.

"WHAT?" he yelled through the phone. I knew Bishop was pissed off but there was nothing I could do.

"The nurse is about to walk back in. I will call you later." I hung up while he was still talking.

"Give me some time. This is federal information so it might take a while," I said. I slowly stood up and Ashanta helped me.

"This shit hurts," I replied.

"This will help," Ashanta said. She gave me a small bottle of pills.

"Thank you," I replied.

"Do you want me to drive you home?" Serene asked me.

Where do all of these nice bitches come from? I asked myself.

"No, I'm fine. It's just a small wound," I said. I walked out of the trailer. Ashanta came out after me.

"Can I ask you something?" she asked me.

"What's up?" I asked her.

"Have you ever been around the woman that Kwenya spends some of his time with? Her name is Shantel. She is an older woman," she said.

"You've been following him, too?" I asked and she looked down in embarrassment. I couldn't blame her because if it was Bishop, I would've been doing the same thing. Matter of fact, I would've been whipping asses.

"I can't see him right now. I can, but then I will have to hide what I got going on from him, and I don't want to deal with that on top of all of this. Kwenya is the take-charge kind of guy and he would want to handle it. I don't want him to interfere with this," she replied.

"I don't know her and never seen her before, but if I ever come across her, I will let you know," I replied. I gave her my number before I headed home.

The way it's looking, my court date with Chasity will be canceled. I hope the bitch is dead before then, I thought to myself.

****

The next day...

I drove around in my white 2015 Maxima. I didn't drive it much but I had to let the BMW go because of all the bullet holes. The pain pills Ashanta gave me worked. I stopped at Kwenya's shop to grab me a caramel iced latte before I got my day started. Poet greeted me when I walked up to the counter.

"I'm so happy that you are okay," she said. The shop was crowded so I didn't say much.

"You know how people can get when they see a woman walking alone by herself at night," I answered before I placed my order. Kwenya came from the back of the shop with an older woman.

So, this must be Shantel. Umph, she is pretty but whomever did her ass and breasts should be fired from doing plastic surgery. At least Ashanta has natural beauty. This bitch is faker than Chasity's bank account, I laughed to myself.

"Good morning, Kwenya," I said to him and Shantel side-eyed me.

"What's going on with you?" he asked.

"Oh nothing, just decided to stop by to get my favorite latte. You must take after your father because you look nothing like your mother," I said. Poet covered her mouth and Kwenya smirked. Shantel cleared her throat.

"He is my client," she spat.

"I'm so sorry. Don't mind me because I have a hangover from last night. I just thought you were his mother," I said.

"Will I see you later?" she asked Kwenya.

"If I don't get too busy," he answered. She waved him off and I tried to study their situation. Usually when a woman walks away, the man would look at her ass or something. Shantel walked away throwing her hips side to side but Kwenya didn't look.

"Yo, I swear you are always starting shit," he said to me.

"Why? Because I thought she was your mother?" I asked.

"Whatever, Desi. Y'all have a good one. I'm out and Poet if you—"

"I know, I know. If I need something, call you. I got this, trust me," she said before he left the shop.

"Girl, that woman wants him," Poet whispered.

"I can see that," I replied.

"I heard them talking in the back and she wants him to fire me. She said that he would gain better business if I didn't look so ghetto. She doesn't like my braids and she said it isn't sanitary while I'm baking. I wear a hairnet when I'm in the kitchen," Poet fussed.

"She is an old-school hoe, that's all. She preys on younger, successful men; helps them expand their business to reap the benefits. She is going to seduce him next, and I hope he doesn't fall for it," I said.

Hell, if he knows what I know, he will stay away from Miss Shantel. Ashanta is out lurking around in the dark, watching him like a crazy person, I thought.

"That bitch needs to go, although she is good at what she does. Kwenya has an app now where you can order things and it will be ready for pick-up by the time you get here. It has coupons on it and everything. We've been busy lately because of her," Poet said.

Ashanta, doll, you might have some competition after all, I thought. I chatted with Poet for a few extra minutes before I left out of the shop.

****

After I ran my errands, I headed back to my home. When I pulled up, Bishop's truck was parked outside of my building. I popped the trunk and, like the gentleman he was, he grabbed my bags for me. I didn't say anything to him as I headed to my building. I unlocked my door and when I walked in, I headed to my wine cabinet. Bishop came in and sat my bags on the counter.

"Why didn't you call me when you left the hospital?" he asked.

"So, now you want to be captain-save- a-hoe?" I replied.

"Cut that shit out, Desi," he spat.

"What's the matter, baby? Just tell yourself that you are in love with a hoe. Stop fighting it," I said.

"I want to know what happened to you. Who tried to rob you?" he asked me.

"I don't know, now can you leave?" I asked.

"Can we talk for a few minutes? Damn, yo, you just been acting like a bitch lately. We need to talk," he stressed.

"We did last night. I'm not good enough for you. You don't want to open yourself up to me. Blah, blah, blah," I said. Bishop jacked me up and pushed me into the fridge. I screamed out in pain because of my wound.

"My side! My side!" I cried. He hurriedly let me go and lifted my shirt up. I could see the pain in his eyes.

"Man, I'm so fucking mad right now. I know you know who did this shit. You are too calm about this situation. If you didn't know, you'd be paranoid right now. You would've wanted me with you last night," he said.

"I don't need you," I said. He pulled me by my hand toward the couch. He sat me down then sat on the ottoman in front of me.

"Tell me who did it," he said.

Nigga, I'm not telling you shit! Ashanta is wearing a mask and is pretending to be friends with people. She's hiding out in a trailer and she saved my life. That broad done lost her mind for a reason and I will not let you, or no one else, interfere with her weird-ass plans! I yelled into my head.

I forced myself to cry.

"I don't know. My life was too busy flashing before my eyes. I thought I was going to die and I just don't know. I don't want to relive that moment, so please stop bringing it up. I was so scared and you weren't there," I said and he stood up.

He took his shirt and shoes off. He went into my kitchen to put my groceries away. I turned on the TV and sipped on my wine. Ro was calling my phone but I couldn't answer it. I didn't feel like arguing with Bishop. After he was finished putting the groceries away, he sat on the other couch and rolled up. I stared at his chest and the way he wrapped his lips around the blunt. I was still mad at him but I was even more mad at myself for allowing him to get my emotions screwed up.

"If you want a nigga to eat your pussy, just say it," he said.

"Boy, please. I'm not thinking about your young ass," I said.

"Boy? I'm grown over here, shorty. And I'm going to be even more grown when I spread those legs," he replied.

"You and I are not on that level anymore. We can be friends, but far as you sticking your fingers inside of my cookie jar, isn't going to happen," I spat.

"That's my pussy and I can stick, fuck, lick and anything else I want to do with it. I'm going to play your little game, though. If you want to be in your feelings, continue to do so, but stop looking at a nigga like that," he said.

He sat the blunt down to reach inside of his pants. He pulled his big dick out and it was standing tall, strong, and hard. I felt like a fiend wanting to hit a crack pipe. Bishop knew he was my addiction and he wasn't being fair. He started to stroke himself.

"Come here, shorty," he said.

"I'm injured," I said.

"I got you. You ain't got to do nothing," he replied before he put his dick back into his shorts.

"What are we eating for dinner tonight?" he asked. I choked on my wine.

"Nigga, you ain't eating dinner here," I responded.

"I'll order something," he replied.

"Did you fuck Monie or Liana? Hell, with your secretive behind, did you fuck the both of them?" I asked him.

"No, but did you fuck ole' boy you had dinner with?" he asked.

"No, I didn't," I said and he got quiet as if he was thinking about something.

"I want you to come to my family reunion with me tomorrow," he said.

"So, now I'm special?" I asked.

"Always been special. That's why I can't stop fucking with you," he said and I blushed.

"You ain't all of that but I was going to go anyway. Ree-Ree invited me," I replied and he started chuckling.

"Yo, you always starting shit," he said.

"You can buy me something cute tomorrow morning. I want that bitch Liana's face to drop when she sees me," I said.

"I bought you a lot of shit that you haven't worn yet," he said.

"And?" I asked and he shook his head. Bishop and I sat up all night, talking. It reminded me of the times before we were intimate. He was everything to me and he knew that. I knew he loved me but I wanted him to fight a little harder for me.

****

I sat in the passenger's seat of Bishop's truck. I was nervous as we sat in the parking lot of the park where his family reunion was.

"All that shit you talked and now you want to be nervous?" he asked. I ignored him as I got out of his truck. My hair was intact; my shoe game was on point and so was my make-up. I looked good on the outside but I didn't feel good. I wasn't comfortable because I had to smile and be friendly to people I didn't know.

"Come on, shorty," he said and pulled me away from his truck.

As soon as I approached his family reunion, the first person I spotted was Liana. She wore a pair of leggings with his family reunion T-shirt. Bishop squeezed my hand because he knew I already felt out of place.

"You look good," he whispered in my ear and kissed it. Liana frowned her nose up at us before she walked off with a plate in her hand.

"There goes my baby!" a woman yelled out. She looked to be in her late-forties. She resembled Bishop's mother a lot so it didn't take long to figure out it was his aunt.

"What's up, Aunt Mary?" he asked before he kissed her cheek.

"I'm fine but who is this beautiful woman you have with you?" she asked him after she hugged me.

"I'm Desi," I replied.

"This is my shorty," Bishop said.

"Let me take her away from you so I can brag about how beautiful she is," she said and pulled me away from him.

"Tell your son he better keep his eyes to himself!" Bishop shouted behind us.

"I see he's a jealous one," she whispered to me. We walked to a picnic table where the majority of his family was sitting and eating.

190

"Freddy, get this woman a shirt, she is family!" Mary called out to one of the guys.

"Freddy is my husband," she said to me. Freddy gave me a hug and he handed me a shirt. He was very light-skinned and had freckles on his cheeks.

"Welcome to the family. Is my nephew being nice to you? If not, let me know so I can kick his ass," Freddy joked.

"He has his days," I replied. I met the rest of his family and I felt welcomed. I always wondered what my family was like but I don't remember them. I was only three years old when my aunt left me at a church and that's all I could remember. Bishop's family was big and everyone got along; it was beautiful. Bishop's mother and Liana were eyeing me and I knew they were talking about me.

"Don't pay that any mind. My sister is trying to replace her with the daughter she lost. She needs to realize that Liana is no kin to us. I don't know why the little bitch is here," Mary whispered to me. Ree-Ree and Jada arrived and Ree-Ree headed straight to me with a smile on her face.

"There goes my baby!" Mary screamed when she hugged Ree-Ree. Ree-Ree kissed her cheek.

"Hey Aunty," Ree-Ree smiled and looked at me.

"So, I see you fit right in," Ree-Ree said to me.

"She sure does," Mary said then handed me and Ree-Ree a drink inside of a Ziploc bag with fruit and ice in it. It reminded me of a Capri Sun.

"Sip on that slow because that will get you fucked up," Ree-Ree said. For the remainder of the day, I kicked back and joked around with Bishop's aunts and uncles. His aunt Mary was drunk and when she did the cabbage patch, I almost peed myself from laughing at her. When the DJ played Beyoncé's *Get Me Bodied,* I had tears in my eyes because Mary tried to mimic Beyoncé. She even went as far as backing it up on her husband.

"Lil' Freddy, you better get yo' mama before her arthritis kick in. The last time she danced like that, she fell on the ground and we had to carry her to the car," Bishop said and everyone laughed.

"Lil' Freddy, get a fan so my hair can blow!" Mary said when she dropped down to the ground. When she stood up, she kicked her leg up.

"You know that's a wig, Ma!" Lil' Freddy yelled out.

"My mommy wants you to take me to the moon bounce," one of Liana's sons said to Bishop when he ran over to the table.

"Tell your mother I'm busy," Bishop said. The little boy started pulling on Bishop's shorts.

"Take me to the moon bounce!" he cried.

"Oh hell nawl. Liana, come and get your son! Bishop ain't his damn daddy!" Mary screamed.

"I know that he isn't but my sons are a part of me and Bishop should be able to accept it," Liana said.

"I'm sick of her, Bishop," I said to him.

"Go over there with your mother, lil' man," Bishop said and the little boy ran off. After Liana's stunt, I wanted to leave because I felt the urge to slap her. I was sick and tired of her pushing her sons on Bishop.

"Are you ready?" Bishop asked me.

"Yeah, I'm tired," I said. We said goodbye to everyone, including his mother, but she just waved at me. I knew she didn't want to but she did it out of respect for Bishop. The drinks Mary gave me snuck up on me. As soon as I got inside his truck, I leaned the seat back as Bishop pulled off.

"Mary invited you to her cook-out next week. Don't mess around with her too much. She'll get you in trouble," he joked.

"Babe, that cabbage patch, though," I said. Bishop roared in laughter.

"You should've seen her last year. She did the Dougie dance and knocked my grandmother out of her wheelchair. My grandmother said she wasn't coming to anymore reunions because Mary do too much," he said. Minutes later, I realized Bishop wasn't driving in the direction of my home.

"Where are you going? I need to go sleep," I said.

"We are going back to my house," he said.

"Nigga, what makes you think I want to go there?" I asked him. My side started to hurt a little bit, so I took a pain pill. Twenty minutes later, Bishop was pulling up in his driveway. I opened the door and almost lost my step. The pill mixed with the alcohol made me feel woozy. He grabbed me around the waist and helped me into the house.

"I hope you tell me who tried to rob you," he said. He helped me up the stairs and into the master bedroom.

"You need to decorate. This house is too pretty to not have a homely feel to it," I said.

"You can decorate after you move in," he replied but I didn't respond as he undressed me. He went into the bathroom inside his room and I heard the shower come on. He came back into the bedroom naked and helped me up. I almost lost my step but he caught me. After I got into the shower, the water started to wake me up. I turned around and his dick was rested on my thigh. I pulled his head down so that I could kiss him. His hands went to my ass and he squeezed it. A moan escaped my lips. I was trapped between him and the shower wall as he sucked on my lip. I jerked him off and I wanted him to enter me. His mouth found its way to my nipple.

"Damn it, baby," I moaned. His hand played between my legs as my breast disappeared inside his mouth. I jerked him off faster and harder and a groan slipped from his lips. I lifted up my leg to wrap it around his waist. I guided him between my tight walls. His girth stretched me open as he pushed himself inside of me.

"FUCK!" he shouted. He was all the way in and when he started to stroke me, my nails dug into his shoulders. He pulled out then pushed further back inside of me. I felt the pressure build up in my stomach and my nipples were hard like pebbles. I sucked on his chest before I sucked on his neck as he moved in and out of me. I was ready to release.

"I'm about to come!" I screamed. With both of his palms on the shower wall, he fucked me harder. My head banged into the wall as Bishop showed no mercy on my pussy. I tried to grab onto him to keep my balance but he didn't allow me to. He held both of my arms above my head by my wrist. His other hand was gripping my ass cheek as he jabbed at my spot. My eyes closed and my head spun as I came. I felt him throbbing and his body jerked. He sucked and bit my bottom lip as he pumped into me. He gripped my ass harder as he jabbed at my spot each time. My legs shook and his chest tightened when he released inside of me. His face rested in the crook of my neck and I hugged him. I was holding on to him for dear life.

Rakita

"Tell that nigga I said walk out!" I shouted at the bitch that Kwenya had working for him at his shop. I went to his shop early in the morning before anyone else arrived. I didn't want to make a fool out of myself in front of a lot of people but Kwenya had cut me off—completely. He and I had gotten into many arguments in the past. The longest we went without talking was a week. It was over a month since he and I had sex on the side of the road.

"Can you lower your voice?" the woman asked.

"For what? Ain't nobody in here but us. Kwenya, get your black ass out here now!" I screamed. He came from the back with a scowl on his face.

"So, I guess you are fucking her, too," I said pointing at the light-skinned girl.

"I didn't know you was still living," Kwenya said to me and my mouth dropped.

"Why are you being like this? We been messing with each other for years. Do you know all of what I went through so that I could be with you?" I asked him.

"Shorty, I don't want you. What don't you get? I don't love you, I don't think about you, and I don't even care about you. Now, get the fuck out of my store before I drag your dumb-ass out," he said to me. I didn't want my tears to fall but they fell anyway.

"You are going to regret this," I said to him and he laughed.

"Hell, I regret not cutting you off any sooner," he said. I stormed out of the shop and headed to work. When I pulled up to the community I worked in, I hurriedly parked and got out. I was running late from messing around with Kwenya. I walked into the leasing office and the receptionist didn't speak to me like she normally did. When I walked into my private office, the owner of the property was sitting in one of my chairs at my desk.

"Hi Mr. Coldwell, how are you this morning?" I asked him.

"I'm fine Rakita, how are you?" he asked.

"I'm fine, what brings you in?" I said as I sat at my computer. Mr. Coldwell was an older white man and he was very attractive. I sometimes flirted with him but I didn't make it not too obvious.

"I came here to talk to you about something. It has been brought to my attention that you used our showcase room for one of your private flings," he said.

"Excuse me?" I asked him.

"You are the only one with the key. Can you explain to me how dirty condoms, booze, and underwear ended up on the living room floor? One of the residents saw you leave out of there Sunday morning. The place is trashed, there are even holes in the walls. I was going to give you a promotion but I am going to have to let you go," he said. He stood up and fixed his tie.

"I didn't do that!" I said to him.

"Give me the keys, clean out your desk, and you shall leave. If you don't leave within the next ten minutes, I will have the police escort you out," he said. I threw the keys at him and cursed him out as I grabbed my things.

"Fucking faggot!" I yelled at him and the receptionist gasped.

"I should tell your wife that you are fucking the receptionist. How would she feel about that?" I asked him.

"Becca, call the police," Mr. Coldwell said to the receptionist. I hurriedly rushed to my car. I drove home like a bat out of hell. When I pulled up in front of my building, Katrice was outside on her cell phone. When she saw me, she hung up. She wasn't as bad as I thought. She was just ghetto at times but other than that, I had grown used to her.

"Back home early?" she asked.

"I was fired," I said.

"Sorry to hear that. What happened?" After I told her what happened she said she had a job for me.

"What kind of job is it?" I asked her.

"I will let you know. I need to get the details first but it pays a lot. My cousin was just telling me about it. Now, how did the talk with Kwenya go? I remember you said last night that you were going to see him this morning," she said.

"He misses me and I'm going to see him later. You should've saw him this morning. He couldn't keep his hands off me. I even got a piece of that dick and, girl, you won't believe he asked me to carry his baby," I lied. I wasn't telling none of them hoes that Kwenya shut me down. Jesula thought I was only trying to get to Kwenya to set him up. But little did she know, her time was running out. I tolerated Chasity but Jesula had to go because she wanted Kwenya to die.

"Between me and you, Jesula was talking about you this morning. She said that she was going to have Chaos's people kill you because she knows that you are really on Kwenya's side," Katrice said.

"That bitch said what?" I asked her.

"She said she was going to tell Chaos everything when he gets off lockdown and gets his cell phone back. She is a snake, and I also heard her talking to someone on the phone last night. She was telling the person how she was going to get someone fired. I didn't know who she was talking about at first but obviously she got you fired," Katrice said.

"That stupid bitch!" I screamed.

"She needs to go because she is a traitor and she knows too much. I have someone that will make her disappear. If word gets to either Chaos or Kwenya that you are playing them, they will see you as a traitor. I don't know neither but Kwenya sounds like someone you don't want to fuck over," she said.

"Kwenya will kill me if he knew I knew someone who wanted him dead," I said.

"Don't say nothing to Jesula about what we know. Continue to be her friend but just watch her," Katrice said.

"Thank you so much. I didn't like you when you first moved in but I'm really glad that you did," I said to her.

"No problem," she said and walked up the stairs.

****

I walked into my apartment and saw Chasity crying at the kitchen table.

"What's the matter with you?" I asked her.

"I miss my son," she replied.

"Why can't you see him?" I asked her.

"He is better off with his father. Look at how I live and I can't trust anybody. Remember I told you how Desi stole my money? Well, it wasn't her, it was Jesula. Look at what I found under her bed," Chasity said then gave me a backpack. I opened it up and there was money inside of it.

Natavia

"I counted it and it is the same amount that was taken out of my bank account. I know I owed her money but my own cousin stole everything from me. I could've used this money to fight for my son in court but I couldn't afford a lawyer. I know her and if I take my own money back, she would kill me. Jesula is an evil bitch," Chasity said. I knew that Chasity was scared of Jesula but I wasn't.

"She got me fired," I said and Chasity gasped.

"What! That bitch did what?" she asked.

"I was fired this morning and it's all making sense. Jesula is a snake and we need to get rid of her," I said to Chasity.

"How so?" she asked. The door unlocked.

"Act normal," I said to her and she hurriedly got up to put the money back. Jesula came in the house with a scowl on her face.

"When are you going to lure Kwenya to me so I can smoke him?" was the first thing that came out of her mouth when she walked in.

"Soon," I lied.

"Good because Chaos has a squad full of goons back home. They will come here if the problem is not solved soon. If they do come, they will take you out, too, because you failed your job. You are supposed to be Chaos's girl. You are supposed to be holding him down. I can't get close to Kwenya the way you can," she said.

Bitch, shut up! Who do you think you are? You shouldn't have called Chaos in the first place and told him Kwenya killed his brother if you knew you couldn't revenge your own man's death, simple bitch, I said to myself.

"I know that," I said. She bumped into me before she headed to her bedroom.

I cannot believe I agreed to Chaos about letting Jesula stay with me. I shouldn't be scared of a nigga that is behind bars, I said to myself but I knew if I would've turned Chaos down, he would've sent someone to kill me.

****

I walked into the gym and spotted Yolo working out. As much as I hated him, I needed him to do a favor for me. I stood next to him as he lifted weights. Kwenya, Jada, and Yolo had been working out together for years on the same days.

"Where is the rest of the gang?" I asked Yolo. He looked at me and sat up. He wiped the sweat off his forehead.

"Busy, now what the fuck do you want?" he asked me. Yolo hated me and I hated him. I hated him because when Kwenya did his dirt on me back in the day, Yolo was the one that covered for him.

"I came to talk to you about something," I said. I couldn't help but to eye the bulge in his gym shorts. Yolo was sexy and his body was amazing. He and Kwenya both had unique looks; Jada was attractive, too, but he didn't possess what Kwenya and Yolo had which were strong, dominant features. Too bad Yolo was borderline insane.

"Bitch, do I look like I want to talk to your hoe ass?" Yolo asked me.

"Someone is after Kwenya. I tried to tell him but he brushed me off. It has something to do with Jesula. She knows that he killed her boyfriend. She is planning on going to the cops. I overheard her telling Chasity that she was going to snitch," I said.

"I don't know what you are talking about," he said.

"You, Bishop, and Kwenya was outside when her boyfriend was killed. How do I know that?" I asked.

"Like I said, Rakita. I don't know what the fuck you are talking about and I don't know this Jesula broad or her nigga. Now, get the fuck out of my face," he said. I was going to ask him about shooting at us the same night we jumped Desi but I thought better of it. I knew Yolo was going to give Kwenya my message, and as paranoid as Kwenya was, I knew Jesula was going to be gone. I couldn't wait for Katrice's plan because Jesula had to go ASAP. I walked out of the gym and headed back home.

Kwenya

"How the fuck does Rakita know anything?" I asked Yolo.

"I don't know, man, but all of them bitches know," Yolo said.

"Then all of them bitches need to go," I said.

"Damn, nigga. All of them?" Yolo asked me.

"Yeah, Rakita, too. I don't trust them bitches and since when did Rakita and Chasity become friends? Rakita has a stick up her ass and that bougie bitch thinks she is too good to hang around people like Chasity. All of those broads scheming and all of them bitches need to go," I replied.

"Okay, it's your word. You want them bitches gone then they will be gone," Yolo said as he sat on my couch.

"I was going to merk Chasity on the strength of Bishop that night when we were at the club but Rakita's big head was in the way. I didn't want to kill the broad because I didn't know how you really felt about her with y'all history and all. But since Bishop said he wasn't sweating what Chasity did to him, I let it go, too, but are you sure you want me to kill Rakita? This will be my second time shooting at them bitches and this time I'm going to make sure I do it," he said.

"They all know too much so take them all out. But check this out, I just got more news on Ashanta. I don't know if I should be happy or mad. I want her to come home but then I want to send her home and I ain't talking about her house," I said.

"What happened?" Yolo asked me.

"The private detective I hired traced the blocked calls that was coming in to my cell phone. The last time she called me, I kept her on the phone long enough for him to trace it. He was able to get the location and the call came from by my shop. She's been spying on me. She's smart, though, because she realized why I kept talking. I called the number that Chase gave me after she hung up and it was changed. Can you believe that? I actually sat on the phone talking to her for three minutes while she just breathed into the phone. I did all of that just so I could get her number and she changed it on me. She knows I hate talking on the phone. Especially talking to someone who isn't saying nothing."

"Maybe she got a plan," he responded. My connect called me and I answered.

"What's good?" I asked.

"Flight will be ready in two hours," the man said and hung up.

"That was business?" Yolo asked me.

"Yeah, I'm flying out for a little bit. Don't kill them bitches until I get back because something is off about that situation. I want to talk to Rakita first because she sounds like she knows something else," I said. I gave Yolo dap before he left my crib. I went upstairs to pack my luggage. My phone rang and it was Shantel.

"What's up?" I answered the phone.

"Nothing. I was just wondering if you wanted to join me at dinner tonight," she said.

"Naw because I got shit to do," I replied.

"Can I ask you a question?" she asked me.

"What?"

"Is it my age?" she asked me.

"Shorty, age ain't nothing but a number. I'm just focused on getting my shorty back," I said.

"What if she doesn't come back?" Shantel asked me.

"Then I will have to deal with that but pussy ain't going to fix that. Let's be honest, you already know if you and I took it there, it will only be about fucking. There will be no dates, phone conversations, texting, nothing. All you'll get is an open pussy and a wet ass crack. Now, if you want that then when I come back, you can meet me at a hotel ass-naked. If you don't want that, stop asking me stupid shit. You help me with my business and I pay you. Stop acting like you are doing a nigga a favor because it's your job to help muthafuckas expand," I said.

"Well, I guess I will see you when you are free," she seductively said into the phone before she hung up. After I packed, I headed out the door to catch my flight.

Natavia

****

"There is my favorite man," my connect said and hugged me.

"What's good with you?" I asked Jesse. Not too many people know that my connect is a woman. Jesse was just as ruthless as most niggas.

"You finally came to see me. You've been a very busy man, huh?" she asked. Her butler poured me a shot of Henny as I sat on her couch in the living room. As attractive as Jesse was, I never saw her as something more than my connect.

"I've been busy with my personal problems," I said.

"I'm assuming you don't want me to know because you would've told me already. Dinner will be ready in an hour. Dress casual because I have a meeting with a few people and I want you to attend," she said before she left the living room. I went upstairs to the room she had for me. Every time I came into town, she would send an exotic woman to my room, sometimes even two. When I walked into the room, a smell of perfume hit me. I looked around and the place was spotless but it didn't feel right. It felt like someone had been in my suite. I took off my shirt and sat on the bed.

"What the fuck is that smell?" I asked myself out loud. I was going crazy because everywhere I went, I was reminded of Ashanta. The room even smelled like her and I couldn't understand it. I got undressed and stepped into the shower. After I washed off, I wrapped a towel around

208

my waist. I sat on the bed and applied lotion on my arms. The bottle slipped from my hand and when I reached down underneath the bed to get it, there was a notebook hidden there. I opened it up and that fragrance filled my nose again…

His Love Was the Death of Me

I have died from loving a man. A man who took me from the most miserable state of my life. A lot of people had crossed me in my old life. A life that didn't belong to me to begin with. I was a coward and I wasn't strong enough to defeat my opponent. But someone helped me cause my death, a woman who is in love with my man, the man whose child I'm carrying inside my womb. I must stop hiding behind my shadows and fear and protect my man from his crazy ex whom is a Federal Agent. She had enough evidence to put me away in jail because of my husband and his wrongdoings. I couldn't give birth to my baby in jail and let her help raise my child with my man. A man that belonged to me before I even knew he existed and a man who stands before my husband. A man that was made for me and the man that I will sacrifice myself for. I was reborn with a stronger heart and I am fearless. I have morphed into a strong woman who will do anything to bring harm to those who cross me. I will protect myself, my baby, and my man. I'm on a path of revenge and I hope those who hurt me, burn in hell. Better yet, I hope those who hurt me suffer before I watch them burn. I want them to feel the pain I have lived with for years because no one understands the hell I have lived in but escaped…

"Damn, this person is crazy," I said to myself as I turned the page over.

Ashanta doesn't exist anymore! The love she had for him, killed her just so that a new woman can come alive, the woman that was made for him.

I tore the page out of the notebook. I hurriedly got dressed and grabbed my gun. I caught the elevator to Jesse's floor. Her butler stood outside of her bedroom door.

"Sir, she is getting dressed," he said but I knocked him out of the way. I opened up her door and locked it. She was still in the shower. I slid the shower door back and grabbed her around her neck with my gun to her head.

"Where the fuck is she?" I asked Jesse as I choked her.

"You want to die?" she asked me.

"I don't care about that right now! Where the fuck is Ashanta and what did you do to her? Why is she talking crazy?" I asked Jesse as I shoved the paper in her face. I yanked her out of the shower so she could read the paper.

"Nice story, isn't it?" she asked me.

"Is this a game to you?" I asked her.

"No, but I think it's quite entertaining, now let me grab a towel," she said. I grabbed her a towel and she wrapped it around herself but before she did, I caught a glimpse of a tattoo she had on her hip. Her bodyguards knocked on the door.

"Are you okay, Jesse?" one of them called out.

"Yes, I'm fine! Go the fuck away before I blow all of y'all's brains out!" she shouted and the knocking stopped.

"You could be dead right now," she said. She walked out of the bathroom and I followed behind her. She sat on her bed and lit up a cigarette.

"What did you do to her? She is carrying my seed. Do you know how crazy she sounded on that paper? I don't even know who that woman is," I said.

"Men don't know shit but where to bust a nut at. Of course you don't know who she is because you never walked in her shoes. You don't know what it's like to love a man and give everything up for him. When I saw her, I knew who she was. I know everyone in your circle. I have eyes and ears everywhere. I invited her here because I was concerned about her. She looked so pitiful sitting down at the table in the hotel eating breakfast. She looked broken and her eyes were empty. Her face was cut because of Rakita. Her and Rakita got into a fight the night Rakita made it look like Ashanta crashed her car. I offered her medical help and she took it after she realized she caught an infection in her wound. I taught her how to stand up for herself and I told her to live through her words. The woman that wrote that paper isn't crazy. That is a woman who was trapped within herself," Jesse said.

"Rakita played a part in this?" I asked.

"Yes, the ex-Federal Agent. She was for falling in love with someone she should have been investigating. Chaos is a hot head who is a part of a small drug organization. He has a twin brother who was just recently murdered outside of a night club. His brother Kemar has been pretending to be Chaos. Chaos didn't want people to know he was locked up because he didn't want to lose his spot on the streets. He lost his spot anyway because Kemar wasn't a hustler, he was just a thief.

Kemar's girlfriend is living with Rakita because Chaos sent her there. Rakita is supposed to help Jesula get close to you so she can kill you, but since you cut Rakita off, she doesn't know your every move. Do you know how I know all of that?" she asked me.

"Ashanta?" I asked and she smiled.

"Yup, she wanted revenge on her husband and on Rakita, but I guess she found out more stuff. Don't worry, Mondo is there with her," Jesse said as if the whole situation was cool.

"You think a pregnant woman roaming the streets, finding out shit about people, is okay? Ashanta can get killed," I said.

"They don't know she is alive," Jesse said throwing me off.

"Man, I'm out. I'm not listening to you and your crazy talk. Tell me where Ashanta is so I can drag her ass to my house where she belongs. I will take care of everything, so just tell me where my shorty is hiding at," I said.

"I cannot do that. I cannot let you interfere with her plan. Let her have her revenge," Jesse said and blew smoke in my face.

"Chaos's situation is not her situation! That has nothing to do with her!"

"If you act now, she won't feel accomplished. Let her have her revenge and just get over it," Jesse said.

"Ashanta is not like you. Let me guess, a man fucked you over? Someone did something to you because you have lost your damn mind if you think my shorty is going to be doing all of this shit. What's up with that tattoo?" I asked her.

"What tattoo?" she asked me.

"The one on your hip. The one that says 'Desi'? I only know one fucking Desi," I spat. Jesse stood up and tried to slap me but I caught her wrist.

"I don't give a damn if your people are here. You better get to fucking talking because this isn't about Ashanta. This is about you. All of this is about you, and just like everyone else, you took advantage of her weakness even if you didn't mean it. You put her in a position that could hurt her and my seed. You are a selfish, miserable, lonely bitch. All you have is the people that work for you but you don't even know if they really like you. You have known me for a long time and instead of you calling me and telling me that you found my shorty, you turn her into a woman that I don't know, who is putting our baby at risk. Bitch, I will break your damn neck," I gritted as tears fell from Jesse's eyes. I pushed her into the wall and she burst into sobs.

"Desi is my daughter! She is my daughter and I abandoned her because her father didn't want her! I gave her to my sister and told my sister to take care of her. Desi's father didn't want any daughters. He whipped my ass every time he found out the sex of our baby and he made sure my babies didn't survive. The last time I lied and said it was a boy just so that I could keep her. When he saw that it was a girl, he beat me so bad I couldn't have children after that. I turned my back on everyone because he didn't want me to have anybody. I was so weak and

213

insecure back then. Over the years, I grew some courage. I drugged him then locked him up in the basement of this house. He yells but nobody can hear him because of the thick, stone walls and he is also underground. I told his people he died and I even planned his funeral and took over his cartel. Desi's father only wanted boys because they could inherit his drug ring if something happened to him. He didn't believe a woman was fit and I showed him that I could do it as a woman and do it better while he sits in a live grave," she said.

"Damn, y'all broads are crazy," I said and stepped away from her.

"I had my family killed after I found out what my sister did to my daughter. She accepted my money but she didn't tell me that she sent my daughter to a fucking orphanage and no one helped her. I have been afraid because I feel in my heart she wouldn't accept me so I stayed away. I'd rather be dead to her than a dead beat mother so I pretended that part of me didn't exist. When Ashanta told me she was pregnant, I told her to go back or she would've ended up like me—lonely," she responded.

"So, your husband is in this house?" I asked her and she shook her head.

"Chained to the wall like a dog. Follow me," she said. I tucked my gun away and followed her. I don't know why I cared but I wanted to see what a woman was capable of and how far they'd go.

I followed Jesse to the basement and she still had her towel wrapped around her. She unlocked a door and we went down a long, dark stairwell. She turned on a light and a man that Desi resembled, stared at us with cold eyes. He had chains around his ankles and wrist. Seeing that nigga chained like that put me in mind of a slavery movie. He had on clean clothes but he was barefoot. There weren't any windows in the basement and all he had was a mattress on the floor and a bucket to go to bathroom in. I'd rather die than live like that.

"Crazy bitch!" he yelled at Jesse and she laughed. He was a few inches shorter than me. His hair was matted around his face and on his head.

"When my brother Mondo figures out what you did to me, he will kill you!" he yelled at Jesse. He turned his head in my direction.

"Who is this man with you?" he asked Jesse. I noticed that he talked with an accent—a Jamaican accent.

"Don't worry about it. You keep on and I will not shave you. It's been, what? Almost a year?" she teased him.

"Suck my dick, bitch! Just kill me and get it over with! Please, just kill me!" he begged her.

"That will be too easy," she said to him and he cried. He didn't stink and he looked healthy weight-wise. I knew she still cared about him because she was taking care of him.

"So, let me get this right. You got the nigga down here just to take care of him? You feed him and bathe him. You have to take time out of your day just to care for someone you don't like? Damn it, Jesse, this doesn't make sense. Just kill the nigga or do you want me to do it?" I said. I wanted to put the nigga out of his misery.

"I tried but I can't! I still love him," she said.

"Do you want me to do it?" I asked her and she put her head down.

"Please, just fucking do it! I'm sick of being chained! I can barely see because it's so dark down here. I'm going blind, Jesse," he cried.

"Just put the nigga out. You had him down here so long he is handicap now. You already took his soul, just kill the nigga," I said. I handed her my gun and her hands shook as she held it to his head.

This nigga was beating babies out of her and she's still trying to hold onto the nigga, I thought.

"Jesse, just do it. I made my peace with God and I apologized for everything I did to you. Just do it," he said. She fell on the floor and started sobbing.

"I can't do it!" she said. I took the gun from her and shot him in the head twice.

"You can move on now. This nigga been a burden on you for a long time. You never let go of your problem," I said to her and she hugged me.

"Thank you so much, Kwenya!" she said.

****

Two hours later…

I was preparing to head back home to find Ashanta. Jesse told me that she didn't know the exact location to Ashanta lived but she told me if I visited Rakita I would find out. I needed to get down to the bottom of everything and I also had to get rid of a nigga that was locked up. Jesse knocked on the door wearing a sweat suit with her hair pulled back. She was a beautiful woman when she didn't look serious. She actually looked normal as she stood in the doorway of my room.

"I have a proposition for you," she said to me.

"What's that?" I asked.

"I want you to run this cartel. I'm sick of it. I want to go back home. The only reason I stayed here was because of Ricardo. I want to see what Desi is like," she said.

"Too damn smart and she is always fighting and running off with her mouth," I said and she laughed.

"It's all yours, Kwenya. My clients and everything. All I ask is that you give me forty percent off your profit. You just need someone to control the shipments but you are a smart man. You will figure it out," she said.

"I don't like handouts, Jesse," I said and she smiled.

"You took care of my problem and I'm repaying you. You did something that took me twenty-five years to do. I feel so relieved and I thank you for that. I could've had you killed when you snatched me out of the shower but you didn't care. Your attitude and everything else about you is rare. You will be a better fit for all of this. I'm tired of hiding behind a lot of bodyguards because I'm a woman and I know people will try me. I'm giving it up to you. It will be the same only you will move more product and your customers will change. I deal with rich people, some mayors, lawyers and doctors who spend very big. Hollywood is my favorite spot and you will be surprised at how many celebrities spend a lot of money. You will have more of a sophisticated clientele, so when you do business try to dress a little less casual. You still have that dope boy edge to you, go more for the Wall Street, tailor-made look," she said.

"I look like a dope boy?" I asked and she smiled.

"You're still caught between, but yes. You were my only client who visited me with jeans and Timbs," she said.

"I don't like handouts, Jesse," I replied.

"Well, technically it's more of a partnership since I'm getting forty percent, so that makes me still a part of everything. I'm not your connect, I'm your partner," she said.

"We can talk about it later," I said. I grabbed my things and headed out the door while Jesse canceled her dinner.

****

The next day…

I knocked on Rakita's door and she opened it up. She was smelling good and looking good but she wasn't shit.

"I'm glad you came to your senses," she said. I called her the night before and told her I wanted to see her and she didn't hesitate to tell me "yes."

I looked around her apartment and she was the only one home.

Bitch must have told Chasity and Jesula to leave, I thought.

"Did you miss me, baby?" she asked and wrapped her arms around my neck. I hugged her back and kissed her neck.

"Of course, I did," I said before I smacked her on the butt. I sat down on the couch and someone knocked on the door.

"Who is that?" I asked.

"Probably Katrice," she said and opened up the door. A weird-looking woman stepped inside. She was attractive but something was off about her face like she had plastic surgery or something. She was a little thick but not as thick as Rakita. She had hips and her breasts were round and full.

"Are you trying to slide through the club tonight?" the girl asked and popped her gum. I caught the gold teeth she had at the bottom of her mouth and I hated when women sported grills.

"No, I have company," Rakita replied. The girl looked around Rakita's shoulder to look me in the face.

"Damn, he is fine! What's his name?" the woman asked and sat down on the couch across from me. She wore a short skirt and she openly showed me the purple lace panties she had on.

"Kwenya, this is Katrice. She lives upstairs," Rakita said.

If you find out where Rakita lives then you will see Ashanta, Jesse's voice came inside my head.

"What's good with you?" I asked Katrice.

"Shit, just chilling. You got some fire on you?" Katrice asked me with a country accent.

Kwenya, think! Who is this broad? It can't be Ashanta, and if so, how? Ashanta doesn't talk like that but then again it's not hard to talk like a hoodrat. The face is throwing me off but those eyes are like Ashanta's, I thought. My mind was in overdrive until Rakita told me she had to go downstairs to grab the Chinese food.

Katrice lustfully eyed me and stood up.

"Tell Rakita to call me," she said and walked out of the apartment.

Ashanta

I hurriedly grabbed my purse and car keys then hauled ass out of Rakita's building. I drove straight to the trailer cursing and yelling at myself. I never expected Kwenya to show up at Rakita's apartment. I parked the car once I got to the trailer. I hurriedly rushed in and locked my door.

He doesn't know it's you. He doesn't know it's you! I yelled inside my head. I called Serene but she didn't pick up. I forgot that she went to South Carolina with her mother for a family event. I called Jesse and her line was disconnected. I threw my phone across the room. I was so close to messing up Rakita's life and it was about to be ruined. That bitch had to pay for what she did to me. I got undressed, took the gold teeth out of my mouth, and stepped into the shower. I slowly peeled the sticky mask off my face underneath the water. Sometimes it stuck to my skin and I had to be careful because of the wound under the Band-Aid I had on my cheek.

"OWWWWWW!" I cried out as I dropped the mask onto the shower floor. I heard glass breaking and jumped out of the shower. I grabbed my towel then grabbed my gun from under the sink. I walked out of the bathroom and was greeted by a gun to my face. I looked at the person who had on a ski-mask. The stranger took the mask off and it was Kwenya. I dropped my gun and backed away from him.

"How did you find me?" I asked him.

"Your eyes always give you away but I followed you. I have the paper you left at Jesse's house, who is, by the way, my connect," he said.

"WHAT!" I said and he smirked.

"We can get back to that later. But your passage stated that you died and was reborn. So it didn't take long to figure out you were disguising yourself. I must say, though, that was a good idea. Jesse is a very smart woman," he said.

"I can explain," I said. He lifted up my towel and touched my stomach. It was hard and firm and I was starting to show. If someone didn't know I was pregnant, they would've assumed it was a beer belly.

"I know everything now," he said.

"You can't stop me, Kwenya," I said. He sat down on my bed and looked around. He brushed his hand down his waves.

"You are staying in the woods while carrying my baby. Look around you, shorty. This is ain't even you. Why couldn't you just kill Rakita's dumb ass and get it over with?" he asked me.

"That's too easy," I said.

"Grab your bags, Ashanta," he said to me.

"I'm not done," I said.

"Can we talk about that when we get home? But as of right now, grab your things so we can go," he said. I thought there was going to be some type of hugging or kissing because of how much we missed each other but I was wrong. I understood him and I knew that he was upset at how I went about things. I didn't blame him for feeling that way.

"I have to meet Mondo," I said.

"I will meet Mondo," he said. He started grabbing my clothes and whatever else he saw and threw them in my duffel bags. I didn't have much clothes or shoes. He left out to put my bags in his truck and when he came back in, I was still in my towel. He stood in the middle of the trailer and his tall frame seemed so out of place. I knew he was uncomfortable.

"Kwenya, can we please just talk about everything?" I asked.

"Let's go, Ashanta," he said.

"But—" I was cut off when he picked me up. My towel came up and my sex was exposed. Kwenya walked me outside and put me inside his truck. He got into the driver's seat and pulled off.

"What happened to Rakita?" I asked him.

"I told her something came up and I hauled ass so I could catch up to you," he said. I stared at the side of his face.

"What happened to that old bitch?" I asked him and he looked at me.

"Your mouth is filthy now. You do know that shit, right?" he asked me.

"You had her holding my damn dog! That bitch was holding my dog, Kwenya! That was disrespectful. I was so mad that day because no woman should be holding my dog. A woman that wants to fuck you anyway," I fussed.

"Whoaaaaaa, shorty. Just chill out because what Shantel and I have going on is just business. I did backtrack once and fucked Rakita a little after you left but that's all I did," he admitted.

"So, you cheated on me while I was in Mexico with a slashed face?" I asked.

"I thought you was dead," he said.

"So, what. You could've at least waited until I turned into a corpse if I was dead," I spat. Kwenya pulled over on the side of the road. He grabbed me by my neck.

"Listen, shorty, don't fuck with me right now. I have almost lost my mind behind you. I'm not trying to hear that bullshit so shut the fuck up! I thought you was dead and so did everybody else. I was out drinking and one thing led to another. It ain't really an excuse but I didn't cheat on you," he said. He let me go before he pulled back off into traffic.

****

"Where are we?" I asked as he pulled up to a gate.

"Our new house. I was going to tell you about it but I never got a chance to," he said. He pulled up the driveway and parked. He helped me out of the truck and I followed behind him. When I stepped inside of his house I was in awe. It reminded me of Serene's house but bigger.

"This is beautiful," I said. Kwenya grabbed the twists I had in my hair and he caressed my face. He took the Band-Aid off my face and traced my scar with his finger.

"I feel so ugly because of it. I think that's why I decided to wear that fake skin on my face," I said. Others would've called it a mask but I called it fake skin. I still had to put make-up on it and all it did was push my cheeks back and change my nose structure. Without the make-up on, you would've known it was me. I had to use gold teeth to dress it up even more. It was too much work but it was worth it.

"You are still beautiful," he said. He pulled me into him and his hand rested on the back my head as he hugged me in his strong arms. His arms almost swallowed my frame while his body towered over mine. He was my protector. I started to get emotional and being pregnant caused a lot of my mood swings. I burst into tears as I sobbed into Kwenya's chest.

"I missed you so much," I cried. I heard barking and Bella ran to me. I hurriedly picked her up and she licked my face.

"My baby!" I said and kissed her little nose. I squeezed her as I hugged her

"I'm jealous. You didn't give me all of that," Kwenya said.

"That's because I wasn't sure what you and Shantel had going on," I replied. Kwenya left the house and came back with all of my bags. One of the bags had all of my money in it and I needed to put it in a safe. I put Bella down and went upstairs. The master bedroom wasn't hard to find because it was the only room that had double doors. I pushed the doors open and was impressed at how neat everything was. He and I used to argue about how he would throw his clothes everywhere. I walked into the bathroom and got inside the shower because the dried soap on my body was making me itch. After my shower, I dried off and climbed into bed. Kwenya came into the room with Bella running behind him.

"This bed feels like heaven," I said as he took his clothes off. He pulled me into him and wrapped his arms around me tightly.

"I still might have to do that time from when Bernie set me up," he said.

"No you won't. I promise," I said.

"You been busy, very busy," he said.

"I know, just trust me on this one," I said.

"Okay," he replied and his hand slid across my stomach. He cupped my breasts and gently squeezed them.

"I might have to keep you pregnant if you come with all of this," he whispered in my ear as his hands roamed my body. I was on fire and I was throbbing between my legs to the point it ached. I'd been craving him for a while and I wanted him to take his frustrations out on me. He turned me over on my back and kissed me as his hands gapped my legs apart. He slid his middle finger inside of me and I was tight—very tight. My pussy almost pushed his finger out. He opened the gate to the flood that was waiting to be released. He captured my aching nipple inside his mouth and almost sucked the plumpness of my breast away from me. I spread my legs further apart as he fingered me. He pulled his finger out of me and spread my sweet essence across my lips. His tongue traced my lips while he tasted me. I sat up to straddle him. His dick was very hard and my heartbeat raced when I thought about how he was going to stretch me open. He gripped me by the butt to lift me up. His bulging head pressed into my opening and it felt like I was losing my virginity all over again. I winced in pain as my pussy swallowed his shaft inch by inch. He bit his bottom lip as he lay on his back with himself planted firmly inside of me so that I could barely move.

"Fuck, I missed this pussy," Kwenya groaned. He moved me back and forth— my body moved like a wave in the ocean. My nails dug into his chest and my moans grew louder. I squeezed my breasts as my wetness dripped out of me. I bucked forward then rose up and came back down on him. I held onto his shoulders as I rode him. I rode him faster because it made me wetter. The headboard banged against the wall as I sped up.

"ARRRGGHHHHHHHH! FUCK! SHIITTTTTTTT!" Kwenya moaned and slapped my ass.

"Get all of this dick, shorty. I know you miss it," he said before he latched onto my breast. Sweat dripped down my chest as I felt an orgasm brewing. He pinched my clit as he fucked me back.

"Look at that tight pussy squirting on my dick," he groaned.

"OHHHHHHHH! BABYYYYYYYYYY!" I said as my body jerked. He rolled me over and held my legs up in the air like I was a baby. He smacked my ass twice.

POP! POP!

He stuck his tongue inside of me and I started to squeal. Everything felt good about him.

Sllllluuurrrrrrppppppppp. Muah.

The sounds that slipped from his mouth while he was eating me out, turned the notch up on my sex drive. I reached down between my legs to rub my clit while his tongue went in and out of me.

"Let it go, shorty," he said between licks. I almost cried like a baby as his tongue savagely drilled into my slit. I was so horny I felt possessed.

"Fuck me. Please, just stick it in," I begged. He turned my body over. I lay on my side with my knees bent in a fetal position. He entered me and it was slightly painful. I held my hand out and he smacked it away.

"I'm tearing this lil' pussy up tonight, shorty. A nigga been having wet dreams about this shit," he said and stuffed all of himself inside of me. I put the pillow over my face as he pumped long, hard, and deep between my walls. I sank my teeth into the pillow when he gripped my waist and slammed me up and down on his dick. He made sure I felt every inch of him.

He smacked my ass and wiggled it. He was fucking me like a man that was deprived of pussy for years. I was squirting bullets of cum as he tore me open. He snatched the pillow off my face and slipped his wet fingers from my pussy into my mouth.

"I'm about to cummmmmmmmmmm again!" I screamed. His testicles slapped against me as he fucked me so deep I stopped moaning. I had one of those orgasms when you almost lift up off the bed as your eyes roll to the back of your head. The only sound that came out of me was a gasp; the type of gasp a person takes when they come up to breathe after being under water so long. I felt like I was urinating myself as cum poured out of me. Kwenya groaned and jerked. His dick slammed into me again and he started throbbing.

"AARRGGHHHHHHHH!" he yelled out as he came inside of me. Kwenya lay on me and kissed my lips. I closed my eyes to let sleep take over me.

****

The next day...

"Where are you going?" Kwenya asked me when he walked into the bedroom. I was putting on a pair of tennis shoes.

"I'm going over Serene's house," I lied. Serene was still out of town.

"How are you getting there?" he asked. I had left my rental at the trailer I was staying in.

"One of your vehicles," I said. "She is pregnant and alone. I have been checking up on her since I came back." Kwenya gave me an uneasy look before he nodded his head.

"Aight," he said. I kissed his lips and he hugged me.

"What do you want for dinner tonight?" I asked him.

"Fried chicken, and fix a nigga some Kool-Aid with it. Add enough sugar to it. You are the only black woman I know that don't know how to make Kool-Aid," he said and I giggled.

"I been around Rakita and Chasity long enough. Trust me, I know how to make it," I replied.

"I got to holla at you about something. I'm not getting out of the game right now. I'm expanding and partnering up with Jesse. I just want you to understand that because I'm about to be deeper than I have ever been," he said. I sat on the bed and looked up at him.

"It's dangerous," I said.

"Living, period, can be. You should know because you were a doctor and you been through more shit than me and I'm a street nigga. All I'm saying is shit out here ain't perfect and will never be perfect," he replied.

"Promise me that you will be extra careful and promise me this isn't forever," I said.

"It ain't forever and I'm always careful," he said. I stood up and kissed his cheek. I was ready to walk out the room but he grabbed my arm.

"When are you going to see a real doctor? Isn't that what pregnant women do?" he asked me.

"I will once all of this blows over. I'm almost done," I said. He crossed his arms.

"What are your plans, shorty?" he asked.

"I can't tell you because it's a secret," I said. Bella followed me to the door and I picked her up. I grabbed Kwenya's fitted cap from off the couch and put it on my head. I took the keys to his Yukon before I left the house.

****

I walked into the house and Damos was still sitting in the chair. I almost forgot about him but he smelled horrible. Jesse told me before I left Mexico that a confined man will think about everything he's done and would eventually break. She told me to strap Damos down like a dog and leave him. She told me that it would break him down and make him weak. I was in control of his life and he was finally beneath me. I grabbed a bucket to put water and bleach inside of it.

"Mondo!" I called out. He came downstairs with his army fatigue pants on.

"About time because he stinks. I had to stay at a hotel last night," Mondo said.

"Drag him to the shower. I'm going to give him a bath. Not that I care but I cannot tolerate that stench," I said. Mondo grabbed a pair of gloves and dragged Damos's chair across the floor and down the hall as Bella followed behind, wagging her tail.

"Take your clothes off!" Mondo said to Damos. Damos was weak and his lips were chapped. When Damos woke fully and saw me he got scared.

"Get that crazy bitch away from me! Get her away from me!" he yelled and Bella barked at him.

"Shut up, rapist! Mondo, make sure he washes himself off. We have a busy day today," I said. I looked at Damos.

"Make sure you wash that ass really good," I teased because I was aware of Mondo's lust for men.

An hour later...

Damos sat on the couch eating McDonald's and drinking water. He was so hungry that I thought he was going to die from choking as he scarfed his food down. His hands were handcuffed and his legs were tied to the legs of the couch. I sat across from him, smiling at him.

"You are a sick bitch. You left me in the house with that nigga. He couldn't keep his hands off my dick. He stopped touching me once I started shitting on myself. Why the fuck did you give me a shower? I could've just used the food," he said.

"You have no clout in here. You will do what I want you to do. The check you received for my death is ready and I want you to pick it up. After that, you will be free to go," I said to him.

"I don't have no money! Bitch, I need that money!" he screamed at me.

"Bitch, that is my money, and newsflash, I'm not dead. So, you will get me that money or I will have Mondo tie you down and fuck you in every hole. He wants to but he is just waiting on me to give him the go," I said.

"I'm sorry! There, I said it, I'm sorry for doing all of that shit to you. Is that what you want to hear?" he asked.

"I used to but your sorry is like the wind. It just breezed on by. You should have been sorry, Damos. Do you think I did all of this just so that I could get a sorry? You are really fucking stupid, no wonder you and Chasity hit it off so well. Two dumb assholes," I replied.

"You are going to jail for this," he said.

"Oh hush," I said and stood up.

233

"Well, the insurance office is open. Mondo, grab him so we can go. I need to be home in time to cook dinner," I said before Bella and I walked out of the door.

****

Mondo sat in the backseat with Damos. Both of them wore a suit to avoid being suspicious. If Damos didn't comply inside of the building, Mondo had the order to shoot him. Jesse told me that Mondo was military trained and could kill in the drop of an eye and get away. Mondo screwed his silencer on as he looked at Damos.

"When we go in here, you will act normal. I will kill you if I have to. I have no real identity and I've lived in almost every country you can think of. I will drop you then be ghost. Now, let's go, baby," he teased Damos. Damos got out of the van with Mondo and after he did, I called Desi.

"Hey, this is Ashanta," I said when she answered the phone.

"About time you called me. I was starting to think you died for real," she fussed.

"I'm sorry, I've been a little busy. Meet me at the trailer in an hour," I said and hung up.

I waited for thirty minutes until Mondo and Damos came out of the building. Mondo gave me the check and pushed Damos inside the van.

"You got what you wanted, so let me go!" Damos said.

"I will after I'm done," I said and pulled off. I headed back to the house that I kept Damos in.

****

I pulled up in front of the trailer. Desi got out of her car with a smirk on her face.

"So, you and the baby daddy reunited. You're driving one of his trucks and now you are glowing. Good dick, I'm assuming," she said and I blushed. She followed me inside the trailer. As soon as we sat down, I pulled the check from out of my bra.

"Oh shit. Girl, this is a big check," she said.

"Can you cash it?" I asked her.

"Of course. I just need to get my little inside buddy to get into the bank system and change a few things before we can," she said.

"It's that easy? Wow, I need to be a hacker," I joked.

"I can do the basic but this will require a genius. I don't understand how they do it but they do and get away with it. Nothing in this world is safe," she said. She made a phone call. She told the person on the other end that she was on her way.

"Okay, let's go," she said.

****

Desi pulled up in front of an apartment complex. It looked decent and it was in a decent area. I got out of her car and followed her up the stairs. I left Bella at the trailer because she was barking too much. The apartment was on the fifth floor. I thanked God I made it because it was a lot of stairs. Desi knocked on the first door to the right of the hallway.

"STEPHEN!" I yelled out when the door opened. He slammed the door in my face. I knocked on the door.

"Stephen! Open up the door," I yelled.

"How do you know him?" Desi asked me.

"He is my brother," I replied.

"Bitch, get out. Stephen is your brother? Y'all got the same parents? He is soooo ratchet," Desi said and laughed but I didn't find it funny. The door unlocked and Stephen opened it up for us. He mushed me in the back of my head as soon as I stepped inside of his apartment.

"Why your ass ain't dead?" he asked me and my mouth dropped.

"That isn't nice to say," I said.

"I didn't mean it like that. I thought you were dead but you are standing here in my face," he replied. Stephen and I weren't close. I was seven years older than him, so we didn't have that bond. He always stayed in his room or hung out with his friends. He looked more like our father— almost identical.

"Why did you shut the door?" I asked him.

"I panicked. I was getting high and I thought I was seeing shit, and stop calling me Stephen. I hate that damn name," he said.
"Wait, so why are you not in school? And I didn't know you lived in Annapolis," I said.

"That's because I don't want our parents to know. I'm not going to law school and don't plan on it. Those college reports I give to our parents are fake," he said. He started eyeing Desi.

"When are you going to stop playing with me and give me some of that again?" he asked her and my mouth dropped.

I would've been better off dead, I thought.

"Never again because you lied about your age. Look, little boy, we came here because we need a favor," she said.

"So you do illegal things?" I asked Stephen.

"I do what I want to do and don't start that 'I need to be a lawyer' bullshit. I don't want to hear our parents' speeches coming from you, too. Isn't what you are doing illegal? You faked your death to cash in your life insurance money?" he asked.

"I have something else going on in my life and I will tell you about it later, but mother thinks you are gay," I said. He fell over laughing.

"That's what she gets for trying to hook me up with bitches that have no breasts and flat asses. The last girl she tried to hook me up with was a ballerina. Her toes reminded me of braille. I told her ass I wasn't blind and I could see all those corns on her feet. Your mother got drunk one night, like always, and came into my room and I started dancing. I bet that scared the fuck out of her," he said.

Jesus give me strength.

"I don't want to know anymore. Can you just do this for me? I have things to do," I replied.

"If Desi gives me some again," he said. She pushed him into the wall.

"My man would fuck the both of us up. Now, get to work, Stephen," she spat.

"Okay, damn. Give me the check so I can see what bank it's from. This will take an hour so give me some time," he said. He walked down the hall of his apartment. His apartment had a feminine touch to it. I looked around and saw a pair of heels on the floor. I wanted to ask him if he was dating someone but I thought better of it. Stephen was apparently secretive and didn't want his family to know anything about him. I thought I was the only one who wasn't happy with the way our father pushed careers on us that we didn't want.

"I guess rich people struggle like poor folks, too, even though the struggle isn't a financial one," Desi said. It was almost like she'd read my mind.

"You are absolutely right. Money doesn't define us. We still go through the trials in life. I'm a pure example of it," I said and she agreed. Desi's phone rang and she turned the ringer off.

"Bishop is going to kill me," Desi said.

"Why?" I asked.

"It's a long story but I kind of did something and it opened up a can of worms," she said.

"Ohhhhh I see, but let me ask you something. Did you really sleep with my brother?" I asked her.

"Yes, a few years ago. He was around eighteen but he told me he was twenty-two. Stephen looks older than he is and he had that nice car and always kept money. He wore expensive clothes and I thought he was a dope dealer. But, anyways, I ran into him at a party and he wanted some pussy. I told him I wanted two g's and that lil' nigga gave me three. Come to find out, he was hacking into shit and that's how I got put onto it. When I found out his real age, I was crushed a little bit. He's a little freak," she bragged.

"Okay, I don't want to know anymore," I replied. Desi and I talked until Stephen came out of the room.

"Everything is good to go. I'm familiar with the bank you need to cash this check at. A teller by the name of Tisha will help you out but there is a fee. She might be a little jealous, so just tell her that y'all are related to me in case she asks," he said.

"Is Tisha your girlfriend?" I asked.

"She's my baby mama. She is six months pregnant with my daughter," he replied and my head started to spin. Stephen was really living another life.

"But you want to fuck Desi again? Wow," I said.

"I'm addicted to pussy," he said. I didn't know what to say after that. I went into my purse and gave my brother a few stacks of money. He handed it back to me.

"I'm good, but the next time you come back, bring a woman that isn't stingy with the pussy, and don't tell your parents shit about me living here and not going to college to be a lawyer. Oh, and I don't want them to know about my daughter, either, Ashanta. They don't need to know nothing about me and I mean it. Your secret is safe with me, too," he said.

"Okay, but what are you going to do with your life?" I asked him. I still wanted the best for my little brother, although he and were like strangers to each other.

"I don't know yet. I'm still young but I'm tired of our father painting our future. It's our life and we should be able to do what we want with it. You made that mistake but I'm not going to," he said.

"I understand," I said and kissed his cheek. "When this is all over, I want you to meet, Kwenya. I want the whole family to meet him," I said and he nodded his head.

"Okay, but don't stay dead too long. Your mother is no longer wearing her wig. She walks around with her hair sticking straight up like a baby orangutan," he joked but it wasn't funny. My mother took her wigs very seriously and she only took them off when she was stressed or angry.

"I won't," I said. Me and Desi left his apartment, and then I headed straight to the bank.

****

Two hours later…

Desi came out of the bank with two large suitcases. I was nervous that she was going to get caught but she didn't. I sat in the car and waited for her because I still didn't want anyone to see me. She had her shades on and strutted in her heels like she just didn't commit a crime. I admired her because she was unapologetic about who she was. She got inside her car and put the money in her backseat.

"I gave Tisha a cut out of your money. That girl almost made me want to slap her. I told her I was Stephen's cousin and she told me that I didn't look like him. That's what took so long. I had to convince her that I wasn't one of his side-chicks. Stephen must really have a stable of hoes," she said.

I'm not surprised at all anymore, I thought.
"Thank you for everything. Did you take your cut?" I asked her.

"As much as I love money, my life is more important, and thanks to you, those bitches didn't get me. I didn't help you out to get paid," she said. I opened up one of the suitcases and took stacks out of it. I placed them inside of a small MCM backpack that was in her backseat while she pulled off.

"This is one hundred and fifty thousand dollars. I still need your help," I said.

"With what else?" she asked. Desi was always down to get her hands dirty.

"Taking down the mean girls. Their time is over," I said.

"You are a bad girl. I think I just found my best friend and wife," she said and I laughed.

******

When I finally got home, Kwenya wasn't there. Bella ran around excitedly; she loved Kwenya's house. I grabbed the pack of chicken he had in the fridge and started to prepare dinner. After I fried the chicken, I made scalloped potatoes, broccoli and corn bread. I added almost a whole pack of sugar inside his Kool-Aid as I stirred it. I heard his motorcycle outside and Bella ran to do the door.

"Shorty, come and get this dog before I boot her little ass across the floor!" he called out to me. He walked into the kitchen with Bella growling as she latched onto his ankle. I hurriedly picked her up.

"She doesn't like men I don't think," I said.

"What other nigga you been around?" he asked me.

"Are you jealous?" I responded.

"You starting shit already," he said and kissed my lips. He took his shirt off and tossed it in the middle of the hallway. He looked at me to see if I was going to say something but I didn't. I was just on cloud nine being around him again. He sat down at the kitchen table and placed all of his phones on top.

"Where my plate at, shorty?" he asked me. I went into the microwave to grab our plates. I sat them down then I grabbed the pitcher of Kool-Aid with cups of ice. He got up and washed his hands. I never understood why he didn't do that soon as he came into the house. He came back to the table with hot sauce, white bread, and Old Bay seasoning.

"What do you know about this?" he asked.

"I never ate it like that before," I said. He tore the meat of the chicken and laid it in the middle of the bread. He sprinkled the Old Bay seasoning and hot sauce on it. He folded it up and told me to taste it.

243

"UMMMMMMM! That is delicious," I said. We ate silently for a few minutes until Kwenya broke the silence.

"Your mother accused me of doing something to you," he said.

"I'm not surprised. I will talk to her later. How is everything with your mother, especially after the Bernie situation?" I asked. I knew a lot from being around Rakita and Chasity.

"I cut her off," he replied.

"Why?" I asked.

"She chose that nigga over me after I told her he set me up. I'm just not feeling her right now. She calls me but I don't answer. I stopped paying her bills," he said. I wanted to say something but I thought better of it. Once Kwenya's mind was made up, that was it.

"Let me know if you start to feel uncomfortable with the way I live. If you feel like you can't do this, just tell me now, and I will put you in a separate home," he said.

"I'm fine as long as you don't bother me when I write. I also don't want to see or know about anything illegal that you do. Accepting is one thing, but seeing it and being a part of it, is another thing," I replied.

"I can respect that," he said. I got up and sat on his lap, facing him.

"Are you finished eating?" I asked him before I sucked on his neck.

"As bad as I want to slide into you right now, I can't. A nigga ain't eat all day," he said.

"I can bring you a plate to bed," I said. I unzipped his shorts and he stood up with me his arms; he carried me upstairs. Moments later, he was buried deep inside of me whispering in my ear about how much he loved me. I loved him, too, more than anyone could imagine.

Chasity

"Yes, I have the drugs, and all you have to do is put it in Jesula's food. Once she goes to sleep, call me. I will come over and my cousin can take it from there. He owes me so he is willing to help out," she said as we walked around the mall. I had to hurry up and get rid of Jesula so that I could get my money back before she spent it. I wanted to get away from Annapolis because of the warrant I had from Desi. I wasn't going to court for the lies she told on me. I wasn't going to waste my money on a lawyer. I managed to save up a few thousand from stripping but it wasn't enough to leave town with. I wanted to start over and that eighty thousand was going to help.

I saw Kwenya coming out of the store and decided to walk in the other direction because I knew he hated me. He called my name and I didn't have a choice but to see what he wanted. If I had run from him, I would've looked guilty of something. I also wanted to clear my name about the Ashanta situation. It was all Jesula's fault.

"What's up with you?" he asked me.

"Nothing," I said.

"Who is your friend?" he asked as he eyed Katrice.

"She isn't from around here," I said.

"Excuse, us. I need to holla at shorty really quick," Kwenya said to Katrice.

"I will be in Macy's," Katrice told me before she walked off.

"You know I spared your life, right? You were responsible for getting my shorty robbed but since nothing happened to her during the robbery, I'll let you pass, but I need a favor," he said.

"What kind of favor?" I asked him.

"I want you to hold this stripper party for me. I got some niggas coming to town and I'm trying to close in on this deal. I'm trying to impress them so I need some of the baddest bitches to come through," he said as his hand slid up and down my face. When his hand brushed against my breast, my legs almost buckled. Kwenya knew he was toxic and how much of an effect he had on women. The way he talked, his physique, his swag, and the way he smelled—everything about that man was just perfect.

"Can you make that happen this Friday?" he asked me.

"I'll see what I can do, but how do I know it's not a set-up?" I asked.

"I know you stay with Rakita. I don't have time to play, shorty. You would've been somewhere stankin' if I really wanted to get at you. All I'm concerned about is impressing my new connect, that is all," he replied.

Lawd, this nigga is fine! Fuck Rakita, I want him to myself. Once I get him, I can tell him about Rakita and her connection to Chaos. Every woman for themselves, I thought. I gave him my number and he gently smacked me on the ass before he walked off.

I met up with Katrice inside of Macy's.

"So, what happened? I saw the way he was looking at you. Bitch, you better hop on that fine chocolate," she said.

"I am Friday night," I said. After we left the mall, we headed back to our neighborhood. When I walked into Rakita's apartment, she was in her favorite spot which was in front of the TV. Jesula was sitting at the kitchen table eating crabs and drinking a beer.

"Hey everyone," I said.

"Hey," Rakita said.

"What's up?" Jesula asked me.

"Nothing," I said. Jesula's phone rang and she handed it to Rakita.

"This is Chaos calling for you. He is off lock-up now," Jesula said. Rakita took the phone then walked to the back. I sat at the table with Jesula and she mugged me.

"You and that bitch, Rakita, is getting too close. This is my last week here. I'm going back to the islands," she said.

That's what you think, I thought.

"Okay," I said.

"You always been a weak bitch. That hoe doesn't like you or me, and the only reason we are here is because that bitch is afraid of Chaos," she said. Jesula was pure evil.

"I thought you were going to take care of Serene for me?" I asked her. I already knew she wasn't when she told me she was when I was in the hospital. I just wanted to bring it up to press a button.

"Bitch, I said that to make you feel better while you were in the hospital. She had every right to beat your ass because you trapped her husband. If that was me, I would've killed you," she said.

This bitch needs to die! I screamed inside my head. I got up from the table and headed back to my room. I locked my door and called Deron. He answered on the third ring.

"Can I speak to Marquis?" I asked him.

"Hello," Marquis said into the phone and I almost broke down.

"How have you been? I miss you," I said to him but he didn't say anything.

"Do you miss me?" I asked him.

"No, where is nanny?" he asked me. He was looking for my mother which was understandable because I never had him.

"I don't know, baby. Put your father on the phone," I said.

"What?" Deron asked when he got on the phone.

"Can I see him this weekend?" I asked him.

"Yeah, at your mother's house. I don't want to see you or even be near you," he said before he hung up. I lay across my bed as tears fell from my eyes. I regretted half of the things I did, but it was too late to turn back.

Rakita

"Who is here with you?" Katrice asked when I opened my apartment door for her.

"Nobody. Jesula been gone since last night and Chasity went somewhere," I said.

"Great, because I need to tell you what happened at the mall yesterday," she said and sat on my couch.

"Okay." I sat down across from her.

"So, Chasity and I ran into Kwenya at the mall—the guy that was here the other night—and, bitchhhhhhhh, guess what? She ran your name through the mud. She told him that you were seeing Chaos. He was so pissed off that he invited her to a party Friday. So, I spoke up and told him that you didn't know Chaos. Chasity been shady toward me since then but I don't care. I think her and Jesula is trying to fuck with you. They are both shady—they are cousins. I think you should go and crash their little party because, from the looks of it, Kwenya was very interested in seeing what Chasity has between her legs," she said. I believed her because females were sneaky and Kwenya was a man whore.

"See, that is why that nigga is about to get locked up. I was going to help him, but fuck him! I did a lot for that nigga and he turned around and fucked another nigga's bitch and got the bitch pregnant.

That is okay because I fixed his ass," I fussed. I got up from the couch and headed to the kitchen. I needed a drink to calm my nerves.

"How did you fix him?" she asked me.

"I set his dumb-ass up so I could get rid of his bitch and so that I could be his down bitch while he did his time, but they spelled his name wrong on the warrant so he was released. He still has a court date and might have to do time. I had his mother's boyfriend, Bernie, eating out the palm of my hand because I slept with him, too. I did a lot to be with Kwenya and this is how he repays me? He wants to fuck Chasity's nasty and homeless ass?" I ranted.

"So, you got him locked up? You screwed his mama's man?" she asked.

"Yes, I got him locked up and I knew Bernie was going to come in handy so I fucked him. His mother stocks his shop up in the morning. Bernie put two bricks of coke in the flour box that was in Kwenya's mother's trunk. Unaware of what was going on, his mother put the box that was in her trunk in his shop. I called the police and told them where they were. He should've kept his dirty dick in his pants," I said.

"I don't feel sorry for him. Niggas ain't shit. Friday you and I both will catch them. He will pay for that shit and so will Chasity," Katrice fussed. She gave me a small medicine bottle.

"Dump this in Jesula's juice that she has in the fridge. When she falls out, call me," Katrice said.

****

The next morning...

I woke up and cooked breakfast for Chasity and Jesula. I felt good because I knew they both were going down. I poured Jesula a glass of her coconut juice with the medicine inside of it and I sat it down next to her. I should've gave Chasity some but I wanted to see if she was really going to mess with Kwenya behind my back. I wanted to see if Katrice had the right information. I told Katrice some incriminating information about myself but I didn't care. Her country ass didn't know anybody in Annapolis. The simple bitch barely knew how to get home because she still wasn't familiar with the area. I sat down at the table and everyone ate in silence.

Y'all bitches will be gone soon and for good. Fuck Chaos, that nigga don't run shit! I said to myself, although I knew he had enough pull to have me killed. Jesula put her plate in the sink and went into the bathroom. The snake didn't even thank me for making her breakfast.

"So, did you give it to her?" Chasity asked me.

"Yes," I said and rolled my eyes at her. She was going to say something else but we heard a crashing noise. Chasity and I both ran into the bathroom and Jesula was on the floor, clutching her throat. I stood and watched as Chasity ran out of the bathroom. I heard her talking to someone on the phone out in the living room. Minutes later, Katrice came through the door with a man I'd never seen before.

"We were in the area when Chasity called," Katrice said to me. Jesula was still clutching at her throat as she tried to breathe.

"Once she falls asleep, we will take her," Katrice said.

"Where is she going?" Chasity asked her.

"My uncle Benny owns a prostitution ring in Mexico. She will go there, but don't worry, none of his hoes escape," Katrice said. When Jesula closed her eyes, the man wrapped her up in a blanket.

"How will you get out of the building without anybody seeing her?" I asked Katrice.

"The laundry room door leads to an alley in the back of the building. He will wrap her up in a lot of sheets. Don't worry, it will just look like laundry," she said. The big man came back into the bathroom with comforters and more sheets. He threw Jesula over his shoulder and left out of the apartment. He didn't say anything to anybody as he moved quietly.

"I can't believe we just helped someone kidnap her," Chasity said as her hands trembled.

"She had to go. Don't worry, she will be doing what the rest of us been doing, and that's selling pussy. I used to work for my uncle and he takes care of his girls. Jesula will be so brainwashed that she wouldn't think about coming back, especially once she sees his mansion and expensive cars. Y'all will become a distant memory. Well, let me get her ready. I'm leaving and will be back Friday," Katrice said and left the apartment.

Chasity and I went back to the kitchen. We sat at the table in silence.

"I feel bad," she said.

"Well, I don't. She deserves everything that is coming to her," I spat and Chasity rolled her eyes.

Bitch, you will get yours next...

Friday night (Two days later...)

"I'm going to ride with Chasity to make sure Kwenya is going to be here. I'll send you a text if he is just so that you don't waste your time coming out here," Katrice said to me over the phone.

"Okay, cool," I said and hung up. I showered and got dressed. I packed all of Chasity's things in garbage bags and took them to the dumpster. I only allowed her to stay longer so that she could help me with Jesula. I didn't want to take the blame by myself but she had to go. When I went back into my apartment, I had a glass a wine. I was ready to get comfortable until Katrice texted me and told me that she was at a stripper party and Chasity took Kwenya into the bedroom. I grabbed my tennis shoes and tied a scarf around my head. Chasity and Kwenya were both going to feel my pain.

Ashanta

"Let me go!" Damos yelled because he was still tied up.

"I will but you have to wait for the party first, baby. You are about to reunite with your boo thing," I said. My phone vibrated and it was a text from Desi. I went down to the basement of the house. Desi was at the basement door with fighting gear on.

"I like the outfit," I said and she turned around to model it.

"This is a beat-a-bitch-ass-first outfit then ask questions later," she said.

"So, what is it that you want me to do?" she asked me. I didn't give her all the details because I didn't want her to reject my favor.

"I want you to tie me to that chair and beat me up. Bruise my face as bad as you can," I said as I got undressed.

"Come again. Okay, now, bitch, you wait a minute. I'm down for you or whatever, but this is some freaky, weird shit. Why are you naked?" she asked me.

"Listen to me. Just tie me to that chair then whip my ass. Go to your car and call the police and tell them that you heard a woman screaming. Mondo will let Damos go, but he will not get very far on-foot, so everything will work out," I said.

"I need a drink and a blunt," Desi said before she tied me to a chair.

"Just hit me in the face a few times to give me a bruise or two. I will be okay, trust me," I said. She slapped me as hard as she could and the left side of my face went numb.

"I don't want to do this. You are pregnant," she said.

"My face is not pregnant, now hurry up before they get here," I said. She balled her fist up and punched me in the nose. Blood dripped down my chin from my nose and onto my chest. Tears filled my eyes but I took it like a champ.

"One more time," I said and she hit me again. The taste of blood filled my mouth.

"Okay, now leave and call the police," I said. She backed away from me and rushed out of the basement door. My face started to swell up as the blood continued to drip. It was painful but the results from it was all worth it.

Damos

Mondo untied me and I didn't understand what was going on. They were allowing me to eat, drink, and take showers since the day I picked up the check for Ashanta. I didn't understand what changed but I didn't care because I was no longer tied up. Mondo touched me here and there but I was thankful the fuck nigga didn't take full advantage of me. All I knew was, I was finally free and it was all over with. Mondo left the living room of the dirty old house they held me in. I didn't know where Ashanta went but I went looking for her as soon as I heard Mondo leave the house. I was going to kill the bitch with my bare hands.

I went into the kitchen first to look for her purse and her keys. I didn't have money or a car to get home with and I was too tired to walk. I barely got any sleep sitting up the whole time they kept me. As I was rummaging through the kitchen, I heard a car pull up. I hurriedly went to the front door and opened it. The lights cut off and a figure stepped out. The figure was getting closer and I started to make out who it was.

"Chasity?" I asked her.

"What the fuck are you doing here?" she asked looking around. She wore a fishnet dress with a lime green G-string and bra set. She wore a lime green bob wig and her make-up was done.

"What do you got on and how did you know I was here?" I asked her as she looked around.

"I didn't know. I was supposed to meet someone here. What is going on? This doesn't feel right," she nervously said. Another car pulled up and the driver hopped out.

"Bitch, I should beat your ass!" a woman yelled as she headed toward us. Something wasn't right and I felt it in the pit of my stomach. Mondo let me go and left without saying a word to me and Ashanta was still somewhere in the house.

"Rakita?" Chasity asked.

"You damn right it's me! So, you came here to meet Kwenya, huh?" she asked Chasity. She didn't give Chasity a chance to respond because she started swinging on Chasity. They both fell into me and all three of us fell into the house on the living room floor.

"Get the fuck off of me!" I yelled as they swung on each other. I heard police sirens outside of the house. I pushed them off and made a dash toward the door. Everything that was happening seemed out of place. More police cars arrived and I was lucky to still be alive. An officer stepped out of the car.

"FREEZE! PUT YOUR HANDS UP!" an officer said. I held my hands up as the police cars surrounded me.

"I was kidnapped!" I yelled out.

"We got a call about a woman screaming for help," he said.

"There are two women in that house fighting. I have been kidnapped by my wife and a man named Mondo," I said while the other officers went inside the house. A police officer slammed me on the ground and handcuffed me.

"I didn't do nothing!" I yelled.

"Shut up or else you will join your father!" the officer yelled at me. An officer walked outside and called for backup. I also heard him asking for an ambulance.

Them dumb bitches inside of that house is fighting till the death, I thought to myself.

"There is a dead body upstairs and there is also a naked woman tied and beaten inside of the basement. She said her husband and the two other women kidnapped her," an officer said.

"I didn't kidnap anybody! Those bitches just showed up! I was kidnapped!" I screamed. Chasity and the girl, Rakita, were brought out of the house handcuffed. The officers escorted them to separate police cars. An officer picked me up off the ground then sent a gut-blowing punch to my stomach.

"Sick son of a bitch! We have been looking for Ashanta Scott for two months!" he yelled before he pushed me into the police car.

****

"I'm going to ask you again. Who killed Jesula Patterson?" a detective by the name of Angela Gomez asked me.

"I don't know!" I yelled.

"You kidnapped your wife to gain insurance money. The proof is all here. Who beat up your wife? You said a man named Mondo let you go but he never went to the basement. It was just y'all three in the house. So, if he didn't do it and you didn't do it, who did? You stated your wife walked into the house and she disappeared but she ended up in the basement. Your story isn't adding up! Who tied your wife up?" she yelled.

"I don't know! I thought she was dead! I was kidnapped, you have to believe me," I said.

"I talked to your neighbor and a man that fits your description has been coming in and out of your old house. The same house you and your wife shared. How is that possible if you were kidnapped?" she asked me.

"I need a lawyer. My wife faked her death so that she could get revenge," I said and the detective laughed.

"Do you think your story is believable? You want me to believe a woman tied and beat herself up?" she asked.

"I need a lawyer," I spat. The detective fixed her blazer and smiled at me.

"Fair enough but I'm going to make sure these charges stick. You will be charged for murder, kidnapping, and fraud," she said and walked out of the room. I screamed at the top of my lungs.

"ASHANTA! YOU ARE A DEAD BITCH!" I yelled. I was screwed and it didn't matter what I said because nobody believed me. Ashanta had charges filed against me and a restraining order before she went missing. In their eyes, she was the victim and always had been and that is how she got away with her plan. I bet the neighbor at our old house was paid to say they saw me going in and out of the house. How could anyone believe I was missing when someone reported that they saw me? I was a goner and I didn't have money for a lawyer.

Rakita

"Who is Katrice? We went to the apartment above yours and guess what? It's vacant and has been for five months now, so who is this woman?" Detective Gomez asked me.

"I just told you who she was!" I said. She went inside of the Ziploc bag and pulled out the bottle I poured into Jesula's coconut juice.

"This is what we found in your car. This bottle has the same poison that killed Jesula. It has your fingerprints all over it, so tell me what happened!" she yelled. I cried.

"I thought it was something to put her to sleep with. Katrice said that her uncle was just going to pimp her out. I didn't know she was dead!" I said. She pulled out a recorder and pressed a button. It had my voice on it...

"See, that is why that nigga is about to get locked up. I was going to help him but fuck him! I did a lot for that nigga and he turned around and fucked another nigga's bitch and got the bitch pregnant. That is okay because I fixed his ass," I fussed.

"How did you fix him?" Katrice asked me.

"I set his dumb-ass up so I could get rid of his bitch and so that I could be his down bitch while he did his time, but they spelled his name wrong on the warrant so he was released. He still has a court date and might have to do the time. I had his mother's boyfriend, Bernie, eating out the palm of my hand because I slept with him,

too. I did a lot to be with Kwenya and this is how he repays me? He wants to fuck Chasity's nasty and homeless ass?" I ranted.

"So, you got him locked up? You screwed his mama's man?" she asked.

"Yes, I got him locked up and I knew Bernie was going to come in handy so I fucked him. His mother stocks his shop up in the morning. Bernie put two bricks of coke in the flour box that was in Kwenya's mother's trunk. Unaware of what was going on, his mother put the box that was in her trunk in his shop. I called the police and told them where they were. He should've kept his dirty dick in his pants," I said.

"We found this in Jesula's purse. I guess she was going to turn you all in because she recorded you. You all knew she no longer wanted any parts of Ashanta's kidnapping, so you killed her. We have her phone and she texted someone telling them that she was scared and that you all threatened to kill her if she told. So I guess you all tied her up and poisoned her. She had evidence on you but too bad you didn't know she recorded you," she spat.

"That was Katrice's voice!" I said to her. The detective slammed her hand down on the table.

"We searched the database for a woman named Katrice with the description you gave me. She doesn't exist. The leasing office don't know her and have never seen her. I talked to Ashanta and she said that you all planned everything. I searched your car and guess what? I found a bloody rag under the passenger seat that matched Ashanta's DNA. She said you cut her face when she tried to get away. You wanted her man, Damos, and Chasity wanted her money so you all planned and schemed to get what you wanted," Detective Gomez said. I had tears fall from my eyes. How could I have been so stupid? I was set up and the evidence was all there on the tape recorder.

"I need a lawyer," I said. Gomez stood up and smiled.

"You all do," she said and left the interrogation room. Katrice was the enemy the whole time. I didn't know who she really was and I was for certain that Katrice wasn't her real name. The moment she moved into the building, she had a plan. She friended us, she turned us against each other, and she learned a lot about us. Katrice was only there for one reason and that was to make sure all of us went down. I wished I would've kept my mouth shut. I shouldn't have invited Chasity and Jesula into my home. I had a feeling Katrice was working for Kwenya because Chasity and I both went to that house for Kwenya who wasn't there. Katrice manipulated me into telling her what I did to Kwenya by using Chasity. She knew I was jealous over him and she played on that.

Chasity

"Bail denied!" the judge yelled as she slammed her gavel down. I broke down and cried because I was being charged with murder, kidnapping, and everything else I could think of. The money that I found in Jesula's room was fake. The police found the money in my trunk and I was charged with that, too. They were also sticking the charges to me from Desi's claims. I didn't have nobody to turn to. Nobody from my family showed up to my bail review because the family got word that I helped killed my own cousin. Jesula texted her mother before she died and told her that she didn't want to help us torture Ashanta anymore. Katrice got ahold of Jesula's phone and sent that text to my aunt. We were framed and nobody believed us.

I held my head up high as I walked out of the court room wearing my jail outfit. I knew it was the end for me. I felt it in my heart that it was the beginning of my new life which I had to accept. After all I had done, it caught up to me.

I went back into my cell and lay on my bunk. Tears fell from my eyes because I knew I wouldn't see my son again. I stared at the bars on the window in my cell. I took my clothes off and stood up on the sink. I wrapped my suit around my neck then tied it to one of the bars as I balanced myself on the sink. I said a small prayer and asked for forgiveness. Ree-Ree's face flashed into my head because she was someone who suffered from one of my schemes. She was also someone who was a good friend and what I did to her finally hit me like a ton of bricks. I leaped off the sink...

Ashanta

Two months later...

After Damos, Rakita, and Chasity were charged, my life went back to normal. My family was happy that I was alive. I didn't tell my parents what really happened to me. They thought I was kidnapped like everyone else. I almost felt bad that I had to sacrifice Jesula to make my plan stick but she was trying to get close to Kwenya for a man named Chaos and I couldn't let her do that. The charge against Kwenya was thrown out after Rakita confessed everything. I was back to writing and, at five months pregnant, I felt complete. I still had the scar on my face from where Rakita cut me but it healed fast and it wasn't as long as I thought it was. My mother wanted me to get plastic surgery but I didn't want it. It was my battle scar and for some reason it reminded me of the strength I had deep within. Chasity tried to commit suicide but wasn't successful. She was found barely holding onto life but she messed herself up mentally. The oxygen that was cut from her brain caused her to be handicap—mildly retarded, I should say.

"Hey shorty, where are you at?" Kwenya asked me when he came into the house.

"In my office," I called out. He came inside my office and kissed me on the lips. He rubbed my stomach.

"How is my down bitch feeling today?" he asked me and I slapped his arm.

"Don't call me that," I said as I tried to stifle my giggles.

"You know you like it. Can you be Katrice tonight for me?" he asked.

"No," I replied.

"What's up with the book? Any news yet?" he asked. I completed my book and sent it off to be edited. I was publishing it myself. I was waiting for my edits to be returned. I wanted to get it out there and I wanted to inspire more women who suffered from emotional, and even physical, abuse from their spouses. Although my story was fiction, it still reflected my life and hopefully inspired others.

"It should be done with editing in a few weeks," I said before I stood up. I looked like I was seven months pregnant because of how much I ate. It was like my weight came overnight.

"I'm still upset that I don't know your mother," I said to Kwenya and he backed away from me. I met his aunts and everyone else a little after Damos, Chasity, and Rakita got locked up. Kwenya threw a party because he wasn't getting time from what Bernie and Rakita did to him. His mother didn't show up and, although Kwenya acted like he didn't care, I knew he did.

"Fuck her," he said.

"That's still your mother and sometimes love can overcome things. I don't think she meant to hurt you," I said.

"Yo, I'm not talking about her. Why is it important to you?" he asked.

"She has a grandbaby on the way. I want her to be a part of the family, too," I said.

"She got her family and he is in jail. She ain't got shit to do with us and I'm cool on her," he said.

"Okay," I said and walked out of my office to get dinner ready.

******

The next morning, I went to Serene's house because she called me. She stated it was urgent. She was almost six months pregnant and didn't look it. She was having a girl but I looked more pregnant than she did.

"He gave up and signed the papers yesterday," Serene said sadly. I grabbed my chest.

"You and Deron are really divorced?" I asked her and she nodded her head. Tears fell down my face because I prayed every night that their marriage didn't end.

"I'm so sorry, Serene," I said. She shrugged her shoulders.

"Don't be. I think it was meant to happen this way. I just hope he and I can continue to get along for the sake of our baby. He has full custody over Marquis and I just don't fit into that. I shouldn't have to force myself to accept it," she said.

"I'm not giving up on y'all two. I still want you two together," I said before I sipped my tea.

"I kind of met someone," she said and I spit my tea out.

"What?" I asked.

"I was shopping a few weeks ago and a guy approached me. He is very handsome, but anyway, he approached me and I told him I was pregnant. He said it doesn't stop anything and pregnancy doesn't last forever. He and I talk on the phone almost every day. We met up a few times to get ice cream and things like that. I just enjoy his company," she said.

"What's his name?" I asked her.

"Quay but there is just one thing," she said.

"What?" I asked her.

"He is twenty-one," she said.

"Bitch, have you lost your damn mind? No wonder he wants to eat ice cream and shit," I spat. Serene fell out laughing.

"You seriously talk just like your baby daddy," she teased me. I couldn't help but to pick up some of Kwenya's vocabulary.

"What does he do?" I asked her.

"I don't know and I don't care. He is just someone to talk to. He is very smart for his age and he acts mature. He just moved back to Annapolis to help his cousin out with some type of business," she answered.

"Just be safe because this is not like you, but then again, I can't say that because this is the first time since I've known you, that you and Deron went through something," I said.

"I'm going to always love my husband but he just isn't good to me. He makes mistake after mistake and let's be honest, mistakes only happen once. After the first mistake, he should've learned his lesson, but I guess fucking someone else was more important than losing his wife," she said.

"I admire your strength," I said.

"I admire yours, too, even more because of what you had to go through to get it. You are my shero and, honey, that stunt you pulled was fucking awesome," she said.

"I can't take credit for that because Jesse talked me into it. But I felt like I had a starring role as the evil villain in a movie," I said. After I talked to Serene, I went to Kwenya's aunt's house because they were having a birthday dinner for her. His aunt Layla was a sweetheart and she was the youngest out of his aunts. I met all of them but she and I clicked immediately.

"About time, shorty. You were supposed to be here an hour ago. When we get home tonight, we have to discuss a few things. I need to know where you are at all times," Kwenya said to me when he pulled me to the side.

"I can handle myself," I replied but I could tell by the look on his face that he didn't care about that.

"We will talk later. Everyone is around back," he said. I followed him outside and there were about thirty or more people in the back of the house. I even spotted Desi sitting next to Ree-Ree. It wasn't like the fancy functions my parents had. Nobody wore evening gowns or suits and there wasn't a butler serving people appetizers. It was a cook-out where kids roamed around and the adults laughed and joked with one another. Being around Kwenya breathed a new life into me that was full of everything I deserved.

"Are you having twins?" Desi asked me and I playfully rolled my eyes.

"I was hoping there were a pair of twins inside of me but all of this comes from eating. I even told Kwenya I was hoping for twins and he almost stopped breathing. Don't tell him I told you but I think he is nervous," I said. Desi and Ree-Ree laughed.

"Jada doesn't want any more kids. I guess him having two already is enough," Ree-Ree said.

"Jada has kids?" I asked and she rolled her eyes.

"Yes and his baby mama irks my nerves so much that I stopped talking to him for a week. He doesn't put her in her place," Ree-Ree fussed.

"He might still be fucking her," Desi said.

"Really, Desi?" Ree-Ree asked her.

"Sorry, Ree-Ree, but after you told me what you told me, I'm not trusting that nigga. Tell Ashanta what he did and why you haven't spoken to him for a week," Desi fussed.

"Jada and Chloe took the kids to Disney World together and he lied to me about it. I found out because his baby mama sent me pictures of them. I confronted him about it and he said that his kids begged him to go and he hates to see them sad," Ree-Ree said.

"I would've caught a flight down there and whipped everyone's ass including the Mickey Mouse who was in the picture with them. Mickey ass would've been guilty by association, shat," Desi fussed. I put my hand over my mouth to keep from laughing.

"That is a little awkward," I replied.

"So, y'all think he is still fucking his baby mama?" Ree-Ree asked.

"I think that situation should be questionable," I replied.

"What am I going to do? I do love him because he helped me out so much. My family tried to help but I felt too embarrassed. Yet, I felt comfortable enough around Jada to tell him. At first I thought he was just messing with me because of my condition and figured he thought I was just a pushover but he stuck around. I was in the grocery store a while back and I had a hard time giving the cashier the correct change. Jada was in line and he paid for my things. We became friends after that and one night he and I just did it," Ree-Ree said.

"That's a beautiful story, Ree-Ree," I said.

"Jada and Yolo both have issues. Yolo ain't shit and Jada is secretive," Desi said before she sipped her wine cooler.

"Bishop sneaky, too, hell, most niggas are," Desi said. After I chatted with Ree-Ree and Desi, I mingled in with Kwenya's family.

Kwenya

"I need to talk to you," Yolo said as I fixed Ashanta a plate.

"Okay, let me feed shorty really quick," I said to Yolo. He looked at the plate and laughed.

"Nigga, Ashanta can't eat all of that," Yolo said.

"I don't know where she puts it but shorty been eating everything. She put her mouth on everything except for where she really needs to put it at," I said.

"She ain't giving you the head?" Yolo asked.

"Hell no. At first I was cool on it but sometimes I just need a quick nut to go on about my day. She was eating an ice cream cone last night. I mean my dick was hard as fuck watching her slurp on it. I smacked that shit right out of her hand," I said.

"Just tell her, nigga, it ain't hard," he said.

"Ashanta might start feeling insecure again if I tell her that. I know her and she might think that since she ain't doing that then I might not be happy with her and a whole lot of other bullshit," I said. I sat Ashanta's plate down on the picnic table in front of her. I went back to finish talking to Yolo.

"So, what's up?" I asked him.

"Jada in the bathroom downstairs drunk and crying and shit. I asked that nigga what the problem was but he told me he couldn't tell me because I think everything's a joke. The nerve of that fuck nigga, so I came to get you," Yolo said. I went inside my aunt's house and headed down the stairs. I knocked on the bathroom door.

"Yo, what's going on with you?" I asked Jada. The door opened and Jada was trying to fix his shirt. I knew something happened because Jada was always a headstrong type of nigga and it took a lot for him to crack. I'd known him since we were young and I'd never seen him shed a tear.

"I fucked up," he said.

"Nigga, we are men. We fuck up all the time," Yolo said and I pushed him.

"Chill out, nigga!" I barked and he waved me off.

"What happened?" I asked Jada.

"Man, she doesn't deserve this," Jada said as his eyes watered.

"Nigga, what the fuck are you talking about?" I asked.

"Chloe is pregnant again and I didn't tell y'all this but me and shorty been engaged for a year now," he said talking about his daughter's mother.

"Ohhhhhhhh, nigggggggaaaaaaa, you in troubbblllllleeeeee," Yolo said.

"How am I supposed to tell Ree-Ree? I mean, I didn't want this to happen but I started off helping her. I felt sorry for her but then I started to fall in love with her. This would crush her," Jada stressed.

"Damn, nigga. You proposed to your baby mama and ain't tell us?" I asked Jada.

"I wasn't sure of it at first so I kept quiet. I kind of felt like I owed my kids that. I thought she was on birth control but she stopped taking them," Jada said.

"Want me to kill her for you?" Yolo asked Jada. Jada tried to swing on Yolo but missed because of how drunk he was.

"I'm trying to help you out!" Yolo said and pushed Jada. I pushed Yolo back.

"Chill out, nigga," I said.

"All you can do is tell Ree-Ree because you know Chloe always been messy and Ree-Ree is going to find out. I'm surprised she didn't tell Ree-Ree y'all are engaged," I said.

"Chloe just thought Ree-Ree was a friend. She said that she knew I wouldn't mess with a retarded broad but recently she found out that me and Ree-Ree was fucking. She told me that if I didn't tell Ree-Ree soon, she was going to do it," Jada said.

"You better tell her now then," Yolo said.

"I can't tell her," Jada said.

"Tell me what?" Ree-Ree asked when she came downstairs in the basement.

"Awww shit," Yolo mumbled.

"Why are you crying? What happened? Did someone die? Are your daughters okay?" she asked Jada when she hugged him.

"I'll let y'all talk," I said. I was ready to walk up the stairs but Jada pulled me back and I knew it was because he knew Ree-Ree was going to jump on him.

"Baby, I got something to tell you. Please know that I love you and I didn't mean to hurt you," Jada pleaded and Yolo yawned.

Ree-Ree pulled away from Jada.

"It's Chloe, isn't it?" Ree-Ree asked. Jada put his head down.

"She is pregnant and she and I have been engaged for a year," Jada said as tears fell from his eyes. Any other nigga would've thought he was being a punk but I knew it was because he loved her.

"WHAT!" Ree-Ree screamed.

"Baby I'm—" was all he said before Ree-Ree clocked him in the mouth. She leaped on Jada like a cat. He held onto her arms as she tried to swing on him.

"I thought you loved me!" she cried. I pulled Ree-Ree off Jada. I placed her over my shoulder while she was kicking and screaming. I almost dropped her because she was pounding on my back as I carried her up the stairs.

"What and the hell is going on?" Aunt Layla asked. When I stood Ree-Ree up, she tried to run back to the basement.

"Not in my house you won't!" Layla said.

"He cheated on me! He is engaged!" Ree-Ree cried.

"Jada?" my aunt asked her and Ree-Ree nodded her head.

"Hell, whip that nigga's ass! Jada, get your ass up here now! Y'all know I don't play that shit!" Layla yelled. She slapped me in the back of my head.

"What the fuck was that for?" I asked her.

"Watch your mouth, Kwenya. I can still beat your grown ass. I know Yolo ain't shit but Jada is supposed to be better than that," she fussed.

"What did you hit me for?" I asked her pissed off that I was even caught in the middle of it.

"Because you should've talked some sense into him. Got this poor girl crying over him. I'm a woman so I know exactly how she feels," Layla fussed.

"I didn't know that nigga was engaged," I said. Ashanta and Desi came into the kitchen.

"What's the matter, Ree-Ree?" Desi asked.

"Jada is engaged and his baby mama is pregnant again!" she said.

"Oh my heavens," Ashanta said before she grilled me. All of the females were grilling me.

"I never fought a group of females before but if y'all are even thinking about jumping me, I'm knocking all of y'all asses out. Baby mama can catch one, too. That nigga is grown and I don't have shit to do with that," I said.

"But you knew?" Desi said.

"Shut the fuck up, Desi," I said.

"Don't talk to her like that, Kwenya. She just asked you a question," Ashanta said. Females will team up on a nigga as soon as he messes up.

"You mind your fucking business, Ashanta. You are my shorty and you ain't supposed to be siding with these muthafuckas," I spat.

"Watch your damn mouth, Kwenya, and I'm not going to tell you again," my aunt said.

"I apologize," I said to her. The women tried to calm Ree-Ree down. After a while, my cousins and my other aunts were in the kitchen. All the females were talking about Jada and most of them didn't know Ree-Ree but was siding with her. Jada came into the kitchen with Yolo following behind him.

"Just go home and I will get up with you tomorrow," I said to Jada.

"Jada always been the most respectful one when it came to women. I'm really shocked that you did that to this sweet girl. I am very pissed off," my aunt Lolita said. She was the oldest out of all of my mother's sisters. Lolita was the mean one. She used to beat me over stupid shit when I was younger.

"Can I talk to Ree-Ree really quick?" Jada asked.

"Go home, Jada. This girl doesn't want to talk to you," my aunt Kim said.

"I swear women always got some shit with them," Lolita's husband, Thomas, said.

"Don't start with me and go back out there before you burn the steaks on the grill. Ain't nobody told your nosey ass to come in the kitchen," she spat at him. He mumbled something under his breath before he left the kitchen.

"I'm going to divorce his ass if he keeps on," Lolita said.

"Aye, shorty. I'm ready to bounce so get your things," I said to Ashanta. Yolo walked Jada out of the house and I followed behind them. We all stood by Jada's Benz.

"Damn, I fucked up," Jada said.

"Hell, yeah, you did. Kwenya's aunts were about to jump you. See, this is why I'm a ain't-shit nigga. People expect for me to fuck up and when I do, nobody cares because they are used to it. But you, on the other hand, are always trying to be the good nigga when you know damn well it ain't in your blood. You took advantage of Ree-Ree, my nigga," Yolo said.

"Yo, get this nigga away from me," Jada said as he balled his fists up.

"I'm speaking the truth, though, my nigga. You know she is too good for all of this. You were supposed to treat shorty like a fucking gem. Fuck yo' baby mama, nigga. You were supposed to get a blood test on your daughters anyway," Yolo said.

"Nigga, you sound shady right now. Now, you are team Ree-Ree? What, you want her or something, nigga?" Jada asked.

"You are talking stupid," Yolo said and waved Jada off.

"Naw, I think you do. You want to fuck her, don't you? I've been peeping how you been looking at her. Since you found out I was kicking it with her, you been saying slick shit," Jada fussed.

"Nigga, I'm not like you, and if I was I still wouldn't do it behind your back like you did me. Thank God Chloe wasn't my number one bitch or else I would've killed you. You still feel embarrassed that you wifed her up. That's why you don't bring her around or your kids. That's guilt, nigga, but I'm not going to let a hoe stop me from being cool with my nigga," Yolo said.

"We been niggas for years and y'all arguing over petty shit like this?" I asked them.

"Naw, it ain't petty. It's real-nigga shit. He fucked a bitch I was messing with but I been forgave him because we grew up together. We are like brothers but this nigga got the nerve to point fingers when his fingers was up in my ex-shorty pussy," Yolo spat.

"You said you wasn't sweating it. So why wait seven years to speak on it?" Jada asked.

"I'm not sweating nothing. I'm your daughter's godfather. It ain't no bad blood over here because you got to deal with it, not me. The sad part is that Chloe is still a hoe and you want to pass Ree-Ree up for her? Nigga, you crazy. We didn't know you and Chloe was even that serious. We just thought y'all was fucking," Yolo said.

"He does have a point, Jada. We didn't know you and Chloe was that serious. We thought Ree-Ree was your shorty and she is a good girl," I said.

"I'm out," Yolo said and walked away.

"Fuck that nigga. He is lucky I don't knock his bitch's ass out. I think that nigga feeling Ree-Ree," Jada said.

"Go home and get some rest. You had too much to drink. Yolo wouldn't do nothing like that," I said.

"Yeah, you are right. I apologize for causing all of this at your people's house. I'm going to go home and sleep this off. I will hit you up later," Jada said. I gave him dap before I walked to Ashanta's truck. I bought her a soft purple Mercedes G-wagon truck. She said it was too much truck for her but once she got used to it, she was always on the go.

"How did you get here?" Ashanta asked me when I got in.

"Yolo picked me up," I answered. I reclined my seat back.

"Where is Bishop?" she asked.

"I don't know. He said he had to take care of something," I answered as she pulled off.

****

"You think I should call Ree-Ree?" Ashanta asked me as we lay in bed.

"Naw, she got Desi and, besides, give her some time to cool off," I answered. Ashanta sat up and started to kiss on my chest. I knew she wanted some but I wasn't trying to give her none until I got what I wanted. I pulled the cover off myself and my dick was hard and standing straight up. While Ashanta was busy kissing on me, I tried to push her head down.

"What are you doing?" she asked when she sat up.

"Shorty, do you not see how hard my dick is? I want you to eat that muthafucka up like you was doing that ice cream last night. I want my shorty to wrap her pretty lips around my dick," I said.

"Is that healthy for the baby?" she asked.

"I don't want to skeet down your throat. I just want you to top me off before I slide in you," I said.

"I kind of get grossed out behind the thought of that," she said.

"I eat your pussy, and let's be honest, women bleed out of it, have babies and get yeast infections, but I don't think about that," I spat.

"Why are we arguing?" she asked me.

"I'm not trying to fuss with you but if I please you all the way, I think you should do the same in return," I replied.

"I'm not ready for that," she said. I got out of the bed to get a drink. She followed me downstairs naked and her nipples were hard. I knew she was horny but I wasn't in the mood. I poured myself a glass of Henny as she stood in the doorway of the kitchen with her arms crossed. Her stomach was sticking out and her hips had spread out. Her breasts were nice and round and I almost gave in when I stared at her.

"Okay, Kwenya. You win, I will suck it," she said.

"Naw, I'm good. The way you said that I already know it's going to be garbage," I said.

"Rude-ass nigga!" she yelled at me and I laughed.

"Go to bed, shorty. If you want to cum, I suggest you play with your pussy," I said before I guzzled my drink.

"Our sex life has been good. Why does it matter?" she asked.

"Why shouldn't it matter? I'm telling you what I'm not happy with and instead of you just doing it, you want to argue about it. Soon as a nigga go somewhere else your mouth will be open," I said.

"Are you cheating on me? You want to go somewhere else? You want someone else to suck your dick?" she raised her voice as she walked closer to me. She balled up her fist like she wanted to swing on me.

"Don't walk up on me like that and no that's not what I was saying. See, I knew you was going to think that as soon as I said something but I been wanting it for a while," I said. I told Yolo how Ashanta was going to feel and I was right.

"Elaborate for me, Kwenya, because I don't understand what the hell that meant!" she screamed.

"Calm down before you get yourself worked up. Why are you trying to put stress on the baby?" I asked.

"I'm putting stress on our baby? You just told me if I didn't suck your dick then you were going to get it from somewhere else," she yelled.

"That nigga really damaged you. If you were smart you would know that's not what I was saying. All I'm saying is appreciate your nigga enough to suck his dick every once in a while because there's some bitch out here that's willing to do what you ain't doing. Just because I said that, doesn't mean it's going to happen, but if I was that type of nigga, I would've been got another broad to suck my dick. But, instead, I told you. I'm communicating with you but I forgot you ain't used to that shit," I said and she slapped me with tears in her eyes.

"GO TO HELL! All I've been through to be with you and you have the nerve to talk to me this way. Just like there is another woman that's willing, there is another man that's willing for me. A man that will be thankful to have me and will look past the fact that I'm not ready for that. I will be damned if you do to me what my ex-husband did to me by making me feel like I'm not good enough."

"Now, if I hit your ass back then I really would be like that nigga, huh?" I asked her before I walked out of her face. I headed upstairs to get dressed.

"Where are you going Dam—" she said but she caught herself.

"Yo, was you ready to call me Damos?" I asked.

"This just seems like déjà vu. I didn't mean nothing by it. I'm so sorry," she said.

"You think I treat you like that nigga? A nigga that raped you? A nigga that tore you down and made you feel insecure?" I asked her. I was so angry that I wanted to explode but I held it in because, at the end of the day, she was carrying my seed. She sat down on the bed and covered herself up with the sheet.

"I knocked you up because I knew how bad you wanted a baby. I wanted you to be happy so I decided to make you a mother. I did that shit out of fucking love. I did something that a nigga never thought about doing and you got the fucking nerve to stand in my face and call me that nigga?" I asked her but she didn't respond. I banged on the dresser and she jumped.

"ANSWER ME!" I yelled at her.

"I don't know why!" she cried.

"Sleep by yourself and figure that shit out on your own. Don't call me or text me. I will come back when I want to," I said. I got dressed and walked out of the bedroom then out of the house. I got inside of my car and went into the glove compartment. I opened up the black box and there was the ring I was going to propose to Ashanta with. I put it back inside of my glove compartment. I was backing up and I stopped when I saw Ashanta on the back-up camera I had in my car. She was barefoot with a robe on. I got out of the car.

"Yo, I almost backed up into you," I said to her.

"I don't want you to leave. It's late, just come back inside and talk to me. We came too far to be fighting like this" she said.

I brushed my hand down my face from frustration. I turned my car off and went back into the house. I kicked my Timbs off and sat on the couch in the living room. I turned the TV on and Ashanta sat down next to me.

"I think we were both wrong but I admit that I played a bigger role in this. It feels different living with a new man and I'm about to be a mom. I need to stop comparing what you and I go through to what me and Damos went through. When I slapped you, it was because I heard Damos's voice yelling in my head," she said and wiped her eyes.

"I didn't mean to come off at you like that. I guess I need to accept that you ain't going to be topping me off. But, shorty, the next time you slap me, I'm slapping your ass back," I said. She lay her head on my lap as I flicked through the channels. Ashanta purposely caused her robe to slide up so that it could expose her bottom.

"You are hot in your ass," I said and chuckled.

"What did I do?" she asked me. She reached across me to grab a book off the end table. Her robe flew open and her nipples were hard. I gently pushed her off me. I stood up and walked down the hall.

"I'm still not sleeping or fucking you until I feel like it," I called out to her.

Desi

"I love it!" I said out loud to myself. The house that I renovated was done and it was beautiful. Everything was new and it even smelled new. I couldn't wait to sell it and it felt good that I did something on my own. I was making money and I didn't have to spread my legs or cook coke to get it. While I walked around the stainless steel kitchen, I heard someone come in.

"Who is there?" I called out. I should've brought Bishop with me but he hated for me to wake him up some mornings.

"So, you been ignoring me?" Ro asked when he came into the kitchen. He'd been calling me and texting me but I haven't responded. I made a huge mistake when I slept with him. I slept with him once after me and Bishop made up. I met up with him to tell him that I decided to work it out with Bishop but I ended up spreading my legs for him…

"I'm working it out with Bishop. I know we were supposed to go on vacation but I decided that it's him that I want to be with. I'm sorry because I was just going through something and I didn't mean to lead you on," I said to Ro. We were having lunch at Ruth's Chris.

"Damn it, Desi. You do this shit to me again? Is it my wife? I keep telling you that she and I are separated," he said. The day before, I went to Bishop's family reunion and I saw that he was trying to change. I knew he wasn't letting me go and I

knew I couldn't stop messing with him. I was cutting Ro off for good because he was too good of a guy to lead on.

"Look, I'm going to the bathroom," I said as my phone vibrated in my house. I knew it was Bishop and I didn't want to answer around Ro. I went inside the women's bathroom and I felt a presence behind me as I dialed Bishop's number. Bishop answered the phone and before I could respond, Ro was snatching the phone out of my hand. He hung up on Bishop.

"What in the fuck did you do that for and why are you in here?" I asked him. He placed a finger over my lips and locked the door.

"I just want to feel you," he said with lust in his eyes.

"I'm in a relationship," I spat.

"One last time," he said as he backed me up into the counter. My purse fell on the floor and my vibrating phone sat in the sink. Ro kissed me with so much passion that I could feel how he felt about me. He stood between my legs while he caressed my breasts and sucked on my bottom lip. His hands slid up my tennis skirt and he pulled my thong to the side. He pushed my legs further apart before his finger entered me.

"UMMMMM," I moaned when he entered another one. I should've told him to stop but temptation got the best of me. I unbuckled his pants to release his big dick. I massaged his shaft as her fingered me. I was wet and I needed him to enter me. I wanted him at that moment but I knew I didn't love him and I never would. My phone vibrated again and it was Bishop. I knew he was worried about me but Ro was putting a condom on and I couldn't answer. He pulled me down to the edge of the counter and slowly slid inside me. Both of us moaned in pleasure as he stretched me open. He held my legs over the crook of his arms as he pumped in and out of me. He

298

freed my breasts from my blouse and hungrily took them inside of his mouth. I held onto him as he sped up; he was deeper inside of me and he reached my spot.

"SHIT!" I screamed out as he fucked me harder. He never was rough with me but he knew it was our last time.

"Damn, this is pussy good. I want you so bad!" he said pumping in and out of me. My cum was dripping down my ass crack as Ro filled me up. He let go of my legs so that I could stand up. He turned me around and grabbed the back of my neck so that I could lean forward. When he entered me from the back I came hard— very hard.

"This is your dick, baby. This will always be your dick. You feel how that pussy grips my dick?" he asked, slamming into me. He spread my ass cheeks to go deeper. His thrusts turned into slow grinds. He was very deep inside of me and pressure shot up my spine. I threw my ass against him; I was sliding up and down his dick and he was very hard. I knew he was about to bust. He started pounding into me and seconds later, I felt him throbbing and he moaned as he came inside of the condom. As soon, as he pulled out of me, I fixed myself and grabbed my phone and purse.

"Can we talk?" he asked.

"I need to go home. Lose my number, Ro," I said and walked out of the bathroom. When I got inside my car, I called Bishop back.

"About time. You called me then the phone hung up. A nigga was worried about you. Where you at? We had plans, remember?" he asked me.

"I got caught up at the house. The plumbing went wrong and I had to make sure they fixed it. I'm on my way home," I said.

"Okay bet, love you," he said and hung up. I pulled over to the side of the road and cried my heart out. I did the very thing to Bishop that I accused him of doing to me. I prayed that it went to my grave...

Ro brought me out of my flashback when he kissed my lips. I pushed him away.

"You need to stop calling me and texting me. I gave you your last time. What else do you want from me?" I asked him.

"I've been thinking about you even more since. I can treat you so much better," he said.

"But I love him and he is trying. Ro, please just let it go," I said.

"Your body says otherwise. You came so hard on my dick," he whispered in my ear.

"Sex ain't better than love, honey. You and I are adults so let's be adults about this. We fucked up and now it's time to move on. Popping up here isn't the answer. Calling me around the clock is not the answer. What do you want me to do?" I asked him.

"I want you to be mine and I'm not giving up. What are you going to do, Desi? Are you going to be with him and doubt yourself? Why do you want to keep questioning yourself, wondering if you are good enough? I accept you and always did. It's hard to give up when I know I deserve you and you deserve me," he said.

"Why can't we just be friends? I love Bishop very much. He and I are in a great place and I just moved in with him yesterday. Even if I'm with you, it will not erase my feelings for him. Why do you want a woman whose heart is in a different place? I don't want you that way," I said and headed toward the door. I hated that Ro had to drive down the same street my house was on.

"Let's go. I'm ready to lock up," I said to him. He sucked his teeth and followed me out of the house. I locked the door and headed toward my car.

"You will come to your senses," Ro called out.

"Dream about, boo," I said as I got into my car. I started my car up and hurriedly sped off.

****

"What's going on? You've been sleeping a lot lately," I said to Bishop when I walked into the living room. When he asked me to move in, I waited a couple of weeks before I agreed. Bishop stopped going over his mother's house but he invited his mother over instead. Me and his mother were on speaking terms but she still found a way to throw Liana up in Bishop's face.

Bishop sat up on the couch and he only had on baller shorts. His body did something to me every time as if it was my first time seeing it.

"I think I'm coming down with the flu, shorty. I haven't been feeling good. I been busy with the new shipment and neglecting my health. Did you have fun the other day at Kwenya's aunt's crib?" he asked me. I didn't tell him about Ree-Ree and Jada because I knew he would've been pissed. It was Ree-Ree's choice if she wanted her cousin to know.

"Yes, it was fun. Kwenya's aunt Layla is loud as hell. She acts like his sister instead of his aunt. His other aunts are well-reserved," I said and he chuckled.

"We all got a ratchet aunt," he said.

"Do you want me to fix you some soup?" I asked him.

"Naw, I'm good, shorty," he said and stood up. He lifted my chin up and kissed my forehead. His diamond grill smiled at me.

"Where you been at? Why is your sexy ass looking single, shorty?" he asked me and I blushed.

"You know I got to look good when I step out of the house. What do you want for dinner?" I asked him as I kicked off my heels.

"I want you to take a pregnancy test," he said. My soul almost left my body. I felt like I had to pass out because I had never thought about being a mother.

"Why?" I asked as I fanned myself.

"You haven't had a period this month. I talked to Kwenya earlier and he said that you might be knocked up. I'm tired as fuck for no reason," he said.

"Ummmm, sorry to bust your bubble but my ass ain't pregnant," I said.

"What if you are?" he asked me and crossed his arms.

"Don't wish bad luck on me. Have you seen the way Ashanta eats? I don't eat like her and I don't want to eat like her. I've gotten chubby since I stopped stripping," I fussed.

"You sure it's from the stripping? Look, I sat a pregnancy test on the dresser in our bedroom," he said.

"Please, stop scaring me. I don't want to be nobody's damn mama," I spat and walked out of the living room. I headed straight into the kitchen. I pulled the ground beef from the fridge. I was making Cajun lasagna, garlic bread, and a fresh salad. Bishop loved lasagna and he could eat it every day.

"What if you are pregnant? Would you keep it?" he asked when he sat down at the kitchen's island.

"I don't know. Look, I don't want to talk about this but who told Kwenya's black ass he was a doctor? That nigga thinks he is all of that because he knocked up a doctor; now his ass thinking he special," I fussed.

"Yo, get on subject. Would you keep it or not? I'm trying to be prepared for when that time comes because I been up in that pussy raw. My pull-out game been weak and there is a possibility that I knocked that ass up," Bishop said. I grabbed the tequila that sat on the counter and poured him a glass. I slid the glass to him.

"Drink that because you lost your mind. I can't get pregnant," I lied.

"Seriously, Desi?" he asked me.

"As a heart attack. I have a disability that won't allow me to get pregnant. I forgot what it's called so let me Google it really quick," I said. I grabbed my cell phone off the counter.

"Get some sense, shorty, and get some now. You will take that pregnancy test tonight. Now, hurry up with my dinner because I'm hungry," he said. He grabbed his drink and walked out of the kitchen. I rushed to the hall bathroom and turned the faucet on. I dialed Ashanta's number and she answered on the third ring.

"Hellllooooo," she sang sweetly into the phone.

"What are you doing?" I asked her.

"Typing my new story up. What's going on with you, and why do you sound like you are panicking?" she asked me.

"Where is your man at so I can curse his big black ass out? That nigga told Bishop I might be pregnant because Bishop ain't drinking enough orange juice," I said.

"What does orange juice have to do with it?" she asked me.

"Not enough damn calcium. Hell, you are the doctor," I said.

"Was a doctor, but anyways, what does orange juice have to do with anything?" She laughed.

"Got damn it, Ashanta. I don't know but I'm scared, oh lord help me. I don't want any kids. Well, I do but I'm scared," I said.

"Calm down, Desi. Babies are a gift from God. Awww all of my friends are pregnant. We all can go out and eat and go baby shopping," Ashanta said.

"Would you just come down from the clouds a little bit? I'm scared, I need a big blunt. I'm not giving Bishop anymore pussy," I said.

"Y'all are in love so it will be fine," she said.

"Remember I told you I opened up a can of worms when we were at Stephen's house? Well, I never told you what I did. I had sex with another man and I'm paranoid that it might be his baby. We wore a condom but it breaks sometimes," I said.

"Ohhhhhh no. You cheated?" she asked me.

"Will you be quiet before Bishop hears you?" I asked her.

"Ummmm, he will actually hear you before he hears me, Desi," she said smartly.

"Look here, smart ass. I don't know what to do," I said.

"Tell him the truth because he will find out sooner or later," she said. I wanted to reach through the phone to choke her.

"Bitch, have you lost your mind? That nigga is crazy and trust me, he will be a whole other nigga if he found out," I said.

"Meet me at Serene's house tomorrow at noon. She can tell you what to do. My mother will be there, too, so you will have more opinions," she said.

"Okay, that's a bet," I said and hung up. I went back into the kitchen to prepare Bishop's dinner. I had a lot on my mind and I couldn't wait to talk about it.

****

The next day...

I rang Serene's doorbell and moments later she opened the door for me.

"Well, look at your sexy ass," she said and kissed my cheek.

"Don't do that. You might put me in the mood," I joked when I stepped inside of her mini mansion.

306

"Ashanta and her mother are in the living room," she said as I followed her to the living room. Ashanta was eating a slice of pizza and it smelled horrible. Her mother sat on the couch holding her nose.

"Hey," I waved.

"Hey Desi. This is my mother, Mrs. Scott and, Mother, this is my other friend Desi," Ashanta said with her cheeks stuffed.

"What in the hell are you eating?" I asked Ashanta.

"Everything but her man's dick, obviously," Mrs. Scott said. Ashanta choked on her pizza and Serene patted her back.

"Mother, that was rude," Ashanta said.

"We are all having girl talk. Didn't you just tell me that Kwenya isn't sleeping in bed with you?" her mother asked her.

"What is on that pizza?" I asked Ashanta.

"Feta cheese, ham, bacon, anchovies, raw onions, pepperoni, sausage, hamburger meat, and pickles," she said and Serene gagged. I wanted to gag, too, because it smelled like feet and ass.

"I hope your baby kicks your ass," I said and sat down. Serene poured me a glass of wine and lit some aromatherapy candles that sat on the coffee table.

"So, are you and King Kwenya having problems in the castle?" I asked Ashanta.

"Yes, we had this big argument and I kind of snapped. He has an issue with me not giving him head," she said.

"Lawd, you are lucky. I know some bitches in the hood that would give away their food stamps to even taste that nigga's sperm. How can you lay next to a man like that and not want to suck his dick? I suck Bishop's dick in his sleep, when he's driving, when he's at the dinner table eating and when he is counting his money. Oh, I'm sorry, Mrs. Scott," I said.

"I sucked my husband's dick at the Mayor's ball last year. We almost got caught but I didn't care. If a man is taking care of you the least you can do is blow his flute," Mrs. Scott said. Serene laughed until she had tears in her eyes and Ashanta placed her hand on her stomach.

"I'm about to be sick," she said. She rushed out of the living room holding her mouth.

"I'm trying to show her tough love now because she really needs it. It's better late than never. Kwenya might be an asshole sometimes but he is a good man. I know this because my daughter's never been this happy and pregnant. He is doing something right so the bastard is alright with me," Mrs. Scott said.

"Kwenya is always an asshole. That nigga cannot go one minute without saying something slick," I said.

"He is gorgeous, though," Serene said.

"You ain't lying about that," Mrs. Scott said. Ashanta came back and lay on the couch.

"Mother, please don't ever tell me about you and Father again. Y'all are too old," Ashanta said.

"Exactly. I'm old and I still suck my husband's dick. I got arthritis in my wrist and I still choke his monkey. What is your excuse, young buck? I might be old in years but, chile, I'm young in the bedroom. I'm a wild buck, baby, and your mama can make him scream. He needs Viagra to keep up with me," Mrs. Scott bragged.

"I like her," I said and Ashanta rolled her eyes.

"I'm going to get a banana. We are fittin' to help her out," Serene said and went into the kitchen. When she came back, she had four bananas.

"Okay, here is the thing. Each one of us will perform on this banana. Mrs. Scott, you go first," Serene said.

"Let me show y'all how it's done," she said. She took her teeth out of her mouth.

"You got fake teeth? Oh my gawd! What happened to your teeth?" Ashanta asked.

"I got them pulled years ago. I was in a car accident when you were a little girl. It messed up my teeth so I just got them all pulled," she said.

309

"This is cheating," I said and Serene agreed. Ashanta's mother put her teeth back inside of her mouth.

"You go, Desi," Serene said. I showed them what I was capable of as they watched me. I made the banana disappear in my mouth as I slowly relaxed my throat muscles to keep from gagging.

"Bitchhhhhh, you got a magician in your throat?" Serene asked me.

"That's what Bishop asked me," I replied.

"Kwenya is huge," Ashanta said.

"Bishop is huge, too, but don't worry it takes time. I started young," I said. Serene did her thing and I was shocked that she almost had me beat. She worked her tongue very good. It was Ashanta's turn and I had to brace myself.

"She is about to embarrass me," her mother said.

"Think of a big ice cream cone with extra fudge and peanut butter. Oh and don't forget the pecans," Serene said. Ashanta put the banana in her mouth.

"Don't use your teeth," I said.

"Relax your throat," Serene said.

"Get some spit on that. Wet it so it can slide into your mouth easier," Mrs. Scott said. Ashanta practiced for thirty minutes until she half-way got it right.

"My jaws hurt," she said.

"It's supposed to hurt," Mrs. Scott said.

"Okay, I want to talk to you all about something. I'm not used to opening up to people on a personal level. But here is my situation. I cheated on my boyfriend. When I went home yesterday, he had a pregnancy test for me. I didn't want to take it because I don't want to be pregnant. The man I cheated with wore a condom but I'm still not sure about it. What would any of you do if you were me? Keep it or get rid of it?" I asked.

"I would keep it because either way the baby is a part of you," Serene said.

"I totally agree," Ashanta said eating the banana.

"What kind of man is your boyfriend? Is he a square? A thug? Or what?" Mrs. Scott asked me.

"He isn't a square but I wouldn't call him a thug, either. I think Bishop's level of thinking is different from what we classify as a thug. He is street and talks his best hood slang, but he knows how to turn it off and that's what is sexy about it," I said.

"So, in other words, if he finds out you cheated, we will be attending your funeral? Don't sugarcoat nothing with me, chile. A thug mixed with gentleman is so dangerous and yet so sexy," Mrs. Scott said and fanned herself. Ashanta shook her head and Serene laughed.

"Bishop has temper issues but I don't want to lose him. I'm really scared," I said. Ashanta sat down next to me and offered me half of her already-eaten banana.

"I should push you off this couch," I said to her.

"I made you smile. Don't be scared, we got your back. I'm against abortions but if you are pregnant and that's something you want to do then that's your call. We are not in your shoes and we don't know how you feel, but you got to do what is best for you and nobody else," Ashanta said.

"Only judgment that matters are God's and He is a forgiving God," Serene said.

"Amen," Mrs. Scott said. I went into my purse and pulled out the pregnancy test.

"I'm going to take this and get it over with," I said. I got up and headed toward the bathroom. My legs felt like noodles.

****

Hours later...

It was two in the morning when Bishop came home. I lay in bed with the TV on. Bishop came into the bedroom and the smell of weed filled the room.

"That stinks," I said.

"So does your attitude. What the fuck is wrong with you?" he asked me as he pulled his diamond chains over his head. He sat them down on the dresser along with his diamond Rolex.

"Where did you go?" I asked him.

"Strip club with Yolo," he answered.

"For what?" I asked.

"To chill," he answered. After he took his clothes off, he headed for the shower. His phone vibrated and I picked it up.

"Who is this?" I asked the caller.

"Liana, tell Bishop he left his hat in my truck," she said.

"What was he doing in your truck?" I asked her.

"None of your business. He can talk to you about that," she spat. I hung up and went into the bathroom. I slid the shower door back and smacked Bishop as hard as I could. He grabbed me around my throat and slammed me into the shower door.

"What the fuck is your problem?" he asked me.

"You was with Yolo? Liana just called and said you left your hat in her truck. How did you end up with Liana if you were supposed to been with Yolo?" I asked him.

"I was with Yolo. I saw Liana at the strip club and when we walked out, she wanted to talk to me about something. Yo, I swear I was only in her truck for two minutes. All she asked me was if I could loan her some money so that she could get her own crib," he said. I snatched away from him and headed back to the bedroom. I got dressed and left out with Bishop's cell phone in my hand.

****

I texted Liana and told her to meet me at the local Walmart. She replied with an "Ok". I couldn't wait to see her face once she realized it was me and not Bishop. I sat in Bishop's truck and waited for Liana. He called my phone and his from the house phone but I didn't answer. A truck pulled up on the side of Bishop's truck and I hopped out. Liana got out of her truck.

"What is this?" she asked. She wore a trench coat and a pair of come-fuck-me red pumps.

"Do you think I'm going to allow you to keep pushing up on my man? Those kids are not his and you are not his. Every time I turn around, you need something from him. Tell me something, Liana, what makes you think he is responsible for you and your kids?" I asked her.

"Bishop still loves me and I want him to accept my children because they are a part of me. You are a hoe whose been ran through. Your pussy is nowhere near as valuable as mine. You have zero education and you need to work on properly speaking. I have a good job and a good background. What can you put on your résumé besides being a stripper?" she asked.

"But I always had a roof over my head. As far as your education, what do you have to show for it? You drive that old truck, your kids wear Spiderman shoes and their clothes are always a little too tight. You are living with your ex-nigga's mama and you need money from Bishop to move out of her house. So tell me what is special about being a beggar? You have nothing that I want, bitch, nothing! I eat meals that cost more than your paycheck and guess what? It doesn't come from Bishop's money. I got my own money and it doesn't matter how I got it, but, bitch, I got it. Look at you, at the local Walmart waiting to get fucked in the parking lot. Even when I was a prostitute, I was fucking and sucking in the Four Seasons and I was getting bent over the rail in the penthouse suite that overlooked the city. So, if you want to get fucked for free at least get fucked in style," I spat. Liana spit in my face and after she did, I lost it. I slammed my fist into her face over and over again as she slid down the driver's side door of her truck. I yanked her head back by her hair and continued to swing on her. I didn't want to fight Liana, I just wanted to talk to her, but she messed up when she spit on me. Spitting on someone is the nastiest thing you could ever do.

"You want to spit, bitch? I will knock your damn teeth out!" I yelled as I hit her again. She started kicking me on my legs and my leg gave up on me. I fell on the ground with her and we were both tussling. She punched me in the nose and I punched her back. I dug my stiletto nails into her face until I felt something wet dripping down my fingers. Liana screamed for help as my nails continued to dig in her face. She bit my wrist and I felt her teeth going through my skin. I pushed her head against the side of her car door and elbowed her in the face. She was fighting me back to keep me off her but I was a fighter. I used to fight the older girls in the group homes and foster homes that I lived in and we used to fight with everything we could get our hands on. I had been hit with bottles, bats, brass knuckles, and a hammer. A few workers and security guards from Walmart pulled us apart. Liana's face was a bloody mess. I hurriedly got into Bishop's truck and sped off. As soon as I pulled into our driveway, I rushed into the house and into the hallway bathroom to look at my face. My lip was busted and I had a few scratches but I didn't look as bad as Liana.

"Why, Desi?" Bishop asked as I cleaned off my face. He was standing in the doorway of the bathroom.

"Because I felt like it. That bitch feels too comfortable asking you for shit and I don't like it!" I yelled at him.

"So you leave out in the middle of the night to fight her? That was really fucking lady-like," he said.

"You wasn't going to check her, so I did. Do you know that she thought I was you? She showed up wearing a trench coat with a pair of pumps. I bet she learned a lesson after tonight," I fussed. I poured alcohol on my wrist where she bit me. I went into our bedroom and took a shower. When I got out, Bishop was lying in bed. I got into bed with my back turned toward him.

"Did you take the pregnancy test?" he asked me.

"Not yet," I lied.

"What's this then?" he asked and turned on the light on the nightstand. After I took the test at Serene's house, I dropped it inside of my purse. I would've been grossed out if I didn't put the pink cap back on the stick. Bishop had the test too close to my face.

"When you left, I went into your purse to see if you only took my phone and left yours and I came across this. Why are you fighting while carrying my baby? And why didn't you tell me as soon as I came home?" he asked.

"I didn't know how to tell you. I'm scared, Bishop. I don't want to be a mother right now. I'm stressed out," I said.

"Why are you scared?" he asked me.

"I don't have family and your mother doesn't like me. I just feel alone with this," I replied.

"You got me and the rest of my family loves you. My mother may not like you, but you are still carrying a part of me that she will have to accept," he said.

"I'm blaming Ashanta and Serene for this shit. But I still don't know if the test one-hundred-percent accurate. I need to make a doctor's appointment. I also feel some type of way that you know about my cycles. You knew I missed my period before I did," I fussed and he chuckled.

"I keep track because that's the only time I can't get none. I know everything about it," he said.

"Are you going to stick by me?" I asked him.

"Always, shorty," he said and I kissed his lips.

"So, did you fuck shorty up?" he asked me.

"Had that bitch's face looking like Freddy Krueger's," I said and he laughed.

"Did you get my hat?" he asked me and I looked at him.

"Nigga, I wasn't thinking about your hat," I said.

"I was trying to call you to tell you don't forget my hat," he said. He scooted closer to me and wrapped his arms around my hips. He pressed his dick into me. His tongue sent chills up my spine when he licked my neck. He and I were already naked.

"Whatcha' got for me tonight?" he asked. I climbed on top of him with my back facing him. I took his dick into my mouth when my pussy touched his lips. He spread my cheeks and stuck his tongue inside of my pussy. My hand went up and down on his shaft as spit coated my fingers.

POP! POP!

He smacked my ass and jiggled it before he stuck his tongue back inside of me. Sixty-nine was a challenge for us. Bishop and I always tried to outdo one another. If I sucked him too good, he would eat me out until I couldn't take it. Everything I did to him, he did better, and I always had to tap out. I played with his testicles as my head bopped up and down on his dick. My mouth was like a vacuum as I sucked on him.

"Shhiitttttt, suck it harder, baby," he groaned. He spread my cheeks further apart and I felt the tip of his tongue lick around my butthole.

"I'm going to make you cum you first," he bragged. He licked my butthole as his finger moved in and out of my pussy. I stopped giving him head because the feeling he was giving me was too intense.

"BIISSHHOPPPPPPPPP!" I cried out. He devoured both holes like he was eating apple pie. His thumb slid into my anus while his tongue was still inside of me. I sat all the way up and straddled his face. He palmed my ass as I rode his tongue. He was ready to make me burst. When his mouth wrapped around my clit, I came on his face. I got up to get him a rag for his face. After he cleaned his face off, he stared at me. I was snuggled underneath the covers. My eyes were closing and he caught an attitude.

"What about my nut?" he asked me.

"I'm tired," I yawned. He snatched the covers off my back and propped my butt up. He rubbed his dick between my slit and my pussy started purring all over again.

319

"Damn it, Bishop. It's four in the morning and I'm tired," I complained. He pushed my head into the pillow and crossed my arms behind me back.

"This is going to be quick," he said before he pounded the life out of me.

****

I was moving around in the kitchen stiffly as I prepared breakfast for Bishop and I. My body was sore and I thought my vagina was going to fall out in the toilet when I used the bathroom. The doorbell rang and when I opened the door, Liana and a few other girls stood in front of me with scowls on their faces.

"So, y'all hoes came to jump me?" I asked.

"You put your hands on my cousin?" one girl asked. Bishop's mother's car pulled up in front of the house. She got out of the car and walked through the grass.

"Wait a minute, Liana! I thought I told you not to bring this mess to my son's house," Bishop's mother yelled at Liana.

"Look what she did to my face," Liana screamed.

"That's between you and her but not at my son's house," his mother spat.

"You don't even like her," Liana fussed.

"Bishop! Come down here and bring my Beretta! I'm about to play Angry Birds with these bitches this morning," I shouted upstairs. Bishop came downstairs in his boxer-briefs with a gun in his hand.

"Who is at the door?" he asked.

"The giraffe and the rest of her Madagascar friends," I said. When he pulled the door back, he cocked his gun.

"Get the fuck off my step before I blow your brains out. Y'all bitches ain't jumping my baby mother," he said with his gun pointed to Liana's forehead.

"Bishop!" his mother said.

"Get in the house, Ma," he said to her and she hurriedly came inside.

"Did you just put a gun to my head?" Liana asked as her friends stood behind her. There were four of them including her.

"Y'all came to my house, now get the fuck away from my door before I light y'all asses up like an old western movie. This shit is dead and I mean that. Y'all can do whatever y'all want to do, but y'all bitches ain't jumping shit that belongs to me and I put that on everything," he spat.

"Let's roll out," Liana said. I shut the door and Bishop's mother was still standing in the foyer.

"I have nothing to do with that. I heard Liana talking on the phone this morning about coming over here and I told her not to do it," she said.

"You need to kick her out," Bishop said.

"Where are her kids going to go?" she asked me.

"All those friends she has and she can't crash on nobody's couch? She is a grown-ass woman and those kids are nobody else's responsibility but her own. What she needs to do is take her ass back to her husband so those kids can wear proper clothing," I fussed.

"Liana came back because her husband started using drugs and she couldn't afford their house. Bills piled up and she could no longer afford them," his mother said.

"But has the nerve to look down on me. Instead of her chasing a man, she needs to chase another job. She wants Bishop's money because of what her husband is lacking. Bishop is your son, why do you want a married woman to trap him into taking care of her and her kids? Why would you want your son with a woman who only wants his money? And you were going to help her. I don't need Bishop's money. I bring enough to the table to add to his money. I'm not trying to take away from your son. I want to help him build so that me and him both can have. No disrespect but I'm telling you woman to woman that your plans with hooking Liana up with him are over," I said.

322

"Today I realized how wrong I have been. I apologize for my behavior and if my son can look past your past then I should be able to also. I will be more understanding with the relationship. All I wanted to do was help her so she wouldn't end up like my daughter. If only I'd known what my daughter was doing, I would've stopped her but I couldn't," she said. Bishop hugged his mother.

"It's all good, Ma. But on the real, Liana needs to go because she is causing too much trouble," he said.

"I know, now put some clothes on," she said. Bishop headed back up the stairs and I went into the kitchen. She followed behind me.

"I'm going to pretend I didn't see my son holding a gun to someone's head," she said as she helped me cook breakfast.

"He is a protector," I replied as I chopped the onions for Bishop's omelet.

"He looks very happy," she said and smiled at me. I smiled back at her but on the inside I felt like scum. His mother was opening up to me. Bishop had been treating me right and I was harboring a secret. I knew I had to tell him but I didn't know how. Everything fell into place for me but I was far from having my happy ending.

Bishop

"What's up with you?" I asked my cousin, Ree-Ree. I took her some leftovers that Desi had made. Ree-Ree didn't look like herself.

"I don't want to talk about it," she said.

"I ain't got shit to do right now, so you better talk. What's up with you? And why haven't I been hearing from you?" I asked her.

"I'm sure you already know," she said.

"Stop beating around the bush. I don't know nothing until you tell me," I said and sat down on her couch.

"Jada has been engaged for a year and his baby mother is pregnant. I thought he loved me and I wanted to start a family with him. No wonder he kept me a secret for so long but I thought it was because he didn't want any confrontation from you. I stopped taking my birth control pills and I ended up pregnant. I was going to tell him but I found out he was engaged. I got an abortion earlier, Bishop, and it was the hardest thing I had to do alone. I feel so stupid. People that I loved crossed me over. Chasity did me dirty and Jada did me dirty. What did I do to get this treatment? Because of Chasity I had to learn all over again. I thank God it wasn't permanent but nobody knows what it feels like to learn everything over again. I was supposed to go to college. I wished I died when I hit my head. This isn't life, this is hell," Ree-Ree said and burst into tears. I hugged her as she cried on my shoulder.

"The situations are temporary, Ree. What Chasity did to you wasn't permanent because you bounced back. I mean, you didn't bounce back right away, but all that matters is that you did. What Jada did to you isn't permanent damage. You will find a nigga that would treat you right. You can still go to college," I said.

"It's too late for me to go," she said.

"It ain't never too late. How about if you go to college, I will go with you," I said and she smiled.

"Really?" she asked as she wiped her eyes.

"Really. I got my high school diploma when I was in juvenile boot camp. I ain't never tell anybody but I got the shit. If you go to college, I will make use of it," I said.

"You are my favorite cousin," she replied.

"You saying that shit now but tomorrow you will be cursing me out," I said.

"You already know," she said. After I chilled with Ree-Ree for a few hours, I headed to the hood.

****

I pulled up on the block and spotted Jada at the dice game. I got out of my truck and walked over to him.

326

"My nigga, let me holla at you really quick," I said. He gave the niggas he was chilling with dap before he walked off with me.

"So, you just shit on my peoples? My nigga, you know Ree-Ree didn't deserve that shit and you know what she been through, and you shame her like this, nigga? You had my cousin thinking she was in love and pull this shit on her?" I asked.

"I didn't plan on it. It just happened but I do love your cousin. How is she?" he asked me.

"Cramping from getting an abortion," I spat.

"Yo, I'm not feeling your tone. What me and your cousin go through is our business," he spat. I slammed my fist into his face and he stumbled. Jada was nice with the hands but I was quicker. He swung and I dodged it. I came back with a punch to his side. I could've been a boxer if I wasn't into the streets but it didn't stop me from knocking niggas out. Jada caught me in the chin and from there on out, there was nothing but fist throwing. He tried to slam me but I kneed him in the face.

"Break that shit up!" someone yelled as I slammed Jada on the car.

"Talk shit now, nigga!" I said. I slammed my fist into his nose. His face was leaking but I didn't want to stop. I couldn't stop as I continued to hit him in the face. I knocked him out with my last punch. He slid down a car and laid out on the ground. I walked away from him and headed back to my truck. I got in and pulled off. I wanted to feel bad about what I did to him but I couldn't. I tried to come up with an excuse as to why he did Ree-Ree like that but I couldn't. He was my nigga and he dogged my cousin out and that was the bottom line.

****

I was sitting in the club chilling with Yolo and Kwenya. I thought those niggas were going to be in their feelings about what I did to Jada.

"Jada let this lil' nigga fuck him up. See, I would've swung a few punches then shot your ass. I ain't got the time to be getting knocked out by a dice game. Those niggas would've went into my pockets and played dice with my money. I can't go out like that," Yolo said.

"That's still our nigga, muthafucka'. He just put himself in a fucked-up situation. If that was my cousin, I would've done the same thing. Jada just got to realize that a real nigga will protect his family," Kwenya said to Yolo.

"I think you should be a professional boxer. It's good money because niggas be betting a lot of money on it," Yolo said to me.

"Naw, I'm good," I said.

"He have a point. You can go legit. If you got a talent, embrace it," Kwenya said.

"Look at that bitch-ass nigga, Rohann. I should fuck him up for dropping the ball and making the team lose. I put money on his team.

Pretty-boy-ass nigga need to be ice skating," Yolo said and Kwenya laughed. Rohann and a few other football players sat in the VIP section next to ours. He looked at me and gave me the head nod.

"That nigga knows you?" Yolo asked me.

"He used to fuck with Desi but I don't like how this nigga keep grilling me," I said.

"Nigga, you should've used that energy on the field. Bitch-ass nigga!" Yolo yelled out. His football friends waved Yolo off but Rohann spoke up.

"I use my energy fucking these hoes. Just ask your boy that's sitting across from you," he replied to Yolo. I stood up.

"What the fuck you say, nigga?" I asked him and he laughed.

"Nothing, bro, just chill," he said.

"Yo, I think this nigga is trying to clown Bishop," Yolo said to Kwenya.

"That nigga in his feelings. He probably fell in love with Desi," Kwenya replied.

Did this nigga just tell me that he fucked my bitch? I asked myself.

"Nigga, do I look like I fucking know you? What are you speaking on, muthafucka?" I asked Rohann.

329

"I just fucked your bitch in some Gucci flip-flops," Rohann said rapping Future's lyrics. His teammates started clowning with him. I was ready to walk into his section but Kwenya pulled me back.

"Chill, nigga. That nigga knows he got bodyguards on his side and you don't want that type of exposure. You don't want muthafuckas to start digging into your personal life because you whipped a football player's ass," Kwenya said. I sat back down on the couch. I picked my blunt up from the ashtray and lit it.

"That nigga dramatic. Yo, Bishop, ignore that punk ass one-year-contract-signing muthafucka. You got more bread than that nigga and he in the NFL," Yolo said.

"Nigga, you must've had on Gucci flip-flops on the field earlier because you were running like a bitch trying to catch some balls and I ain't talking about a football," Yolo called out to him. Kwenya roared in laughter and I choked on my weed smoke.

"Aye, come here really quick," Kwenya said to the waitress. She came over with a pen and pad.

"You see that section over there? Send them six bottles of Ace of Spades. Put it on my tab," Kwenya said and the waitress walked off.

"Nigga, you crazy," Yolo said. Minutes later, three waitresses came out holding two bottles each inside of a bucket of ice.

"That's for playing hard on the field today," Kwenya said to Rohann and his team. Rohann bit his bottom lip and grilled Kwenya.

"You see that white woman with the long, blonde hair wearing a black dress with the diamonds around her neck? She is standing by the bar. That's his wife," Yolo said. I looked at Rohann's wife and she was bad.

"I would fuck the pink off that pussy," Yolo said.

"Nigga, you fuck anything," Kwenya said.

"So did you," he replied.

"What happened to Poet?" I asked Yolo.

"She cool but it ain't nothing. I was into her and I stopped being into her," Yolo said.

"After you harassed her to mess around with you?" I asked.

"Yeah, she lives with a nigga and when I was up in that pussy that nigga came home. He walked into the room to get a bar of soap and left right back out. I asked her who that was and she told me it was her ex-nigga and he sleep in the other room with his girlfriend. I was turned off after that," he said.

"She told me about that. She said that him and her been broken up for three years and didn't want to give their place up, so they stayed and became roommates," Kwenya said and laughed.

"I was cool with that but that nigga walks into her room without knocking just lets me know they are still fucking. I'm cool on shorty but she can still give me the goodies," Yolo said. Kwenya and Yolo was clowning around but Desi was on my mind.

Did she fuck that nigga again? I asked myself.

"I'm ready to go home. I will holla at y'all niggas later," I said and stood up. I gave Yolo and Kwenya dap.

"Don't go home and knock Desi out like you did Jada because of that fuck nigga," Yolo said and I waved him off.

"Naw, I just got things to do in the morning," I replied before I headed out of the club.

****

When I got home, Desi was on the couch in the living room with just a wife beater and thongs on. She was eating a bag of onion rings and watching TV.

"You went to the club and made it in before midnight?" she asked me.

"Yeah, I was getting tired. But let me holla at you really quick," I said. I grabbed the remote and turned the TV off.

"What's the matter, babe?" she asked. I knew shorty like the back of my hand and I could tell she was nervous about something.

332

"Why are you nervous?" I asked her.

"I'm not," she lied.

"Did you fuck that nigga Rohann? That nigga was feeling himself tonight at the club. He said some slick shit and now I feel like he got one up on me," I said.

"I told you I didn't," she said.

"And what is that supposed to mean to me? Bitches lie all the time," I replied.

"I'm a bitch?" she asked me and stood up.

"I'm not talking about that. All I want to know is what really happened because that nigga was ready to catch one to the dome," I replied. Desi sat down on the couch with her arms crossed. Tears welled up in her eyes and I knew at that moment she did it. I knew as soon as I asked her that she did it. I probably took her for granted in the beginning but I ain't stepped out on her. Even though I still had feelings for Liana, I didn't act on them. Monie came on to me more times than I could count but she got nothing—I was faithful to Desi.

"When did you do it?" I asked her.

"The day after I went to your family reunion," she responded.

"BITCH, WHAT!" I yelled at her and she jumped.

"It could've been understandable if it happened when you cut me off but the day after we made it official? The day after I asked you to move in with me? The day after I took you around my family because I wanted to show you how much I wanted you and you went and fucked that nigga? You moved in with me knowing that you shitted on me. So much for trying to turn a hoe into a housewife. Bitch, you ain't shit for that. All that crying and fighting you was doing because you thought I was fucking around but it was you," I said.

"It was a mistake," she yelled.

"You are too grown to be making that type of mistake! What happened? You slipped on his dick? It wasn't a mistake and the nigga got feelings for you. My niggas noticed it and so did I. You fucked a nigga that's in love with you and now you are stuck with him. Is that why your phone been going off?" I asked.

"Calm down!" she cried. I flipped the coffee table over. Desi got up and ran down the hall and I chased her. I caught her by the back of her neck.

"I will kill your ass in this house! I'm not done talking to you," I said.

"You are hurting me," she cried.

"Good! You were with him when I kept calling you that day, weren't you? But that didn't stop you because you went and did it anyway and lied about it. You are a dirty-ass hoe," I spat and pushed her into the wall.

"That ain't my seed. I don't want shit to do with it," I said.

"We used a condom," she replied.

"Get out of my crib," I told her.

"No, I'm not leaving! We are going to talk about this," she said and I laughed.

"Oh, so you don't want to leave?" I asked her. I went into the hall closet and grabbed the jump rope I exercised with. I grabbed Desi and tied the rope around her while she tried to fight me off. After I got the rope tight around her, I tied it in a knot so she couldn't get out of it. I laid her down on the floor as she kicked and cursed me out. I went into the kitchen to grab some tape. I wrapped the tape around her ankles.

"Now, all I got to do is throw you in the river so you can drown," I said.

"You are insane! You are fucking crazy! Let me go," she screamed and rolled around on the ground.

"Goodnight, shorty," I said before I walked upstairs. Desi was screaming and crying all night while I laid in bed. I felt like choking the life out of her but I loved her too much. Desi grew on me quick and I fell for her hard. If only she knew how much she messed my head up.

****

After I woke up, I took care of my hygiene and headed downstairs. Desi was sleep in the hallway and I almost felt sorry for her. I walked over her and fixed myself a breakfast sandwich. I took my food into the living room. I forgot that I broke my coffee table. I sat my plate on the couch and turned the ESPN channel on. When I was ready to bite into my sandwich, Desi started yelling at the top of her lungs.

"This is so uncomfortable! Bishop, let me loose!" she screamed.

"Call your man up and tell him to let you loose and shut the fuck up because I can't hear the TV!" I shouted.

"I have a doctor's appointment today!" she screamed. My doorbell rang. I got up to open the door.

"Good morning," my mother said when she walked into the house.

"What are you doing here, Ma?" I asked her. Before she could respond, Desi was screaming at the top of her lungs again. My mother dropped her purse and ran down the hall.

"Watch your step, Ma, before you trip over that pile in the hallway!" I called out to her. I went back into the living room. I heard my mother cursing me out as Desi cried about her legs going numb. While I was sitting on the couch eating my sandwich, I felt a blow to the side of my face. Desi was on top of me swinging on me. My mother pulled her off and they both fell on the floor.

"That bitch busted my lip," I said to myself as blood dripped on my wife beater.

"What in the name of God is going on here? And what are you trying to do, Bishop? Get locked up for kidnapping or something?" my mother asked me.

"We were role-playing cops and robbers," I said. Desi got up off the floor.

"He knows damn well I'm pregnant!" she yelled.

"That ain't my baby so I don't give a fuck about you or the pregnancy. If you know what I know, you need to do less talking and worry about packing," I spat.

"Where is she going to go, Bishop?" my mother asked me.

"With you. You took Liana in and she got kids by another nigga. Well, this one does, too," I said.

"She is carrying your child and she gave up her place to live with you. People make mistakes but you don't kick a pregnant woman out in the streets!" she replied. Desi walked up the stairs and when she came back down she was dressed in sweat clothes and had a bat in her hand. She opened the front door and walked out. I heard my alarm going off and when I ran to the door, Desi was beating my truck with a bat. She pulled out a pocket knife and flattened my tires.

"Yo, what the fuck!" I yelled out before I grabbed her. I snatched the bat from her and threw it in the yard.

"I'm going back home," my mother said when she walked passed us. She got in her car and pulled off. I pushed Desi away from me and went inside of my house.

"You hogtied me!" she yelled behind me. I went upstairs to the master bedroom. She walked into the room behind me.

"Get your shit out and put it in the room down the hall. The relationship is dead. I'm never fucking with you on that level again. But since that might be my baby, I'm not going to do you that dirty and kick you out," I said.

"I don't love him. I love you," she replied.

"But you opened your legs for a nigga that is married. You let a married nigga ruin what we had. He goes home to his bitch every night but who will you be coming home to? Y'all females always want a real nigga but don't appreciate shit. You fucked that up, not me! So, all of that crying and apologizing shit don't matter to me. I guess you fall in the category with the rest of the dumb broads. You just will be another baby mama added to the bunch with a ran-through pussy. I should've pulled out and nutted on your face. Matter of fact, here you go. Thank you for your services," I said. I picked the money up off the dresser and tossed it in her face. She stormed out of the room sobbing. I paced back and forth inside of the bedroom frustrated. I started punching the wall.

"FUCK!" I yelled out. I had a feeling shorty was going to do me dirty and I was right—I was always right.

338

Damos

I sat at the table playing cards with a few niggas I was locked up with. I had a court date coming up. I was going to serve over thirty years if I was found guilty.

"That nigga Kwenya took the DMV over I heard. When he gets out, I want to link up with that nigga but I heard it was hard to get on his team," the inmate Brisco said.

"Lower your voice, I'm trying to read this book!" the older inmate Carl said.

"Nigga, you always reading but let me borrow that book when you finish. What's it about?" Brisco asked Carl.

"It's hard to explain the story. The author's name is Ashanta Scott. She released it almost two weeks ago and my wife said she couldn't put it down. It's about some broad being in an abusive marriage with a king-pin. But anyways, the husband's side-chick thought she killed the wife but she didn't. This broad went missing for years and got plastic surgery done. She changed her name and everything. She went back to get revenge on her husband and the side-chick by becoming friends with the side-chick who is now married to her husband. Well, anyways, the nigga doesn't know it's his ex-wife he's cheating on his new wife with. Mannnnn, if women could pull this shit off, I don't think a nigga in his right mind would cheat. This broad in this book is making his whole empire crumble but the plot thickened. The nigga she thought she was getting revenge on is a twin. The man she originally married was killed but she didn't know. Well, her husband's brother was pretending to be him to have his empire. This book right here is like a big mystery and I don't think you will understand it," Carl said.

"Hurry up and finish. I like mystery books," Brisco said.

"Wait a minute. Isn't Ashanta Scott your wife?" Brisco asked me.

"Yeah, that bitch is my wife," I answered. I laid the cards on the table and went back to my cell because it was time for count down. I lay on my bunk and Brisco came in. It was me and him to a cell. It was another inmate in our cell, too, but he was in lock-up. The C.O. locked our cell and walked away.

"Word around the house is that your father was a cop and he set Kwenya up," Brisco said.

"My father isn't a cop. They got me mixed up with someone else," I lied.

"That's what I said when I heard it. Cops' children get killed around these parts," Brisco said. I turned my back toward him and dozed off.

****

I was pulled off my bunk and slammed onto the floor. When I looked up, Brisco was standing over me with a shank.

"What are you doing?" I asked him.

"Sending you a message from Kwenya. I told you I was going to join his team when I got out. But I'm trying to collect the bounty on your head," he said.

"Come on, man, don't do this to me! Help me! Somebody help me!" I screamed. A guard came to our cell.

"What is wrong, Bennett? Why are you making a lot of noise?" the C.O. asked me. She was a black female that was in her late-twenties. Her name was Officer Stewart. She only let certain inmates get away with certain things and I heard from Carl it was because she was sleeping with a few of them.

"He is trying to kill me!" I cried. She smiled at me.

"The boss said your time is up so your time is up. Brisco, hurry the fuck up before someone else comes," she said to him and walked away. Brisco stabbed me in the stomach and I tried to fight him off but he kept stabbing me. Blood was all over the cell as I fought for my life. I lost the battle when the shank went into my throat.

Ashanta

I stood in the middle of our bedroom as I fixed Kwenya's tie. We were having a big dinner for our family and for my success with my book. It was the talk all over and I had a few interviews lined up. Within the same week that it was released, I had received a lot of feedback. My book had some of what I went through inside but I added a lot of things and changed things. It was a hit and Kwenya supported me through it all. He had my book in all of his bakeries.

"This is getting good, shorty," Kwenya said as he held my book in his hand.

"Put it down so I can fix your tie right," I said.

"Let me just finish this one page," he said and pulled away from me.

"The nigga Otis ain't dead, is he?" he asked me.

"I can't tell you that," I said. I grabbed my clutch and he sat the book down. I stood in the mirror admiring my baby bump. I wore a black dress that clung to me. The dress dragged the ground and fanned out. I wore a pair of black and silver Jimmy Choo stilettos and my hair was in an up-do. My diamond choker and diamond earrings Kwenya bought me, brought out the plain black dress I wore. Kwenya stood behind me wearing a black suit that fit him perfectly. He rubbed my stomach.

"Don't wear any panties. In the limo on our way back home, I'm trying to slide into something wet," he whispered in my ear before he pulled away from me. He slid my dress up and pulled my panties down. I stepped out of them and he tossed them on the bed.

"I feel naked," I said.

"That's the point, but the limo just pulled up, so let's go," he said.

****

"This is beautiful! You planned this all by yourself?" I asked my mother when I looked around the ballroom.

"Yup, all by myself. Your father is being an asshole tonight so be aware. He didn't want to come at first because he said that being an author isn't a good career. I'm glad you decided to chase your dreams but honestly I was getting tired of keeping track of your life. Your father needs to just accept that we cannot force you and your brother to do what we want y'all to do. I'm just glad that you are here and alive. I lost my mind when you were gone," she said.

"There is my beautiful daughter," my father said and hugged me.

"Hey Daddy," I said.

"Can I talk to you?" he asked me. My mother rolled her eyes and walked away.

"Is everything okay?" I asked.

"I don't approve of this. Being a young doctor is an accomplishment. Not too many doctors can say that but you were determined to get finished early. You studied day in and day out. You didn't take any breaks, and for ten years straight, you were on the right path. You busted your ass just to become a writer? That book is nothing but ghetto trash and I'm ashamed of it. A young and intelligent woman gone away just to be a stay-at-home pregnant woman," he said to me.

"Get the stick out of your ass and look around you. This is not your life, it's mine, and my old job depressed me. You are busy trying to impress your rich friends and they don't even care about you, Father. All you are to them is a black man that made it. You think speaking properly and having social events is the higher life? Well, it's not because you are not even happy with it. You have to put on a mask just to fit in. I'm sorry if I no longer want to wear mine. I like to curse sometimes, I like to act ignorant sometimes, and yeah, I know it sounds crazy but I like the feeling of being free. I don't have to impress anybody and guess what else? I listen to rap music. You used to ban me from that 'garbage' you called it. I like to get in touch with my black culture from both sides; from the rich to the ghetto. Down to the fried chicken and cherry flavor Kool-Aid, I love it all. My book became a number-one bestseller within a week. A young black woman made that happen and you should be proud of that," I spat.

"I worked my butt off so you can have everything and you need to appreciate it. You need to be more reserved like your mother. You should've learned to leave trash behind after you were kidnapped. If you were on the right path, that wouldn't have happened," he gritted.

"Father, everyone wears a mask but you don't know who they are until it is taken off. Read my book and you will find out that behind all of us, there is a person that we are afraid to show. One day you will figure it out, but my guests are coming in so I hope this conversation can be saved for a later date," I said and walked off.

Desi and Ree-Ree both walked into the ballroom.

"Well, don't you two look remarkable," I said and hugged them.

"This place is really big," Desi said.

"Yes, it's beautiful," I replied. Bishop walked in dressed in a suit and he looked very handsome. He kissed Ree-Ree on the cheek before he gave me a hug.

"You look beautiful," Bishop said to me.

"Thank you, you clean up well yourself," I said. He smiled and walked off. He didn't say a word to Desi and he didn't look at her.

"That was awkward," Ree-Ree said.

"It's been two weeks and he still has not said one word to me. When we are home, he says nothing to me. I talk to him and he actually ignores me. The doctor confirmed that I was already pregnant when I slept with Rohann. I just turned nine weeks and I slept with Rohann six weeks ago. I just don't know what to do," Desi said.

"Bishop is very stubborn—too stubborn," Ree-Ree said. Jada walked in and my mouth dropped because he was with his wife. He got married a week prior to the party. He had a secret wedding with just his family and his wife's family. I told Kwenya I didn't want Jada to come but it wasn't fair because Jada was someone he grew up with. His wife was very pretty; she was tall and slim and her baby bump showed. Her thirty-inch weave was bone straight and her ring could be spotted from across the room. Ree-Ree's eyes welled up with tears.

"You'd better not cry or look sad in front of that nigga. Stand up tall and hold your head up straight," Serene said. I didn't know she was standing next to us. I was too busy scoping out Jada and his wife. I met Ree-Ree through Desi the same as she met Serene through me. We all clicked and it felt good to have other female friends instead of just one.

"He has been calling me a lot lately. He sent me flowers and a diamond bracelet last week. I will get over it," Ree-Ree said.

"What and the hell is Quay doing here?" Serene asked me.

"Where?" I asked.

"He just walked in with Yolo," she replied. We all stared and I could see why Serene was smitten by the young man, he was handsome. He resembled Yolo in a lot of ways.

"Is that Yolo's brother? They almost look like twins," Desi said.

"No, that's his cousin. He said he was going somewhere with his cousin but he didn't tell me where," Serene replied.

"I haven't seen him before," Ree-Ree said.

"He is from Trinidad but the majority of his family is over here," Serene replied. My brother Stephen walked through the crowd in my direction. He looked uncomfortable because he hated to be around a lot of people.

"Lighten up," I said and hugged him.

"I'm trying to but all of these people are smothering me. Hey ladies, y'all look lovely tonight," Stephen said as he eyed Ree-Ree's hips.

"Let me talk to you for a second," Stephen said and pulled me away.

"What's going on?" I asked him.

"You didn't tell them anything, did you?" he asked me.

"No, I can keep a secret but I do think you should go back to college. It doesn't have to be for that but you shouldn't completely drop out," I said to him.

"I am going back once I figure out what I want to do. I've been so into school because of our pops that I haven't had the time to think about what I really want to do. I am going back, though, I promise," he said and he touched my stomach.

"You really got something in there don't you?" he asked me I and laughed.

"Yup," I replied.

"Where is Tisha? She was invited," I said.

"She is home and I don't want our parents to meet her until the baby shower," he said. Stephen was complicated and I thought about asking more questions but I didn't. It was obvious that he wasn't into Tisha like that because he roamed around like a free man. I talked to Stephen for a few more minutes before he excused himself.

As more guests arrived, the ballroom filled up. People I went to high school and college with, Kwenya's family, and a lot of my parents' friends were in attendance. It was the most fun I had ever had. The waiters and waitresses were walking around with trays of drinks.

"What a fucking time to be pregnant. I need a drink and a blunt really bad because Bishop is irking my nerves. Who is that bitch he is talking to?" Desi asked me.

"That's Ashley. She and I went to Med School together," I replied.

"That hoe is going to need some medical attention if she doesn't keep her fucking hands to herself," Desi said and stormed off toward Bishop. The DJ played Miguel's song *Adorn*. I walked across the floor and grabbed Kwenya's hand. I pulled him to me and he wrapped his thick arms around my waist.

"You got rhythm," I said to him and he whispered in my ear.

"How do you think I knocked you up? Don't be surprised."

I kissed his lips and my nipples started to ache. Every time Kwenya's body was in proximity to mine, a jolt of passion shot through me. His hands slid down to my bottom and he gently squeezed it.

"You want it, don't you?" he asked.

"Naw," I answered.

"Are you wet?" he asked.

"Behave yourself. We have a lot of guests here," I responded.

"I will wait, I don't want your pops fucking me up," he joked. After the song went off, I excused myself. I had to go to the bathroom. I walked down the hall and pushed the door open.

"Oh shit!" Yolo yelled out. Ree-Ree was sitting on the counter in front of the mirror with her dress hiked up. They weren't doing anything but kissing but I was still shocked. Yolo pulled away from her and he slid her dress down. He wiped the lipstick off his lips.

"Uh, yeah. I will holla at y'all later," he said and hurried out of the bathroom. I looked at Ree-Ree and her light-skinned cheeks were red.

"Wait a minute. Were you and Yolo just making out? Oh my heavens," I said.

"Girrlllll, I'm fine," she said and fixed herself in the mirror.

"Be careful, Ree," I said to her and she looked at me.

"I have no attachments to anyone. Men do it all the time and, besides, we were just kissing. Have you ever noticed how fine Yolo is?" she asked and giggled.

"Yes, he is very easy on the eyes but when did all of this happen?" I asked.

"We sorta been talking on the phone lately. I ran into him at the liquor store last week. He is very easy to talk to, believe it or not. He isn't all that bad, but, anyway, he is just a secret friend. I came onto him first," she said.

"Well, I can't talk. I started messing with Kwenya while I was married and that was wrong but it was a beautiful wrong. Maybe yours will be a beautiful wrong, too," I said.

"That doesn't sound bad at all. I will see you on the floor," she said and walked out. I handled my business and washed my hands.

"Your dress is really clinging to you. You look amazing," a voice said from behind me. When I turned around, it was Jesse dressed in a long, black dress that hugged curves I didn't know she had. She looked to be in her thirties and her make-up was flawless. Her long, Chinese-bang wig set the look off.

"You look amazing, too. I didn't think you were going to come," I said.

"I've been taking care of business. I had to make sure I tied up a lot of loose ends before I came back home," she said.

351

"Great, now let me introduce you to my friends," I said. I grabbed her hand and she followed me.

****

"Serene, Ree-Ree, and Desi, this is Jesse. Jesse, these are my friends," I said. Serene and Ree-Ree waved but Desi didn't. I had to remind myself that Desi didn't like new people.

"Well, aren't you going to speak?" Jesse asked Desi.

"I don't know you. What am I speaking for?" Desi asked.

"Ummm. He was right about your attitude but we can work on that," Jesse said. I was confused and I could tell by the look on Desi's face she was confused, too.

"What?" Desi asked.

"Oh, nothing, honey. I'm just an old woman who tends to talk out of her head. Ashanta, I'm going to go and talk to Kwenya," Jesse said and walked off.

"I don't like her," Desi said.

"You don't know her," Ree-Ree said and Serene agreed.

"Something about her I'm not clicking with and I knew that when the bitch walked in here. She sticks out from everyone in here, and not in a good way," Desi said.

"Look who just walked in and she brought a date with her," I said.

"Shantel? Why is she here?" Desi asked.

"I invited her. I help Kwenya with the books to his shops and the money has really increased because of her. She did a lot for his company, so why not keep her around?" I asked.

"You are a better woman than me because my man would not be working with someone like her. She seems sneaky," Serene said.

"He doesn't deal with her. When it's something pertaining to his business, I'm the one who meets with her. She and I talked and I told her that things are changing and she will not be contacted by Kwenya anymore. She understood and kept it professional," I said.

"I can dig that," Ree-Ree said.

****

"What were you and Jesse talking about?" I asked Kwenya.

"I'm not discussing that part of my life with you. We had an agreement, remember?" he asked me.

"Well, in that case, I don't want to know. Desi doesn't like Jesse and told me to stay away from her," I said to Kwenya as we headed back home. He took off his tie and jacket. He brushed his hand down his waves.

"Desi is Jesse's daughter. It's a long story but that's why Jesse came back. She doesn't know how to confront Desi," Kwenya said.

"I'm not surprised. I always knew Jesse hid a lot from me. She is so secretive like she is always planning," I replied.

"It's called 'staying ahead,'" Kwenya replied. I knew Kwenya still kept things away from me, too, but he showed me enough and I couldn't complain. I unzipped his pants and his eyes followed me. I got down on my knees in the limo as I released his thick, long dick.

Slurp on it like an ice cream cone, I told myself. I licked the tip of him and kissed it. He was impatient and I knew I had to hurry up and get to it. I added spit on the tip of his dick and slowly slid my mouth down inch by inch. A groan escaped his lips when he threw his head back. My head went up and down as spit flowed from my mouth and down my hands. I relaxed my throat and when I looked up at him, I could see the muscles in his chest tighten. He was my king and I was serving him. It turned me on a lot because I was in control.

"UGGHHHHHHHH!" he moaned as I sucked him. My hands went up and down his shaft and my tongue played with the tip of his dick. When he grew harder inside my mouth, my pussy clenched. His hand went to the back of my head. He gently pressed my head down as he slowly pumped in and out of my mouth. I grabbed my breast and squeezed my nipple. My pussy got wetter because of how hard he was.

"Shit, shorty, suck that shit," he groaned. I started to moan when he grabbed my breast. He massaged my breast and my wetness dripped down my inner thigh. I had a mini orgasm from the pleasure we were giving each other. He lifted me up and pulled me down to straddle him. He hiked my dress up and entered me.

"ARRGGHHHHHHHH!" I moaned. I pulled his shirt apart and his buttons flew across the limo. His hands gripped my ass as he leaned back into the seat. My fingers traced the outline of his abs while I rocked my hips. I leaned forward to suck on his neck. His fingers were buried into the skin on my ass while I rocked my hips back and forth. My nails dug into his chest as I sped up.

"Make that pussy talk, shorty! Make it curse a nigga out! Fuck that dick!" he said loudly and I bounced up and down on him. My pussy was making sloppy, wet sounds and I knew the limo driver heard it all but that's what made it more spontaneous. He ripped my dress at my neckline and slid the straps down on my bra. He sat up and started sucking my nipples. I grabbed my breasts and stuck them further into his mouth as his dick pushed up inside of me and against my spot. My clit jumped and he knew what that meant. He flicked his tongue across my nipples while his thumb circled my clit. I moaned out loud and squirted everywhere on the backseat of the limo. I felt him throbbing while exploding inside of me. I fell down onto his chest and he kissed my neck.

"Keep still," he said. He was still releasing semen and the slightest move from me would've caused him to get hard again for another round and I was too tired. The limo came to a stop and we were in front of our house.

"My dress is ruined and the seat...this is so embarrassing," I panicked. I tried to close my dress. Kwenya gave him his suit jacket and his black pants had a lot of our essence on them.

"This is a lot," he said as he fixed himself. The driver got out and opened the door for us. I stepped out first with my head down from embarrassment. Kwenya stepped out the limo with scratches on his chest and his pants falling down. I covered my mouth with my hand when I looked at the wet seats we were sitting on. Kwenya went inside his pocket and peeled off one-hundred-dollar bills. He gave them to the older black man.

"This is for the mess. We apologize for that," Kwenya said and the man smiled.

"Ain't nothing wrong with that, my brother. You and the lovely lady have a wonderful night," he said and titled his hat. When he pulled off, I fell out laughing.

"That was insane!" I said and he smiled.

"That mouth is beautiful, shorty," he said.

****

The next morning...

I sat down at the kitchen table eating the breakfast that Kwenya made for me. I dropped a piece of bacon on the floor for Bella while his back was turned. He hated that I fed Bella table food because he thought it caused her to beg. I read the newspaper and there was a stabbing at the detention center.

Damos Santos Bennet, age 31, was found dead in his cell from multiple stab wounds. There were no witnesses and the case will be further investigated. This is the fourth homicide this year...

I stopped eating my food because I felt bad for what happened to him. I didn't want death for him. A tear slipped out of my eye and I hurriedly wiped it away before Kwenya saw me.

"Are you straight before I leave? I got to meet Poet at the shop to help her with this big order," he said before he kissed my lips.

"Yes, I'm fine," I said.

"Okay, cool, and don't tell Desi about Jesse. Don't get involved in that because Desi is going to want answers that nobody can give her but Jesse," he said.

"Yes, Father," I joked.

Kwenya

"How was the party last night? I'm mad I missed it," Poet said.

"It was straight. It wasn't really my thing but I had to make baby mama happy," I said.

"What did I do to Yolo? He just stopped talking to me. Is he seeing someone?" she asked.

"Come on, shorty. You know that ain't a real nigga thing. I'm not getting into that," I replied and she sucked her teeth.

"Y'all niggas stick together," she said while rolling up the fresh dough. The door chimed and someone walked in.

"I will go see who it is," Poet said and walked out of the kitchen. Moments later, I heard arguing and I went to the front.

"You need to leave!" Poet screamed.

"That nigga killed my brutha!" a man yelled at her as I approached them. It was the nigga Chaos. I remembered his twin brother's face.

"You killed my brutha!" he yelled and pulled a gun out on me. I hurriedly pulled my gun out from the back of my cargo pants and we both shot at the same time. I felt a burning sensation pierce through my shoulder as I fired my gun. Poet hid under the counter and started screaming. Chaos ducked down.

"This is the welcome home greeting I get?" he asked and a bullet flew over my head. He stood up and started shooting at me again. I let off a couple of rounds and he flew back across the table. I shot at him again.

"KWENYA, LOOK OUT!" Poet yelled. When I turned around, a few bullets caught me in the chest. Another bullet went through Poet's head. I only had one bullet left. I went to my office in the back of the shop. I pulled out a shotgun from underneath my desk as blood poured from my mouth. I knew I wasn't going to make it but I couldn't let a nigga kill me so easily. There was someone else in the shop. I sat in the chair at my desk and waited for the person to come in. I heard someone walking to the back and they were getting closer. The door slowly inched open and I fired my gun.

"Kwenya," my mother said and fell down to the floor.

"MA!" I choked up but I knew she was dead before she hit the floor. A masked man stood in the doorway with a gun aimed at my head. I dropped my gun and coughed up more blood. I killed my mother and at that point I didn't care about my life. I was going to leave my baby and shorty behind but I couldn't live with what I did to my mother. I closed my eyes and welcomed death. I heard two gunshots and a thump. I opened my eyes and Yolo was standing behind the fallen body. He rushed to me and pulled me out of the chair.

"Naw, nigga! Naw! Don't go out like this! We were supposed to hit the gym. I was on time this morning, come on, nigga!" Yolo cried.

"Take care of my seed and Ashanta for me," I said.

"No, nigga, no! Fuck that! You are a G! We don't go out like this!" he yelled but my body was getting cold and I knew it was it for me.

****

I jumped up and looked around and I was in my office. I fell asleep in my chair and that dream messed my head up. I had to get to that nigga Chaos first. At the party, Jesse told me that Chaos was released from jail because his charges were dropped. I also had to see about my mother.

"Kwenya, are you okay in there?" Poet asked me. It was good to hear her voice. I got up and opened the door and she was standing in front of me with flour all over her.

"You were yelling. Are you okay?" she asked.

"Yeah, I'm good. It's good seeing you, though," I said and she frowned her nose up.

"What were you smoking?" she asked me.

"Get back to work, girl, and stop being nosey, damn," I said. She walked away mumbling underneath her breath.

That was some good kush, though. It put a nigga straight to sleep. I didn't know I was asleep until I woke up, I thought.

****

"So, you had the nigga killed just like that?" Yolo asked me. Yolo, Jada, and I were sitting by the pool in the back of my crib. Him and Jada squashed whatever small beef they had but Bishop and Jada still wasn't rocking with each other.

"Had that nigga shanked and he was still considered Ashanta's husband. In order for me to marry her, I had to do it because he wasn't trying to sign the divorce papers. She is going to cash out on his death because she had life insurance on him. But word on the street is that Bernie got caught slippin' in jail. I heard he got turned out in the shower room," I said and Yolo chuckled.

"We got a big shipment coming in tonight. It's bigger than the one we had last month. Oh, and Jada, check out the young dude Kobe that you got working for you before you put anything in his hand. He is a hothead and loud niggas draw too much attention. You either tell him what it is or he can bounce," I said and he nodded his head.

"Babe, look who is here," Ashanta said when she opened the sliding door. I looked behind me and Jesse was standing next to her.

"I'll be inside in a minute, now close the door," I said and she closed the door.

"I still can't believe that old broad was your connect. I would've been hitting that all day, every day," Yolo said.

"How is Quay doing with his part on your team?" I asked Yolo.

"Good. He is a smart lil' nigga and he don't talk much but he observes a lot," he replied. After we discussed business, I walked with them to the garage where they were parked. Jada had to hurry home but I still had to holla at Yolo about something.

"Tomorrow is Rakita's birthday. Don't forget to send her that cupcake we talked about," I said as we dapped.

"Oh, nigga, I look forward to it. I will get up with you later," he said and got on his motorcycle. When I walked back into the house, Jesse and Ashanta were sitting down in the living room talking.

"I'm going to check up on the roast," Ashanta said and got up. Jesse sat on the couch sipping her wine.

"That shipment that comes tonight, I want to be there. I want to see how your team operates," she said.

"Don't worry about that," I replied.

"Bossed up, I like that, but we are partners and I need to know these things," she said.

"And I've got everything running smoothly so you don't need to worry about anything," I replied. She smirked at me.

"I want to be there," she said and stood up.

"I will see what I can do," I said.

"You are the boss," she replied. She walked over to me and kissed my cheek.

"I'm going to say bye to Ashanta then I'm headed out," she said and walked out of the living room.

****

Two days later...

"I still can't believe how much you grew up," I said to Quay. We were at the basketball court shooting hoops. He was seven years younger than us. I didn't want him to get caught up in the streets but Yolo said there was nothing we could do about it. Quay wanted to make his own decisions and that's what he did.

"Y'all think I'm still a little boy. I'm a man," he said as he dribbled the ball.

"Nigga, you still piss in the bed," Yolo joked with a blunt hanging out of his mouth.

"I'm old enough to shoot yah, though. Keep running that mouth," Quay said and Yolo laughed. Yolo knew how to provoke someone. Quay's phone beeped. He looked at it and started smiling.

"You haven't been in the US for a whole month yet and you are already in love. Who is the woman?" Yolo asked Quay.

"None of your business and it ain't like that. She is just cool to chill with. She is different from the girls back home," Quay said.

"Leave him alone, Yolo. If he doesn't want to tell then that's his business," I said.

"He needs to be careful who he lets in his circle," Yolo replied.

"She is your woman's friend. She was at the party," Quay said to me.

"Ashanta only has three friends. I know it ain't Desi or Ree-Ree. Only one left is the pregnant, ghetto one. What's her name? Cereal?" Yolo asked Quay.

"Her name is Serene," Quay said.

"What do you want with a pregnant broad? Yo, are you serious? You came all the way back home to play daddy to a stranger?" Yolo asked.

"I met her at the mall and I thought she was one of the prettiest women I've ever seen. She and I are just friends. She ain't checking for me like that and I'm cool with it," Quay said and Yolo shook his head. Serene was a cool person but her situation was too much for Quay—the nigga was just turning twenty-one.

"You see those lil' thots over there? The ones sitting on top of the Jeep? That's what you should be worried about. That and getting money until you are ready to settle down. Women like Serene are already established. That's a big step, lil' nigga," Yolo said.

"Shut the fuck up. I'm grown and I ain't going to keep telling you that. Those girls over there can't even suck my dick. They probably slept with every nigga on this basketball court. Loose women don't turn me on. A woman with brains and her own bank account does. I bet one of them are looking for some nigga to buy the new Jordans or they probably want to suck some dick for Beyoncé tickets," Quay said and I laughed.

"He does have a point. After a while, hoes will be just hoes," I said and Yolo waved me off. The sun started to go down. We headed back to our vehicles. A girl walked over to Quay's two-door Audi.

"These broads are going crazy over that lil' nigga. I need to go back home to get my accent back," Yolo joked.

"Did you get a chance to see Rakita?" I asked Yolo.

"She couldn't have any visitors because her and another inmate was fighting in the cell," he replied. The cupcake had poison in it. I wanted to put her out of her misery.

"It's cool, it just wasn't her time to go," I replied.

"When are you going to pop the question? Are you still holding onto Ashanta's ring?" he asked me.

"I got this, nigga. I'm going to propose to her when she has the baby shower," I replied and he gave me dap.

"I will get up with you later," he said and walked off.

Desi

"It's late," I said when I walked into the master bedroom. It was five in the morning and he was just getting home. Bishop and I still weren't sleeping together. He smelled like perfume and he had pink lipstick on the collar of his shirt. It felt like a ton of bricks hit me. He took his clothes off and got in the shower.

"I'm moving out," I called out to him but he didn't respond. I went through his phone while he was in the shower. I saw the girl's number, the one who packaged up his product. Her name appeared in his call log a lot. Him and Monie was talking over six times a day. I checked his messages but it was empty. I heard the water cut off so I put his phone back where I got it from. Bishop came out of the bathroom with a towel wrapped around his waist.

"Did you find what you were looking for?" he asked me.

"Are you screwing Monie?" I asked.

"Call her and ask her. I'm ready to go to bed so I will holla at you in the morning," he replied.

"This situation is stressing me out. I'm getting sick behind it and I need for you to be a little understanding," I said.

"You did this to yourself," he spat. After he dried off, he got into bed. He grabbed the remote and turned on the TV.

"Do you want to know why I cheated?" I asked. He muted the TV but he didn't take his eyes off it.

"He knew I was a stripper and a prostitute but he always respected me. You don't say it but I can tell by your actions that it bothers you and you will not accept me as a whole. You only accept the person I am now but you have to accept the person I was and that's what was missing. I own up to my mistake but I just wanted a love I have not experienced in all my twenty-six years of life," I replied.

"Move on and be with the nigga. Just because a man shows his love differently than the next nigga doesn't mean shit. You think I went raw just to the feel the pussy? I went raw because I didn't want to be protected from you; sexually, mentally and all that other soft shit. That was my way of letting you know you had me. You saw improvement and you still fucked another nigga. I'm not trying to hear none of that bullshit you are spitting. If that was me, you would've been locked up. If I would've told you that I fucked another woman because she made me feel better, you would've stabbed me and her. I'm taking this situation light because you are pregnant. Lock the door and close it when you leave out of my room," he said and closed his eyes. I got up and went into my bedroom. I left his door wide open.

****

"How many bedrooms does this home have?" the middle-aged black coupled asked me. I was showing them around the new renovated house that I was renting out.

370

"It has four but the basement is fully-finished, so you can set it up as another bedroom. It's up to you how you want use it," I replied.

"This is a beautiful home. We have five children and it's very hard to find a place for a big family," the wife said.

"How much is the rent?" her husband asked.

"Sixteen hundred," I said.

"That is what we pay for our three-bedroom home in Annapolis," he replied. I stood in the kitchen as they continued to look around. I didn't feel too good and my head started to spin.

"Are you okay, Desi? You don't look too good," the woman asked. I was so out of it that I forgot her and her husband's names.

"I'm fine. I will be okay," I said.

"Me and Nate want to live here. It is a beautiful home and it makes me feel like I'm living someplace far because of what you did with it. The floors, the chandelier, and everything else about this home is immaculate," she said.

"Okay, great. I have an application for you to fill out," I said and pulled one out of the folder in my purse.

"We have to head to our daughter's school, so can I fill this out at home then fax it to you?" she asked me.

"Sure, that will work. It was nice meeting you two and I will talk to you soon," I said. We shook hands and they left. I turned off all the lights in the house. I had to meet with my real estate agent to look at another house. Everything was coming along great but my love life was in shambles. When I walked back into the kitchen, Rohann was standing by the fridge with his arms crossed.

"Are you spying on me? This is very fucking creepy! Shouldn't you be practicing on how to kick a field goal or something?" I asked him.

"Very funny, but I have people around that know you and someone told me you were here. These are my stomping grounds and you know that," he said.

"What do you want?" I asked him.

"I want you, and a little birdie told me that you were pregnant," he said eyeing my purse. I had my prenatal pills sitting at the top of it.

"Yes, I am," I replied.

"Is it mine?" he asked me.

"You wore a condom so why would you ask that?"

"I was fucking you very hard and it broke. I forgot to tell you that," he said. My stomach started to turn. I ran to the sink and threw up. I ran the water to wash it down after I was finished.

"I was already pregnant, dumb-ass," I said.

"I need proof because I do want to be in my child's life if it is mine. I don't want that thug you mess with around my child because I know he thinks the baby is his," he said.

"It is his, so you can stop trying to scare me because I'm not biting. I have proof he is the father so get the fuck out before I call your wife and tell her that you are harassing me," I said.

"She knows about you. Go ahead and tell her. As long as I pay the bills at home, she doesn't give a shit," he said.

"That was really a mistake. The day we had sex in the bathroom has made my life a nightmare. You are becoming an issue and it's turning me completely off. Do you think I will want you after the creepy shit you've been doing?" I asked him.

"You belong to me! I've always been in your corner and now because you are dick-whipped by some young street nigga, you want to cut me off. What is he doing with his life? What can he offer you?" he yelled.

"Happiness, and let's be honest. I don't need a man to take care of me. I have my own hustle now and you are standing in it. You want me to leave my child's father to be with you because you think you can offer me better? Your pockets are not that interesting to me. Only when I was fucking for it. Bishop has exposed me to a lot, and I mean a lot, in everything," I spat. I grabbed my purse and a sharp pain shot up through my back. I tried to ignore it as I rushed out of the house. I lost my footing and fell down the steps. The cramps were getting worse as I lay on the ground.

"What happened? Are you okay?" Rohann rushed down the steps.

"It hurts!" I screamed. He gently pulled me up and he grabbed my purse. He helped me inside his truck and the pain started to come again. I threw up over my clothes as tears fell from my eyes. Something was wrong with my pregnancy but I tried to ignore it. I was being punished for wanting to get rid of it when I first found out. I didn't want the baby until I saw my first sonogram. I was afraid to become a mother at first. I didn't have a mother to show me motherly love and I thought I wouldn't be able to show my baby. When he pulled up in front of the hospital, he got out and rushed me out of his truck.

"What's the matter?" the nurse asked at the front desk.

"My pregnant girlfriend fell down the steps and now she is cramping," he said. If I wasn't in pain, I would've sucker punched that fool.

"Would you shut the fuck up and get me a doctor! I feel like my stomach is about to fall out of my ass!" I screamed at Rohann.

****

An hour later...

I lay in the hospital bed waiting for a tech to come and give me a sonogram. There was blood in my panties but the doctor wasn't sure if I had a miscarriage. Rohann left and I was glad because I had one of the nurses call Bishop and tell him that I needed him with me. There was a knock on the door it was the nurse and Bishop. It didn't surprise me how fast he came. He was crushed because of what I did to him but even a blind person could see that he still loved me.

"What happened, shorty?" he asked when the nurse left the room.

"They are trying to see if I had a miscarriage. I won't be able to live with myself if I did. I've been a horrible person," I said as tears threatened to fall from my eyes. Bishop sat down beside me and rubbed my stomach. He didn't respond but it felt good for him to touch me.

"I had to make a phone call but I'm back," Rohann said when he came into my room. Bishop stood up.

"What the fuck are you doing here, nigga?" Bishop asked him.

"I'm the one who brought her here. Like always, I have her back! That could be my baby, too," Rohann said. Bishop's nostrils flared and he pulled out a gun.

"Bishop, we are in the hospital. Please don't do this. You can get locked up," I said.

"I will serve that time like a muthafuckin' G for blowing this nigga's brains out," Bishop spat.

"This is the man you want, Desi?" Rohann asked.

"Can we all talk about this like adults?" I asked.

"You call him an adult?" Rohann asked me. Bishop's finger slowly started to squeeze the trigger.

"BISHOP NO!" I screamed…

Ashanta

"Are you sure you don't want me to stay with you?" I asked Kwenya as he lay in bed. He was sick with the flu and I had an interview for my book. I wanted to stay home and take care of him but he didn't want me to.

"I'm cool, shorty, now go ahead. I don't even want you around me because it's contagious. I don't want you to get sick," he said and coughed. I felt his head and he had a fever.

"I'm going to cancel my interview. I can't leave you like this," I said. The doorbell rang. I looked on the screen on the kitchen wall before I opened the door to let Jesse in. She stepped inside and kissed my cheek.

"You look lovely. I stopped by to talk to Kwenya. He hasn't been answering my calls and we have something important to discuss," she said. It didn't bother me that Kwenya's partner was a female because I trusted Jesse.

"He has the flu. Follow me," I said before we headed up the stairs.

"Kwenya, Jesse needs to speak with you about something," I said when we walked into the bedroom. He sat up but I could tell he was uncomfortable. His body was also sore from the flu.

"You need anything?" I asked him.

"Some water," he replied. I went downstairs to get him the water.

"Ohhhh," I said as I placed my hand over my stomach. I felt the baby kick. At six months pregnant, I was excited that I only had three more months to go. I didn't want to know the sex until birth. I wanted to be surprised but Kwenya was impatient and he wanted to know. I headed back up the stairs and I could hear Kwenya and Jesse talking about Chaos from the hallway. When I walked into the bedroom, something didn't sit well with me. Jesse had a rag and she was wiping Kwenya's forehead. She was looking at him the same way I looked at him. Kwenya was coughing and he didn't notice it. I gave him the water and he gulped it down.

"I'm good now, Ashanta. I don't want you to miss your interview. I'm ready to take a nap anyway," he said.

"Jesse, can I speak with you in the hallway?" I asked her. She stood up and followed me into the hallway. I closed the bedroom door behind her.

"What's going on?" she asked me.

"You didn't come back home for Desi, did you?" I asked.

"What are you talking about? And I don't like to be questioned," she said.

"The fact that Desi still doesn't know that you are her mother. You don't care about Desi. You came back because you fell in love with Kwenya. I saw the way you looked at him," I replied.

"Why would you accuse me of something like that? After I helped you out. After I made you into a stronger woman and you come at me like this? Do you know what I did to bitches that back-talked me? I used to cut their tongues out," she said.

"Something happened between you two the last time he was in Mexico. You will not pull the wool over my eyes. That has happened to me too much and I'm not standing for it. I know he is a remarkable man, but he is my man. I went through hell and high water to be with him and nobody is going to come between that. Especially a woman that is old enough to be his mother. Who do you think I am, Jesse? Did you think I was going to become that little pushover bitch again after my payback? You must've thought it was temporary. Oh wait, you must've thought I was going to bow down to you because you helped me. I thought you were a smart woman. I admired you and your strength but you are a snake," I spat.

"I don't like being called a snake and you are walking on thin ice. Too bad I don't want to kill you for disrespecting me. It will crush him because of how much he cares about you. I don't want to hurt him, but then again, he might not miss your boring ass," she replied.

"What can you offer him? He wants a family and I'm sure your eggs have expired," I said.

"I can offer him everything and I did. He is on his way to having the biggest drug cartel throughout the US, and guess what? I'm the one who is helping him run it while you sit on your ass and write books. A man like him needs a female that can grind the same way he does. I didn't intend to fall in love with him. The last time he was in Mexico he opened my eyes. He did something for me that took me years to do. He was so passionate about my situation and it made me realize he is the type of man I need in my life. Even though I thought about your feelings, I still can't control mine," she said.

"Does he know that?" I asked. The door opened and Kwenya was standing in the doorway.

"Can a nigga sleep? And what is all of this about?" he asked.

"Nothing, me and Jesse were discussing the baby shower plans that she will be planning for us. Go back to bed, honey," I said and kissed his lips. He shut the door and I looked at Jesse.

"You can take care of him while I go on my interview," I said before I walked off. As soon as I got inside my truck, I made a phone call.

"Hey Stephen. I need a favor from you," I said when he answered the phone.

"What is it?" he asked.

"I need to know about someone. Family history, medical records, and everything else," I said.

"Okay, cool. Give me the name and I will start now," he said.

"Jesse Carter," I replied and hung up. Jesse taught me how to be vindictive. She made a big mistake!

Chaos

"What are you doing here?" she asked when she walked inside the apartment.

"Is that the way you talk to your cousin?" I asked Poet.

"You are nothing but trouble and you need to get the fuck out of my house. Did you break into my apartment? I told you I was not going to help you with your little scheme. I have a good job and you will not jeopardize that," she spat.

"You tink yah too good now? You cannot escape the family. You are one of us and when we are against someone, you are, too. Why do you work for that nigga? You shame your family! He has my brutha blood on his hands. You fucked his friend? Yolo has my brutha blood on his hands, too. Jesula told me it was three niggas that killed my brutha," I spat.

"Kemar was evil and he was up to no good. He came into this city and started robbing people. Well, he robbed the wrong person and I don't feel sorry for him. He is good dead! I hate this family and I came here to get away from y'all but it's hard!" she cried. I put my feet on the coffee table.

"You don't want to help me?" I asked her.

"I'm not getting involved. Kwenya gave me a job and I send money back home to my mother. I need that job so I can help some of our family back home. What have y'all done for the family back home? Y'all have done nothing but take and take and not give. If you don't leave my house, I will call the cops," she said. I pulled out my gun from my pants. I pointed it at Poet.

"Call that nigga that you were fucking. I will get him first," I said.

"Yolo?" she asked.

"Call him over so I can blow his brains out. Kwenya will know what's it like to lose a brutha. He can feel how I felt," I said. Tears fell from Poet's eyes.

"Please don't make me do that," she sobbed. I cocked the gun.

"Call him or else I will blow yah brains out!" I yelled at her. She grabbed her cell phone from out of her purse. Her hands shook as she dialed his number.

"Speakerphone and sound normal," I said.

"What's up, shorty?" Yolo answered the phone.

"Can you come over here? I need to talk to you about something and it's urgent," she said.

"You can't tell me over the phone?" he asked.

"It's very important and I want to talk face-to-face," she said.

"Aight and fix me something to eat because I'm hungry. I will be over there in twenty minutes," he said and hung up.

"How did you find out about Yolo and I?" she asked me.

"Joel told me when I called the other day. He doesn't like the nigga, neither. I don't know why you and Joel still live together because he tells everything about you," I said. Joel was Poet's ex-boyfriend that she was roommates with.

"Did Joel let you in?" she asked.

"Yeah, before he left out for work," I replied and she cried.

"Yolo doesn't deserve this," she said.

"Sit down and wait for yah boyfriend with me. You can watch him get his brains blown out. You did very good," I said.

To Be Continued...

CPSIA information can be obtained
at www.ICGtesting.com
Printed in the USA
LVOW01s0844021016
507014LV00022B/1318/P